A Jersey Dreamboat

The Jersey Scene Book Three

Georgina Troy

Published by Accent Press Ltd 2015

ISBN 9781783757091

This book is a work of fiction but the idea was inspired by a trip my friend, Carol McQuillan O'Regan, and I took in our early twenties. We were invited to a joint 21st birthday party and introduced to the two older brothers of one of the birthday boys. They invited us on a cruise to make up a group of ten people. We were the only English girls. We had no idea they were Counts, or that we would spend the first couple of nights of our trip staying in a magnificent chateau … It is therefore to Carol that I dedicate *A Jersey Dreamboat.*

Acknowledgements

Grateful thanks to my talented and supportive friend, Christina Jones; to my brilliant editor, Cat Camacho; to Hazel Cushion and her excellent team at Accent Press especially Beth, Stephanie and Greg. To the Romantic Novelists' Association and the Jersey Writers. To non-writer friends, Fee Roberts for being the first one to buy my books, to Josette Lindsey for her help with the French phrases used in the book, and to Laura Ransanz González, who I will probably be asking to help me with Spanish phrases for a future book. To my long-suffering husband who has to listen endlessly to ideas and self-doubt and get used to generally being ignored a lot of the time. To my wonderful family, especially my lovely children, James and Saskia, and to the newcomers to the household, Jarvis and Claude, who have been very patient when their walks have been delayed.

Chapter One

'Sometimes I just want to grab life by the bollocks and kick the hell out of it.' Izzy Le Lievre slammed down her mug, splashing the bank's rejection letter for an overdraft with cold coffee.

'And other times?' asked her mother, Cherry, not bothering to hide her amusement. She was busily creating another of the huge sculptures which were her source of income.

'I just grab the nearest Toffee Crisp and eat it.'

'It's just money, darling, and there are other banks you can approach.'

Izzy frowned, thinking back to all the paperwork she'd collated for the meeting. 'I gave them everything they asked for. He laughed at me as if I was some silly woman playing at building up a business.' She flicked several drops of liquid from the form where they'd left a stain. 'Why didn't he take me seriously?'

Cherry shook her head, causing the mop of blonde hair on the top of her head to wobble. 'Maybe you tripping over your own feet as you entered his office wasn't the sort of entrance he expected from a professional businesswoman.'

'He's still a git. And he was a bit pompous, now I come to think of it.'

'I guess. Make me a tea, darling.' Cherry indicated her well-used kettle on the recycled melamine work surface.

'Raspberry leaf?'

'No, Isabelle. This is me you're talking to. You know I only have that in the cupboard for the odd occasion. Make me some proper tea.'

Izzy walked over to the small cluttered worktop in her mother's studio and put the kettle on. Her mother had been on a diet for as long as Izzy could recall, which was probably why she kept various boxes of tea she'd almost certainly never finish.

Izzy made the tea in one of her mother's pottery mugs and carried it over to her, placing it on a small messy table next to her elbow. Studying the sculpture her mother was working on, Izzy narrowed her eyes. It looked a cross between a man in pain and a yeti, but whatever it was someone must have commissioned it.

'Can I open the windows a little wider?' Izzy asked, fanning herself in the July heat and wishing she didn't have the next ten weekends booked up for weddings and birthday parties. This was the third summer she and her best friend Jessica Moon had been kept busy building up their vintage hire business, Lapins de Lune. She loved her work, but it would have been nice just to have one weekend dozing lazily in the sunshine in their back garden instead of creating works of art for the weddings and milestone parties for Jersey locals throughout the summer months.

Her mother nodded. 'Yes, do.' She held up a photo, studied it with narrowed eyes, and altered the aquiline clay nose in front of her slightly. 'Strange-looking man, but rather charismatic in his own way.'

'Who?' Izzy asked, shrieking as the studio door was flung open and her business partner and best friend, Jess, burst into the room like a manic fairy. She looked furious. 'What's the matter?'

'Sorry to burst in,' Jess panted, pulling a pained expression in Cherry's direction by way of an apology. Cherry waved her over for a peck on the cheek. Jess hurried over and, leaning forward to ensure her lacy crop top didn't connect with Cherry's clay-smeared hands, kissed her. Spotting the letter next to Izzy she raised her eyebrows. 'Bank?'

Izzy nodded. 'No go, I'm afraid.'

'Bastards.'

Izzy waited for her to tell them the reason for her unexpected visit and when Jess picked up and read the bank's letter but didn't elaborate, she couldn't hold back any longer.

'Well? Is something the matter?' she asked trying to keep the sarcasm out of her voice.

'Apart from this, you mean?' Jess waved the letter in the air. Her shoulders slumped. 'Yes, something has happened.'

'Go on,' Izzy urged, when Jess hesitated.

'You'll never guess what that cow Catherine de St Croix has done?' She pursed her lips and folded her arms in front of her chest.

Izzy could tell by Jess's nervous foot tapping that she wasn't going to like what was coming next. 'What?' she asked, not sure she really wanted to know.

They had been asked by Catherine, only daughter of the local Seigneur, to hire their entire collection of vintage party décor including linens, bunting, and crockery for her forthcoming wedding to a wealthy London hedge fund manager. The booking had been for three consecutive weeks, including the stay of various houseguests at her father's manor house for the lead up to the wedding, the celebration weekend, and the following week.

Dread seeped through Izzy. 'Please don't tell me she's changed her mind about getting married.'

'No,' Jess snapped, hands now perched on her slim hips.

Izzy sighed. 'Thank heavens for that.'

'They've only gone and bloody eloped.'

'Why?' Cherry asked, stepping away from her masterpiece, intrigued.

'No idea, romantic though, don't you think?'

Izzy waved her hands in the air. 'Er, hello? Never mind her love life, what about our business?'

Jess seemed to deflate in front of her. 'We're screwed.'

'Snot-nosed little madam, I never liked her.' Cherry pulled off the pink and green silk scarf she tied around her hair when she was sculpting and threw it on the floor. All three watched it glide down slowly, not giving Cherry the dramatic effect Izzy suspected her mother had been after. 'No one treats my daughter like that and gets away with it!'

Izzy bent down and grabbed the scarf, motioning for her mum to sit down on a nearby clay-splashed stool.

'Mum, calm down.' Izzy didn't like Catherine's fiancé very much, but suspected he wasn't going to have an easy life being married to someone as demanding as she could be. 'It's our own fault for only having one booking for the three busiest weeks in the year – we should have settled on a few smaller ones.'

Jess sniffed. 'I blame myself.'

'Don't,' Izzy said, stroking her friend's arm. 'These things happen.'

As devastated as Izzy was at this news, she didn't like the thought of Jess feeling so guilty. They'd argued about this booking for days before accepting it.

'But I insisted it would be a brilliant opportunity,' Jess said, her eyes looking rather watery. 'I thought it would help us,' she made quote signs with her fingers, '"cultivate a professional relationship with the attendees who would be staying at the manor house".'

Izzy shook her head. The last thing she was going to do now was be negative and make her friend feel any worse than she already did. 'Your intentions were good.'

'How much money have you lost?' Cherry put down her knife and photo and crossed the stained floor to give Jess a big hug. 'There must be a cancellation clause in your terms and conditions?'

Jess began to cry. 'She didn't sign the contract.'

'What?' Izzy stared at her in disbelief, all thoughts of remaining positive vanishing at this revelation.

Cherry's arms dropped to her sides. 'Jessica, please tell me this isn't as bad as I presume.'

Izzy glared at her mum and hurried over to Jess. She tried to push away the memory of when she had relented about the job and made Jess promise to ensure Catherine would sign their contract.

'She never signed it?' she whispered, just in case she'd misheard.

Jess shook her head.

'But all our clients are supposed to sign the contract before we agree to take them on and mark their date, or in this case dates, into our diary system.'

Jess nodded her head rapidly. 'Yes, I know.' Turning to Cherry, she explained, 'Ordinarily we'd have been covered so that in the event of a last-minute cancellation her father would still have had to pay us a cancellation fee.'

'Yes, with the amount increasing on a sliding scale as each day passed closer to the wedding.' Izzy took a deep breath, desperate not to give into the panic rising in her chest. 'Jess, I thought you said it was all in hand.'

Jess sniffed, and pulling a tissue out of her denim shorts pocket, gave her nose a good blow. 'It was, sort of,' she explained. 'I'd been phoning her every day and Catherine kept promising to get the contract back to me. This morning, knowing it was getting really close and that you'd have a fit if you knew she still hadn't signed it, I drove to the manor to find her.' She groaned covering her face with her hands.

'Go on,' Cherry urged, going back to sit at her stool.

'That's when they told me she'd bloody eloped.'

'Oh.' Izzy blinked away tears. 'We did take a deposit though, didn't we?'

Jess nodded between gulping sobs. 'When I confirmed the initial booking.'

Light-headed with relief that their hard work hadn't all been for nothing, Izzy grinned. 'Thank heavens for that.' She gave her mother a reassuring smile.

Cherry's expression remained stern. 'How much?'

Jess winced. 'Ten per cent of the total estimate.'

'Is that all?'

Izzy understood her mother's shock. She was pretty shocked herself and couldn't believe what she was hearing. Only ten per cent?

She didn't ask in front of her mother why Jess had lowered the deposit from their usual twenty-five per cent and was unable to understand why her friend had done such a thing. It wouldn't make up for having no bookings at the busiest time of the year. Hadn't Cherry nagged them time and again about needing to toughen up if they wanted Lapins de Lune to survive?

'She ground me down,' Jess said eventually, not looking either of them in the eyes.

Izzy spotted her mother's tight-lipped irritation and not being in the mood for one of her tirades, decided to back Jess up. 'We were hoping to make contacts from Catherine's wealthy family and friends for more weddings and parties, so only asked for a smaller percentage.' Izzy explained. 'It was stupid.'

'It was extremely stupid.' Cherry snapped, shaking her head, causing her blonde curls to bounce wildly around her head. 'Honestly, girls, you're supposed to be professional event planners. When will you learn?'

Izzy couldn't help feeling indignant at her mum's words. 'We did learn, Mum,' she argued. 'Don't forget we'd initially intended hiring out our crockery and linen as our business. Now that's just our sideline. We soon learnt we needed to offer more if we wanted Lapins de Lune to work.'

'That's true,' Cherry's voice softened slightly. 'But you can't afford to keep making mistakes and expect to survive financially.'

'This is the first big mistake we've made.' It was. Up until now their business had gone really well. They both loved collecting the vintage décor and when Jess's granny had died several years before and left her cottage to Jess, they'd both been stunned to discover that she'd left her linens and crockery sets equally between Jess and Izzy.

'She hated that you didn't have a gran of your own to leave you special mementos,' Jess recalled Izzy telling her when the will had been read. 'She always said we should relish the past when we plan for our future. Although I didn't understand what she was going on about at the time.'

Izzy had been deeply touched that Jess's gran had thought of her. Apart from Cherry and Jess, of course, the old lady had been there to offer her much support after her boyfriend David's unexpected death four years before. She still felt the excitement when they'd discovered the abundance of linens stashed in two cedarwood chests, each separated with a layer of tissue paper. The linens had been the inspiration for them to start the business they'd always talked about.

'Yes, but this mistake could be the one that ruins you,' Cherry said, in her typical matter-of-fact way, before turning her attention back to her work. She studied the picture once again. 'What will you do now? You could advertise for other bookings, I suppose.' She dampened her index finger and thumb in a small bowl of water and made a miniscule adjustment to the bust's square chin. 'I doubt anyone who's anyone would leave their planning until this late in the summer though.'

She was right, Izzy thought miserably. What where they supposed to do now? She watched her mother, willing her to come up with an ingenious plan.

7

Cherry kicked a spatula out of her way as she moved around the figure in front of her. Izzy could see she was trying to hide her fury and hoped her mother didn't take it upon herself to go and have words with the Seigneur about his daughter. Cherry Le Lievre was well known on the island for her no-nonsense attitude to people and this wouldn't be the first time Izzy experienced her marching off and causing chaos at some function or other.

'I have no idea what to suggest,' Cherry said eventually, looking from one to the other of them and shaking her head. 'It really is too bad of Catherine de St Croix. Just because her father is the Seigneur doesn't give her the right to mess about with other people's lives so thoughtlessly.' She closed her eyes briefly. 'Seigneur. What is that anyhow?'

Izzy wasn't sure. Cherry, who refused to go by her original name of Ingrid, had moved to the island from her native Sweden nearly thirty years before. She'd told Izzy many times how much she'd hated the work as a waitress for one of the local hotels. Despite her own parents being socially important in her home town, she still found the whole idea of anyone thinking they were higher up the social chain than others extremely nauseating. Not that the Seigneur probably saw himself this way, Izzy thought. Catherine certainly did though. Izzy loved her mother – and since her father had died when she was ten, she was her only parent – but her fierceness when protecting Izzy and her older half-brother, Alex, was legendary.

'If only she'd given us more notice,' Jess said, her voice tight. 'A week doesn't give us any time to salvage this mess.'

'I know,' Izzy agreed, stroking her friend's back. As bad as she felt right now, she would have hated to be poor Jess. 'We'll think of something, don't worry,' she soothed.

She heard whistling as someone came down the lavender-lined pathway towards the studio. It stopped as

Alex entered the large sunny room and saw her.

'Hey, munchkin, what are you doing skulking in here with Herself?'

'Don't be rude,' Cherry said, flicking a piece of wet clay at her beloved son. 'Can't you see the girls are upset?'

He seemed to notice Jess for the first time. 'What's up?' he asked looking awkward and moving over to the sink on the other side of the studio to them.

Izzy wasn't ready for a post-mortem about the unexpected cancellation. It was her cue to leave. 'A bit of a business disaster,' she said, leading Jess towards the door. 'I'll leave Mum to explain everything; we need to get on.'

'But I might be able to help,' he said, concern on his tanned face.

Jess's step faltered and Izzy had to pull her gently along. She was aware of Jess's attraction to her brother, but as much as she loved Alex, she wasn't sure Jess could cope with someone whose life was ruled by the tides, especially a professional surfer who had as much female attention as he did.

'Thanks, but we're in a rush,' she fibbed. 'Bye, you two,' she said, giving her mum a quick peck on her mucky cheek and nodding in Alex's direction. 'Mum can tell you all about it.' She propelled Jess outside. 'We've got work to do.'

She could hear Cherry launching into a tirade about the de St Croixes and left them to pick over the bones of their disaster.

'What are we going to do now?' Jess asked, sniffing miserably as they walked to the back door.

'I have absolutely no idea,' Izzy replied. 'But I do know we're not giving up this business without a fight and certainly not because Catherine's let us down.'

As they walked up the garden path, Alex bellowed for them to stop.

Izzy groaned. She wasn't in the mood for his usual teasing and motioned for Jess to go back to their place. 'You make us a couple of drinks, I'll catch up with you in a sec.'

'Hey, I was calling you,' Alex said, running up the path towards her, his sun-bleached, floppy blond hair falling over one eye.

'I heard.'

He pushed his hair out of his eye and gave her a hug. 'I'm sure it's not as bad as you think, Iz.'

She shrugged him off, bending to pick a stem of lavender from her mum's chaotic garden. 'I hope not.'

Alex gave her his brightest smile. 'If you don't want me to try and help, how about filling some of your time this weekend by helping me celebrate my birthday?'

'Bugger, I'd forgotten.'

He laughed. 'That's fine, little sis,' he said ruffling her hair and making her scowl at him.

'Get off, idiot.'

'Agree to come to my party then.'

'Why?' He never usually asked her to join him at parties.

'It's a party, Iz, you might enjoy yourself.'

'Party?' Jess said, appearing next to Alex, blowing her nose and looking a little less forlorn.

Izzy pulled a face at her friend; she guessed she wouldn't have gone too far.

'Yeah, it's tomorrow night at the Dive,' he said smiling at her appreciatively.

Jess dabbed at her damp eyes with a corner of her tissue.

Izzy could tell she was perfectly aware she was showing her enviably long legs off to perfection in her tiny denim shorts. She sighed, causing Alex to grin knowingly at her.

'It'll do you both good to have a bit of fun for a

change,' he said, winking at Izzy and trying his best to be persuasive.

She barely contained a groan. Watching her brother and Jess was almost like seeing two peacocks showing off. 'We've got so much to do though, Alex,' Izzy argued.

'You're always working too hard.'

Unlike him, she thought. 'Great. I suppose all the people you've invited will be surfers and beach bums,' Izzy teased, beginning to warm to the idea.

He laughed. 'Of course. Who knows, you might surprise yourself and like one of them, or even,' he widened his eyes in mock shock, 'have fun.'

Jess giggled. 'I think we should go, Iz. We can have a few drinks, a bit of a dance, and forget about this bloody mess for a bit.'

Izzy thought for a moment. What else would they realistically be doing on a Saturday night? All they could do was phone around their contacts, update their website, and put the word out on social networking sites that they were now available for last-minute bookings. It was all so humiliating and not the sort of image they were hoping to project. So much for the well-organised business image they were hoping to build locally.

'I suppose we don't need more than a few hours to get everything in place,' she admitted. Jess was right, it would do them good.

Later that afternoon, after spending a couple of hours trying unsuccessfully to drum up business, the two girls were repacking the linen for Catherine's wedding into boxes in the tiny living room of their Rozel Bay cottage.

They worked quietly, each lost in their own thoughts, till Izzy felt compelled to check, yet again, if anyone had contacted them about a booking. She stood up and stretched, glancing outside. Their lawn was awash with daisies and buttercups.

'We really need to mow soon, you know?' she said, reaching for the laptop and opening up their website.

'Never mind the garden,' Jess said nervously. 'Anything online?'

Izzy shook her head. 'Nothing.'

Jess sighed. 'It's all my stupid fault, I should've listened to you.' She placed the lid over the last box and carried it over to the table at the far side of the room. 'I'm sick of being miserable,' she said, a hint of the Jess Izzy knew seeping back. 'Let's go for a walk along the harbour wall and treat ourselves to a big fat hot chocolate.'

Izzy smiled, even though it was too hot to enjoy a warm drink. 'With cream and a flake,' she added, desperate to keep the positive vibe going.

Jess pushed a tenner into her back pocket and they headed outside. She leaned against the low garden wall, which boasted ormer shells along the top. Grazing her hand lightly across them while Jess locked the door, she turned her face up to the early evening sunshine. She couldn't imagine ever tiring of living in this pretty island.

'Bloody Catherine, eloping like that,' she said, almost to herself. 'I know it was stupid not to get her to sign, but there's no point in us wallowing.'

'Exactly,' Izzy agreed, linking arms with Jess as they turned and walked along the narrow road towards the pier, the sun warming their bare arms. 'We knew we'd have to take a few chances and sometimes they don't pan out. This was one of those times.'

'I suppose it was,' Jess said, smiling for the first time that day.

The wide granite pier was busy with others making the most of the summer weather. Izzy loved this place, with its pretty little houses and huts on the left and the tiny C-shaped bay to their right. She looked down onto the tourist-packed sandy beach.

'I love living here,' she said, recalling when Jess had

asked her to consider moving into the cottage soon after her grandmother had passed away. Izzy hadn't even taken the time to consider the pros and cons of moving in with her best friend before saying a hearty yes. Looking back, Jess had always been so supportive of her when she'd lost David. Her friend had never felt sorry for herself because her own mother had died giving birth to her. Jess had always insisted she loved her gran like a mother anyway, but Izzy suspected Jess's toughness came from her putting on a brave face about not ever knowing her real mother.

Izzy realized it all could have gone horribly wrong, ruining the friendship they had enjoyed since primary school, but everything had worked out nicely in the cottage that was so different from her mother's cool, simplistic tastes. It even had a mysterious room they'd discovered shortly after she'd moved in. Izzy had been outside and noticed a window at the top of the building. When they'd tried to discover how to get to it, they'd unearthed a locked door behind a wardrobe in her bedroom, but despite searching everywhere still hadn't discovered where Jess's gran had hidden the key – and Jess was loath to damage the house by breaking down the door.

'Despite the lack of parking?' Jess asked. Parking was a nightmare through the summer when they needed to bring their small van to the cottage and load it up for parties.

'Even that is worth coping with to live here.' She breathed in the warm salty air. 'How many other people can say they have a slip on to a beach at the end of their road? We'll find a way round this, you know, Jess.'

'I hope so,' Jess squinted out to sea. 'I feel so guilty about this mess.'

'Don't,' Izzy smiled. 'It'll be OK.'

'But what if it isn't?'

Izzy stopped walking and grabbed Jess's arm. 'The

only people we have to prove ourselves to are ourselves, Jess. So what if this doesn't work out?' she said. 'I believe we'll only fail if we don't try, and we are trying, so no more negativity. Let's enjoy this gorgeous evening and make the most of going to a party.' She laughed and pulled Jess on towards the hut once again. 'Let's face it, we're never free on a Saturday night.'

Jess nodded. 'You're right. We don't get to do this very often.'

They reached the red-painted snack hut and ordered their jumbo hot chocolates.

'We're going to be enormous if we keep on having cancellations,' Jess laughed.

'Only if we treat ourselves to these each time they happen.' They leaned over the metal railings while they waited for their order, looking down on the groups of families and teenagers sharing picnics, making the most of the summer. 'Or, we could start walking along the cliff paths when the weather cools, like we said we'd do last winter.'

Jess nudged Izzy to let her know their drinks were ready. Thanking the café server, they carried their cardboard cups further along the pier.

'We should do that, you know. We're always moaning about needing to do more exercise and there are some gorgeous walks around the island.' Izzy pictured the cliff path on the north of the island she'd walked several months before with her mum. 'One of the people I was talking to at a party mentioned a good book of paths.'

Izzy pulled the chocolate flake from her drink and bit into it, moaning happily. 'I think it's a good idea. I'd rather burn off calories walking, these drinks are far too delicious to give up.'

They sat on a bench, lost in their own thoughts. Izzy looked across the beach to the hill, with its pretty houses dotted all the way up, partially hidden by pine trees and the narrow road wending its way towards the rest of the island. There really was no place like home. She'd enjoyed travelling to India and the Far East with David during a nine-month getaway when they'd both worked as English language teachers, and there was her original ambition to be a horse trainer, but his death weeks before she was about to go away to study had crushed her ability to focus on anything much.

After giving in to Jess's coaxing to join her with the venture they'd chatted about over the years, and with her friend's constant urging her to meet prospective clients and keeping her busy, Izzy had come out of herself. They worked hard building up Lapins de Lune and eventually she'd stopped cursing fate for stepping in and guiding her on a different future to the one she'd expected.

'We're pretty lucky, Jess,' she said, taking a tentative sip of her hot drink. 'I know things are a bit lousy at the moment, but we've got a lovely place to live in and we will find a way to claw back some money, I'm sure of it.'

Jess shrugged. 'We'll give it a go and we can always go to Plan B if we don't find a solution.'

Intrigued, Izzy raised her eyebrows. 'And that is?'

Jess laughed. 'I haven't figured it out yet, but I will.'

Chapter Two

The club was packed but it wasn't hard to locate Alex and his cronies. All were confident and tanned, and even the less attractive of his friends seemed to have some appealing quality about them. Jess elbowed Izzy sharply in the ribs.

'Ouch, what?' she said, wincing.

'Look, who's he?'

She gestured towards a tall, dark-haired man who had olive skin and slate-black hair, and was laughing with her brother He looked like a 1920s silent movie star. He and Alex were talking to a taller man with fairer hair, but there was something strikingly similar about the two strangers. 'They look like brothers,' she said to Izzy. 'Hmm, I don't recognize either of them.'

Izzy did. 'I've seen him at the manor where Catherine lives,' she said, indicating the fairer-haired man. 'I think he works there in the gardens or stables or something.' She didn't mention she'd spotted him galloping across one of the fields a few weeks before as she was dropping off a wedding plan to Catherine. She'd nearly had palpitations at the sight. It was like something out of a period movie, very Darcy-esque. She sighed at the memory.

'Poor sod, working for that cow. Gorgeous though,' Jess said, flicking her long dark hair. 'Mind you, he's not as pretty as your brother, a bit too rough and ready for my liking.'

'Please don't go there, Jess. Alex is fine as a brother, but he makes a horrible boyfriend. I don't think he understands the concept of one man for one woman.' Izzy had known about her best friend's crush on Alex for years. She'd even teased her on the odd occasion, but secretly hoped they wouldn't ever get together. Someone would end up getting their heart broken, and she'd be stuck right in the middle.

'Come on,' Jess said, grabbing her by the elbow. 'Let's go and introduce ourselves.'

By the time they reached the table the darker man had gone. Izzy stifled a sigh. She spotted Alex waving at them and pushed their way through the crowd to get to his table. He stood up to greet them. 'Hey, shortie, you came.'

She refrained from telling him where to go. She wasn't short at all, in fact growing up she'd been teased about her long, skinny legs and height, although thankfully her friends had pretty much caught up with her by the time she was eighteen, but his teasing never ceased. 'I keep hoping you'll get bored of making fun of me,' she said as he grabbed her wrist and pulled her towards him.

'Never. I enjoy it far too much.' He grabbed her cheek between his index finger and thumb and squeezed it. 'Little Cheeky Chops.'

She swiped his hand away. 'Get off me,' but she forced a smile onto her face, since the fairer-haired guy had just appeared from the bar.

'Meet Ed, he's an old schoolmate,' he said. 'He's been telling me all about a trip he's going on with a group of friends.'

'Are you going too?' Jess asked.

'Too busy, unfortunately.' He smiled at Jess and motioned for her to sit next to him. Poor Jess, Izzy thought, aware her friend was going to take this attention a little too much to heart.

Izzy said hello to Ed and sat down next to him.

He narrowed his eyes slightly. 'Haven't I seen you at the manor?'

Izzy nodded. Not wishing to think about Catherine and

their awful dilemma, she forced a smile. It wasn't difficult to pay him attention, he was incredibly handsome. 'So, tell me about your trip then.'

Alex disappeared over to the bar, leaving Jess and Izzy to listen to Ed. He was very well-spoken, which wasn't surprising if he'd attended the most expensive school in the island, as Alex had done. 'Ten of us are picking up a yacht at La Vielle Port in Marseille and sailing down to Nice over the next three weeks.'

'Sounds amazing,' Izzy said truthfully. 'Have you done this sort of thing before?'

He shook his head. 'No, but a close friend delivers yachts to people as part of his job. He's delivering this one for a friend of his, and the friend suggested he take some people along for the ride.'

'I wish I could do something like that,' Jess said, looking across the room at Alex leaning over the bar as he gave his order to the attentive barmaid. She crossed her long, bare legs when he turned to look in their direction. 'Has Alex told you about our disaster?'

Izzy glared at Jess, not wishing to insult Ed's boss's daughter at a party.

'Ahh, Catherine's elopement, yes I heard about that,' he said, looking slightly awkward. 'How did it affect you two?'

Izzy explained about their event planning and hiring business, and their stupidity at not making Catherine sign their contract. 'So, you see, we're a bit stuffed at the moment work-wise, and this is supposed to be our busiest time of the year.'

'I'm sorry you've been left in such a difficult position. Catherine can be very thoughtless at times.'

That's an understatement, Izzy said to herself, but nodded.

He stared at them both for a bit in silence. Unsure how to end the awkward pause, she asked, 'When do you go?'

'Go?'

'On your cruise,'

'Bastille Day.' He laughed. 'We thought it would be a perfect way to celebrate. Any excuse.'

Alex arrived back at the table carrying a tray of drinks. 'I thought it would save us going back too soon for refills.'

Typical Alex, always ready to save any time he could, Izzy thought. 'Cheers,' she said taking a vodka and tonic. Jess gave him a wide smile that went on for rather a long time, Izzy thought, though he didn't appear to mind.

'I met your father recently with Alex,' Ed said. 'He's a fun guy.'

'He's not my dad, only Alex's.'

Ed looked mortified. 'Hell, I'm sorry; I never think before opening my mouth.'

She didn't believe that for a second. Wishing to put him at his ease, she placed a hand on his forearm. It was impossible to miss the hard muscles under his blue shirt. Working outside had a lot to answer for, it seemed. 'It's fine. Alex's dad was Mum's husband and mine was a boyfriend she met when he was away on business.' She smiled to soften her words. 'I'm surprised you don't know that bit of scandal, it's still very much on the locals' lips.'

He shook his head. 'Must have been before I came over here.'

'I'd have loved my dad to be a flash businessman like yours,' Jess said to Alex, her head tilted to one side.

This was getting a little worrying. 'Jess?' Izzy said widening her eyes for emphasis. 'Can I have a quick chat in the Ladies'?'

'What? Oh, all right then,' she said getting up.

'We won't be a sec.' Izzy ignored Alex's amusement as they left the table and grabbed hold of Jess's arm, pulling her into the Ladies'. 'What are you doing?'

'Nothing.' She looked so angelic that if Izzy hadn't known her quite so well she'd believe her.

'I know my brother is only a few years older than you, but he has so much more experience than you do and I just know that he'd end up hurting you. I'd hate for that to happen.'

'I'd be fine,' Jess said dreamily.

'But don't you think you'll be a bit out of your depth with him?'

'Don't get mad.' She laughed and pushed Izzy's left shoulder. 'He's great fun.'

'Well –' Izzy said, about to continue when Jess interrupted her.

'I'm a big girl, Iz. You don't have to look out for me any more. All that business with Shaun was a big fuss over nothing.'

It hadn't seemed like it at the time, Izzy recalled anxiously, or for about a year after Jess's first love had unceremoniously dumped her by text on her birthday two years before. Izzy sighed. 'I'm just worried about you,' she explained, disliking the tug of guilt as she tried to persuade Jess that Alex wasn't someone she should bother with. 'Alex might say all the right things, Jess, but he's no Prince Charming.'

It wasn't like Jess had ever taken her advice over anything anyway, so she freshened up, reapplied her pink lip gloss, and they returned to the table where several others had now congregated.

'Don't you think, Iz?' Alex shouted, waving them over. 'I was telling Ed about Mum's latest creation in her studio. 'I thought it looked like an ugly bear.'

Izzy laughed. 'He's right, but someone will be paying a small fortune to own it.'

'We'll never make a fortune now, small or otherwise,' Jess pouted. 'Bloody Catherine, eloping like she did.'

Izzy noticed Ed tense and glared at Jess. Didn't she realize how awkward this must be for him? Although aware he and Catherine probably got along, it was hard to imagine someone as snobby as her spending time with a bloke who worked at the manor. Then again, Izzy thought, taking in his handsome face and broad shoulders, you would have to be a nun not to appreciate Ed's physical attributes.

Ed downed the remnants of his pint. 'Why don't you two come with us on the yacht?'

Izzy frowned. 'Sorry?'

'You said you had nothing on for the next few weeks, so why not come with us?'

Jess squealed and beamed up at him. 'We'd love to.'

Horrified by Jess's acceptance, Izzy asked. 'But how much will it cost?' She ignored Jess's loud groan. Someone had to think about money. Hadn't they only this afternoon been fretting about their lack of it?

'Um, not much,' he said. 'We don't have to pay to charter the yacht, so it'll be your contribution towards food and fuel, oh and your travel costs to Marseille. We'd go via Paris, where you can meet the others at my parents' house nearby.' He gave them both a smile. 'Yes?'

Jess and Izzy exchanged glances. When he put it like that, it did seem do-able. She contemplated his words for a few more seconds. She had a small balance in her current account and it wasn't as if they had anything else to do in Jersey at the moment. She could see Jess studying her face. Without speaking, both smiled and said 'Yes' at the same time.

His lips drew back into a wide smile. 'Two of the people coming are here tonight – I'll fetch them for you, so you can meet before we go.'

He left them and walked into the crowd.

Jess squealed. 'Oh my God, I can't believe what we've just agreed to do.'

Neither could Izzy. She looked across the room at Ed, now stopped in front of two guys who were being chatted up by a group of girls. One of them was the man they'd seen talking to Alex earlier.

'Are you two nuts?' Alex snapped.

Alex rarely shouted at her and never at Jess, so they both stared at him in shock at his outburst. 'What's the matter?' Izzy asked, noticing Jess's crumbling expression.

Alex leaned closer to them. 'You don't know these guys.' He narrowed his eyes. 'Why would you agree to go on a cruise with them and their friends?'

'But you said you went to school with Ed,' Izzy snapped, furious with him for stating the obvious and making her consider something she'd rather not. 'Are you saying Ed is someone we should steer clear of?'

Alex sighed heavily. 'No, he's a great guy, but you don't know the others, do you?'

She shook her head, miserably. 'No.'

'Look,' shouted Jess. 'Here they come.'

The three of them sat silently watching Ed lead two friends over to their table, one dark, one blond. They were smiling and seemed friendly enough to Izzy.

'Izzy, Jess, Alex,' Ed said. 'This is Roman and Xavier.'

Jess put her hand out for them to shake, but was pulled off her stool by the darker-haired Roman and kissed three times on her cheeks. 'Ooh, *bonjour*,' she said realizing he was French.

Izzy stepped down when Xavier took her by the shoulders and did the same.

'Ed, he tells us you are willing to sail wiz us to the Côte d'Azur next week.'

Izzy nodded. 'Yes, if that's OK with you both?'

'*Mais, oui, c'est* un pleasure.' He looked at Ed. 'You have explain the girls the details?'

'*Non,*' he said, immediately rattling off a string of sentences Izzy couldn't decipher, despite having studied French at school.

Realizing what he'd done, Ed looked at them. '*Pardon,* I am being rude.' He took the party invitation from his

23

pocket and Xavier passed him a pen. 'I'll write down our phone numbers and the address where we'll stay before travelling to Marseille. I have an email address too, so please email me tomorrow and I'll forward all the details.'

Izzy took the invitation from him and read it.

'If you decide not to join us, please don't worry, we will understand. I don't want you to feel pressured to go.' He smiled at each girl. 'Please let me know if you do change your minds though.'

She noticed Alex glaring at Ed and his friends with irritation. Izzy stood next to her brother.

'I think we need to all have a bit of a chat, don't you?' Alex said quietly, bending his head down to her level.

Izzy nodded. The last thing she wanted was her brother kicking off and embarrassing her, and after all, he did have her best interests at heart. Her mood towards him softened. She moved to sit next to him to allow the others space in the banquette around the table and gave Alex a nudge. 'I'll be fine, I promise,' she whispered in his ear.

He put his arm around her and Jess, and smiled at her friend. He cleared his throat. 'Ed, I know you well and you're a good mate,' Alex began, staring from one to the other of the three guys sitting around the table. 'Xav and Roman, I've only met you this evening, but I want you all to know that Izzy is my little sister and Jess is like my little sister.'

Jess gave a pained whimper. Izzy concentrated on not looking at her, but at the reactions of the three men.

'I expect you to treat these two as if they were also your little sisters.' He gave each one a pointed glare. 'Any funny business and I don't care where you happen to be, I'll come and make your lives a living hell.' Xavier swallowed and Roman nodded rapidly several times. Ed smiled. 'Understood.'

'Good. That's settled then.' Alex said. He peered down at Jess and then at Izzy. 'You two make your arrangements, but if you change your mind at any time, you contact me and I'll bring you back. OK?'

The girls nodded. Izzy could see Jess was still devastated by Alex referring to her as his sister.

'You wish to dance?' Xavier said to Izzy. She instinctively glanced at Ed, though wasn't sure why. Maybe it was because as handsome as the Frenchman was, she couldn't help feeling drawn to Ed. He gave her a hint of a smile.

'Yes, OK,' she said taking Xavier's hand and being led onto the dance floor.

Jess and Roman followed close behind them and danced to 'No Church in the Wild'.

'You have been to France before?' Xavier shouted over the music. The girls nodded.

'Yes, many times, but not to the south of France,' Izzy said.

'Nor on a yacht,' Jess added.

Xavier pushed his floppy blond fringe back off his tanned forehead. 'I am certain you will like the two other guys who are joining us, and the other three girls. We know most of them since we were children.'

Roman laughed when Jess got carried away, as she often did on the dance floor, and twirled around him giggling. 'They will love you girls, you are so, um, how you say …'

'Fun?' Jess offered, waving her arms in the air.

'Exactly. You are fun.' He laughed and copied her.

Izzy smiled at Xavier who shook his head in mock horror. 'Roman is always like this when he has consumed one or two drinks.'

Izzy nodded in Jess's direction. 'They'll get along well then.'

He leaned closer and in a loud whisper said, 'Do not worry. I know we are strangers to you now, but we are good people. I am sure you will feel happier when you meet our mother and father at our home where everyone will stay before leaving for La Vieux Port in Marseille.'

Izzy made a mental note to relay this snippet of information to Alex. He would be much happier knowing that. 'I look forward to meeting them,' she said honestly.

Chapter Three

Izzy leaned over the back of the ferry, feeling more seasick than she could have ever imagined and wondered what the hell she'd been thinking agreeing to spend almost three weeks on a boat. She said as much to Jess.

'It's two and a bit,' Jess said from behind her. 'Remember we're staying a couple of nights with the guys' parents, though what we're going to do there I can't imagine. How will they fit ten extra people into their home?'

Izzy didn't care right now. She simply wanted the boat to dock in St Malo so she could get off and stop feeling so nauseated.

Three-quarters of an hour later, they carried their rucksacks off the metal gangplank and walked the fifteen-minute trek to the train station. The French road signs didn't look much different to those at home, but then again they were only one hour away by sea from Jersey. The only difference was the architecture, but even that was familiar to Izzy after so many trips with her mum to St Malo for birthday lunches and short weekend stays in Dinard.

It had been difficult to fit everything they'd hoped to take into their bags, but eventually they'd cut it down to one dress, one skirt, and a couple of tops each for going out when they were in port, and the rest of their luggage consisted of several bikinis, sarongs, shorts, and underwear. Izzy hated her blonde hair being wavy, but Alex was so amused when he'd discovered she'd packed her straighteners, she'd reluctantly left them behind.

'I'm going to look like a real munter,' she moaned as they arrived at the small shop by the rail tracks. 'I just hope I can top up the vague tan that I've got.'

'You will, don't worry,' Jess said, grabbing two baguettes filled with cheese and ham and two bottles of water for their journey. 'We're going to need these, who knows what time the guys will pick us up?'

They watched the small hamlets and villages clustered together along their route to Paris over the next two and a half hours on the immaculate, air-conditioned train. Jess ate her lunch within the first half an hour and then fell asleep, leaving Izzy to ponder spending so much time on a yacht that would be tiny compared to the ferry they'd just taken. She hoped the sea was calmer than it had been between Jersey and St Malo.

She pulled the invitation out of her jeans pocket and turned it over, re-reading it for the twentieth time. She'd also printed out a few emails from Ed, giving them exact instructions about the train and where to wait for Xav and Roman when they arrived at Gare du Nord.

Izzy wasn't surprised when her mum had been concerned about her going on this trip. She'd always been a little over-protective and Izzy knew it was because of her dad dying so suddenly. Alex had been good enough to stand up for her and eventually their mum had calmed down, although had remained far from impressed.

'You barely know these men,' Cherry said, slamming down a handful of wet clay.

'I'm twenty-four, Mum, I can look after myself,' she said, trying not to let her annoyance show.

'She's got a mobile phone, Mum,' Alex said. 'Don't forget they'll be staying with the guys' parents before they set off on the boat. That should give them a chance to get to know everyone a bit. She's promised me that if she feels at all uncomfortable, she'll call me and I'll get her home again.' He looked pointedly at Izzy. 'Didn't you, Iz?'

'Yes, Mum, so please stop fretting. I'm also more than capable of making my own way home without needing Alex's help. I have been away before you know, and further than the South of France.'

'Yes, I know,' Cherry said. 'But I can't help worrying about you. Your father was always impulsive,' she added, pushing her thumbs into the latest work of art taking shape in front of her. 'I remember him carting me off to some moss-covered hut in the Outer Hebrides when we were first together.'

Izzy frowned. 'So how is that different to what I'm doing now?'

'Isabelle,' her mother said, clay-covered hands on her hips. 'I was with your father at the time. You, on the other hand, are going away with a group of people you barely know.'

'Alex knows Ed, he went to school with him. And Ed works at the manor, so I'm sure you can always contact the Seigneur for information about him if you feel the need.'

Pacified a little, Cherry relented. 'I'm sorry, I know you're an adult and more than capable of looking after yourself,' she said. Izzy nodded. 'Give me a hug. I know I shouldn't ask, but will you contact me every few days?'

'Mum, I'll be fine, I promise. I'll make contact as often as I can, but don't forget I'll be at sea a lot of the time, so I might not be able to do so as often as you'd like.'

Jess grunted, bringing Izzy back to the present. She watched her friend yawn as she woke up.

'Are we there yet?' Jess asked, rubbing her eyes.

Izzy shook her head. 'No, another twenty minutes I think.'

Jess stretched and drank some of her water. 'Right, make-up time then.'

'You look fine without it,' Izzy said. Jess really didn't need any make-up at all with her long dark lashes and perfectly arched black eyebrows. She, on the other hand, did need something to define her features, being so fair.

Jess raised a dark eyebrow. 'Fine isn't the look I'm aiming for though.' She squinted at Izzy and shook her head. 'I think you need to make a bit of an effort too.'

Izzy pulled a face and laughed. 'Thanks.'

'Joking.'

By the time the train pulled into the station, both girls had freshened up, plaited their hair, and made themselves up, though not enough to look like they were trying too hard. Izzy scanned the area and pointed to the exit. 'I think we go out through there and wait somewhere on the left.'

The noise of the station was exhilarating. Jersey could be fun, but since the Germans had taken up most of the tracks during The Occupation in the forties there hadn't been any trains, and there certainly weren't any huge stations like the Gare du Nord, so this was an exciting experience. The tinny voice over the tannoy and the rattle of suitcase wheels along the platforms delighted Izzy.

Excitement coursed through her. 'I think we're going to have a ball,' she said, putting an arm around her friend's shoulders. 'Maybe Catherine's elopement wasn't such a terrible thing to have happened after all.'

They checked the signs and made their way to where they hoped someone would be waiting to collect them. There was no one there. 'They're not coming,' Jess said, panic filling her voice. 'They've forgotten.'

'No they haven't,' Izzy said with more certainty than she felt. She scanned the area several times, and just as she was thinking that maybe Jess had been right, she spotted an older man waving at them from across the parking area.

'Who's he?' Jess asked, doubtfully.

'Let's go and find out, shall we?' Izzy ran over. '*Bonjour*.'

'*Bonjour*,' he said, getting out of the car and dropping a cigarette onto the pavement. '*Isabelle et Jessica?*' They nodded. '*Je m'appelle de Lys*. Err, the boys, I have collect you.'

'Sorry?' Jess glanced at Izzy.

Izzy smiled at him. 'You're taking us to the boys?'

'*Oui, Xavier et Roman.*'

'He's taking us to their home now, I think,' Izzy said. Both girls nodded. De Lys loaded their luggage and Jess quickly got into the back of the car, leaving Izzy to join the older man in the passenger seat.

He drove off so quickly their heads shot back and Izzy was grateful for the headrest.

They'd been driving for almost an hour when he drew up on a bridge and stopped. A couple of gendarmes came over and Izzy was surprised when they didn't reprimand him and make him drive on. '*Venez ici*?' he said smiling and motioning for the girls to follow him.

Jess glanced at Izzy.

'Come along,' Izzy said, grateful to be out of the car for a bit. 'Let's just follow him. I think he wants to show us something.'

They walked behind him as he made his way over to a wall on the side of the stone bridge and waved at someone below. Izzy and Jess peered over at a noisy crowd below them, stunned to notice that they were cheering up at him and frantically waving flags.

'What the hell?' Jess said.

'*Le Maire. Le Maire*,' the crowd chanted as the older man waved at them and bowed his head.

'Bloody hell, I think he's the mayor of this place,' Izzy said, remembering that today was Bastille Day. 'I thought he was a chauffeur.'

Jess giggled. 'So did I.' She moved closer to the edge of the wall and waved down at the crowd, who immediately cheered louder.

Izzy laughed. Typical Jess, loving the attention. It didn't seem to be worrying the mayor either. In fact, he grabbed her by the wrist and held her hand up in the air and the cheers got louder. He must be well loved, she thought looking down at all the beaming faces as they clapped and waved up at him.

'This is your village?' Izzy asked, fascinated by this surreal experience of adoration.

He nodded. 'Is in my family many years.'

She wasn't certain if he'd misunderstood her, but smiled anyway.

'We go,' he said giving the crowd one last salute and bustling them over to the car. 'Is Bastille Day, er, *déjeuner avec ma femme et mes fils.*'

'His wife and son,' she whispered to Jess who looked confused. 'We're having lunch with them.'

'Bum, I want to go and see Roman and Xav.'

'We can't be rude,' Izzy said. 'Not after he's driven us all this way. We'll soon catch up with the guys, Jess.'

'Fine, but I hope this lunch doesn't take too long, I'm getting more and more nervous about meeting up with Roman and Xav again and I want to get it over with.'

Izzy was feeling the same way, but didn't add to Jess's anxiety by saying so. They got back into the car and quickly fastened their seat belts when the old man sped down the narrow roads and out of the village. A short way down a grass-banked lane, he shocked them both by slamming on the brakes just as the car reached two huge stone pillars.

'Château de Lys,' he said, indicating the worn stone name on one of the pillars.

'Château?' Izzy heard Jess murmur from the seat behind her.

The car took them down a lengthy gravel driveway with elms in rows down each side, like soldiers standing to attention. The trees reached across from one side to the other, their branches touching above the driveway making a shaded, leafy archway for them to travel through with lupins clustered along each side.

Surely he couldn't own this place, wondered Izzy, unable to shake off the vision of this mayor standing on the village bridge. What had they agreed to, she wondered, when they said they'd go on this trip?

He slowed down slightly and Izzy held her breath as the aged Peugeot turned in through more gates, this time ornate iron ones with a gold-painted crest. He slowed near to the double oak front doors, slamming on the brakes once again.

'*Et voilà*,' he said, looking pleased with himself for delivering them in one piece to the château.

'*Merci, Monsieur*,' Izzy said, stepping shakily out of the car, relieved to be on terra firma again. She stared open-mouthed at the creamy, majestic building in front of her, with its very own tourelle, and wondered what it must look like inside. 'It's like something out of a historical novel. I didn't realize mayors lived in such splendour.'

'I wonder what their linen is like?' Jess said.

'Their linen?' Izzy nudged her sharply in the side. 'Is that what really springs into your mind when you look at this place?' She stared up at the tower with its rounded tiled roof on one side of the building and the eight-foot-high blue shutters framing each of the windows. She'd never seen anything like this before and it was hard to imagine she and Jess would be walking up the sweeping stairway to the front door any moment now to enjoy lunch.

Jess shook her head. 'No, but it's a little overwhelming, don't you think?'

Izzy needed to gather her thoughts. Having grown up with an artistic, yet practical, no-nonsense mother, it was difficult to step into this parallel universe. It was like nowhere she'd ever been to before. Jersey had some beautiful manor houses and in the three years she and Jess had been building up their business they'd been lucky enough to work in a few, but nothing came close to this.

She walked over to the back of the car to fetch her rucksack when an excited bellow came from the huge double front doors.

'Ahh, *Izzy et Jess*, welcome.'

She couldn't help grinning as first Xavier and then Roman marched over to them arms outstretched. It was good to see familiar faces in such surreal surroundings, especially as they seemed genuinely delighted that they were there. Izzy smiled and relaxed a little.

'Hi,' she said, stepping forward to hug first Roman and then Xavier.

'Great to be here,' Jess said joining them. 'Mind you, he drives like a maniac,' she nodded her head to indicate the tall, skinny man who watched the boys proudly. 'I'm not sure I'd let him collect any more of your guests.'

Both men laughed, their heads thrown back in amusement. Xavier rattled something off in French to their driver. The only word Izzy could make out was 'Papa'. She quickly sidled up to Jess and leaning over to her, whispered, 'Crap, he's their dad.'

Jess looked pained and Izzy held her breath for the man's reaction. 'Great first impression I'm making.'

The older man laughed and patted both boys on the back, saying something to them and indicating Izzy and Jess, before leaving them to enter the vast building. The boys watched him go and then kissed the girls three times on their cheeks.

Roman linked arms with Jess. 'It is OK, he is amused by your comments.'

She immediately cheered up and winked at Izzy.

'It is very good to see you here,' Xav said. 'We will show you to your rooms and then eat lunch, yes? You must be very hungry.'

'Famished,' Izzy said, waiting as he collected both rucksacks and slung one over his left shoulder, carrying the other with his free hand.

'You like the château?'

She nodded. 'How could I not: it's incredible.'

They followed Roman and Jess into the marble-floored hallway and Izzy couldn't help widen her eyes at the scene in front of her. They walked with the men up the curved, creamy stone staircase to the first floor.

'Wow, this is so beautiful,' she said as they turned left and walked along a seemingly endless corridor. 'What is it like working here?'

Xavier shrugged a shoulder. 'It is very quiet most times. I live in Paris in an apartment, but come home to see my family when *ma mère* holds parties. I always love returning home.'

'You live in Paris?' Izzy asked, confused. She looked sideways at Jess, sensing she was having trouble coming to terms with the situation they'd found themselves in.

'So your parents live here then?' Jess asked as they walked along the wide stony corridors.

The boys stopped and swapped looks. '*Oui, mes petites,*' Xavier said. 'This is our family home, *le château.*'

Izzy was aware her mouth was open and had to make a conscious effort to close it so she didn't look entirely stupid. '*Le château?*' Had she heard right?

He nodded at her speck of French. '*Oui, le château.*'

'Holy crap,' Jess said, looking first at Izzy and then around the high-walled corridor.

'You are OK with this?' Roman asked.

'Well, I mean,' Izzy struggled with what to say next. Then it dawned on her how concerned Roman seemed that they'd still be willing to stay with his family and she added. 'Yes. Yes, of course.'

'Don't mind?' Jess looked at her in astonishment. 'This place is like something out of one of the stories that my gran used to read to me. I'd love to stay here.'

Izzy couldn't wait to explore. 'I hope we remember which way to go, this place is huge.'

Xavier laughed and linked arms with her. 'We will give you, how you say, um, tips? Then you will find your route to meet us later.'

Roman and Jess followed them, laughing at something he'd just whispered to her. She could tell Jess liked him and could see why. He was good-looking and attentive and Jess needed someone who wanted to please her. Alex, she mused, would expect her to spend time hanging about waiting for him to finish surfing, come home late all the time, and generally flirt with anything in a skirt or bikini.

'I live near Paris also,' Roman said. 'It is good to return home and spend time with our parents.'

'*Oui*,' Xavier said. 'We do not manage this very often. I have been looking forward to coming back here.'

'I'm not surprised,' Izzy said 'I can't wait to see everything. I hope we have enough time.'

'You are in here,' Roman said to Jess, holding the door open and waiting for her to walk in. 'I will see you later when you have had time to be refreshed,' he said before hurrying down the corridor,

'Izzy, come and look at this,' Jess shouted from inside.

She went to join Jess, amused to see her friend's eyes widening as she stood in the large, airy room. Light flooded in from the tall windows. Jess didn't seem to mind that Roman had made a quick exit, but gazed at the room around her, her mouth making an 'O'.

'This is my room,' Jess announced unnecessarily, flinging her arms wide to encompass the space where the wallpaper, bedding on the ornate four-poster bed, and carpets were different shades of yellow. It was like walking into sunshine.

'It's perfect for you,' Izzy said, moving out of the way when Xavier came in. He held up the two rucksacks, wanting to know which one to leave behind.

Jess took her pink rucksack, thanking him. 'This place is amazing,' she said.

Roman came back into the room carrying towels. '*Pardon*, these were forgotten,' he said, placing three on the bedspread and handing the other three to Xavier. 'The bathroom, it is down the hallway at the end *à gauche*, um, to the left.'

Both girls nodded.

'Your room is next door,' Xavier said, waiting by the bedroom door for Izzy to follow him.

Within a couple of strides she was walking into the prettiest bedroom she'd ever seen. Izzy gasped. 'Oh, Xavier, it's gorgeous.'

Her room was slightly smaller than Jess's, and painted ice-blue, but much more to her taste. She walked over to the open window and rested her palms on the thick windowsill, staring across the vast lawn to the wooded area behind a large lake. 'I can't believe I'm going to wake up to this view tomorrow morning.'

'I am happy you like it here,' he said smiling as he leaned out of a nearby window to talk to her. Izzy giggled to see him there. 'My parents have spent many years to bring the château to this level of appearance.'

'They've done a wonderful job, it's like walking into a dream.'

He stood away from the window and took her hands in his. 'They will be very happy to hear you say this, Izzy.'

She wasn't sure quite what to say to this, so tried, 'Your English is very good.' She wished she had bothered to become a little more fluent in French. She had no excuses, having learnt it at school like all the other Jersey children did, and coming across to France to stay at the holiday homes of school friends through the years. Hearing someone else speaking – if not perfect, then very passable – English, was sobering.

'Thank you, I do not speak as well as my brother, but he was sent to boarding school in Jersey and so his English is perfect, I'm told.'

Izzy raised her eyebrows: she hadn't realized Roman had been educated in the island. 'Why him, and not you?'

'His godfather doesn't have a son, but he lives in Jersey and offered for my brother to do this. My parents, they think it is a good idea and so he moved to Jersey from age fourteen.' He placed her rucksack down on the settee at the end of the bed. 'I will leave you now and go to visit with my mother. We shall meet in one half hour in the hall? I shall introduce you to my mother and we can enjoy lunch together.'

She thanked him and watched him leave. As soon as the door closed behind Xavier, Izzy kicked off her shoes and fell backwards onto the bed. It was like lying in a fabric cloud. She sighed. This was going to be great fun, once she'd got past the meeting with his mother. She would have been much happier with a sandwich and a walk around the grounds, but if she wanted to spend a couple of days as a houseguest in a place like this, she would have to do as expected.

Her door opened silently and Jess popped her head around it. 'You alone?'

Typical Jess innuendo. Izzy laughed. 'Yes, come in.'

Jess ran in barefoot. She shrieked and leapt onto the bed, landing next to Izzy. 'I suppose this is how Catherine de St Croix's guests feel when they stay at her dad's manor house.'

Izzy wriggled her toes and stared up at the intricately embroidered material making up the bed's canopy. 'I suppose so,' she said, not wishing to think about Catherine at this moment. 'I could do this more often,' she murmured, closing her eyes.

'You're not the only one.'

They lay there in silent contemplation for a few minutes. Izzy watched the dust motes dancing in the sunbeams from one of the windows. She imagined that, as perfect as this place was on summer days like this, it must feel a bit spooky on dark wintry nights.

She felt Jess get up.

'Come on, you don't have time to lie there. The guys are going to be waiting for us downstairs soon and I'm going to change,' Jess said. 'I made a crappy first impression with their dad, so I don't want to do the same with their mum.'

'Good point,' Izzy agreed, getting up and pulling off her T-shirt and shorts. 'I think I'll wear that summer dress I packed.' She opened her rucksack and pulled out a creased cream garment. 'Bum, it looks like a dishcloth.'

'Hang it up and wear something else then,' Jess said. 'Roman told me the guys were wearing casual trousers and shirts,' she added. 'so I'm sure we don't have to be smart.'

'That's a relief,' Izzy said, tipping out the meagre collection of clothing she'd packed for the trip. 'I wish they'd told us we'd be staying somewhere like this.'

'Me too.' Jess went to turn the door handle, but stopped and rested her back against the door, eyes closed. 'He's so cute, don't you think?'

'Who? Roman?'

'Well, both of them, but I meant Roman, yes.' Jess opened her eyes. 'What do you think? Maybe we could make a foursome for the trip.' She hugged herself. 'Wouldn't it be perfect to fall in love and spend the holiday seeing all those places with these guys?'

Izzy liked the idea, but it was a fantasy. 'Firstly, Jess, I thought you had the hots for my brother,' she ignored Jess's protestations. 'Secondly, has it occurred to you that we're only going to be with them for a couple of weeks and if they don't already have girlfriends, these guys live in Paris.'

'So?'

'We live in Jersey.'

Jess pulled a face. 'So what? You need to relax and not be so practical for once, Iz. OK, so I might be daydreaming, but there's no harm in that. Anyway I can't see us getting a chance like this again in a hurry, so I for one am going to make the most of what fun I can have, and I suggest you do the same.' Without giving Izzy a chance to reply, Jess opened the door and left.

Maybe Jess had a point, Izzy thought, as she pulled a cotton skirt out of her bag. Giving it a good shake, she decided to try and go with the flow for once and not worry about the future. She was on holiday and doubted she'd be having another one anytime soon. That settled in her mind, she studied her skirt. It would have to do; it was the second smartest piece of clothing she had with her.

She washed her hands, changed, and went into Jess's room, surprised to see her re-plaiting her hair. 'Hurry up, I thought you didn't want to be late.'

They hurried downstairs and, after a bit of confusion as to where the others might be, found Xavier and Roman waiting patiently for them in a hallway. The guys smiled when they spotted Jess and Izzy hurrying down the staircase.

'Sorry we're a bit later than expected,' Jess said. 'She couldn't decide what to wear.'

Izzy narrowed her eyes at her best friend. It was typical of her to shirk the blame when she'd been the one to take for ever on her hair.

'It is no problem,' Xavier said. 'Come. This way is the family dining room.'

Family dining room? Izzy wondered how many they could have.

They walked down a seemingly endless stream of stone corridors with large windows dotted along one side, letting in the golden summer sunlight. Eventually they arrived at a set of doors which Xavier opened, stepping back to let the others inside.

'Maman, Papa, this is Jessica and Isabelle, our friends from Jersey.'

The parents stood up and shook the girls' hands. 'It is very good to meet you,' their mother said, placing her cool, free hand over Izzy's. 'Please, let us sit. Xavier tells me he will show you around the grounds after lunch.'

The girls nodded and sat where indicated.

There was a gentle knock on the door. '*Entrez*,' their father said.

A middle-aged man in chinos and an open-necked shirt walked into the room carrying a serving dish, followed by two women each bearing a tray. '*Madame la Comtesse, Monsieur le Comte, excusez-moi*,' he said.

'*Oui?*' their mother asked.

He spoke too quickly for Izzy to make out much of what he was telling them, but she did pick up that there had been a telephone call from someone.

The first course of pâté and crispy melba toast was served. It was a few moments before Izzy registered how the man had addressed the two parents. 'Comtesse et Comte de Lys?' she murmured.

'*Oui?*' the Comtesse replied.

Izzy forced a smile. She could almost hear the cogs whirring in Jess's brain and prayed she wouldn't elaborate on her own faux pas. 'I ...'

'Blimey, does that mean you two are counts?' Jess asked Xavier, a little louder than Izzy would have liked.

Roman laughed. '*Bien sûr*, of course. In fact our mother was born a baroness, but she married beneath her station.'

Izzy was a little thrown by his announcement, but relaxed when the entire family laughed.

'It is true,' the countess assured her. '*Mais*, I have forgiven my 'usband for my change of title now.'

Izzy laughed, relieved to see they all had such a good sense of humour. Today was turning out to be more surreal by the second, Izzy thought. She doubted any of her friends were ever going to believe what was happening to her and Jess, whom, she noted, looked perfectly calm, as if this was the sort of company she always kept. It made her even more certain that Jess had been right to suggest she should relax and enjoy everything this holiday gave to her.

She cleared her throat, wanting to thank the Count and Countess for letting her and Jess stay at their home. She opened her mouth to speak, but before she managed to say anything the door opened and in walked Ed. The sight of him, so tall, his broad shoulders seemingly taking up most of the space in the doorway, took her breath away.

'You're both here, great,' he said, smiling at Izzy and Jess and looking very much at home.

'You are late,' the Count said, not looking very impressed with Ed's untimely arrival.

Almost before Izzy registered the tone of the older man's voice, Ed said. '*Pardonez moi, Papa, Maman.*' He strode across the room straight to the older couple and hugged them both affectionately.

'Edouard, chérie,' the Countess shrieked, opening her arms wide to embrace him.

Chapter Four

Izzy and Jess stared at each other. 'What the hell?' Jess mouthed.

Izzy shrugged. She had no idea what was going on here, or she did, but wasn't sure she was comfortable with the knowledge slowly dawning on her. 'I still can't believe you're the brother Xavier said was educated in Jersey.'

'Why not?,' he said, his eyes narrowed as he glanced over at Xavier.

'Because you sound so English. You don't have a hint of a French accent when you speak,' she said without thinking.

He nodded, taking a seat opposite the girls.

'You're a count too?' Jess whispered, as soon as his parents began speaking to Xavier about something.

He looked over at them and smiled. 'I am,' he said, holding up a jug of icy water to see if either of them wanted their glasses filled.

Izzy nodded. Her throat was dry. She picked at the skin around her left thumb, trying to process what she'd just learnt.

Izzy pictured him at Catherine's home. 'I thought you were a gardener at the manor!'

He shrugged, filling his own glass before placing the jug back down onto the table. 'I am, of sorts. I work in the gardens and the stables.'

A grim thought occurred to her. 'Is Catherine's father your godfather? I thought he was your boss,' she said feeling foolish.

He tilted his head. 'He's still my boss.'

'So you're connected to Catherine.' Jess glared at him. 'I'm not sure we should really have come now.'

Izzy didn't dare open her mouth. He'd known how Catherine had almost ruined them. 'You obviously know Catherine well then?'

'Of course.'

'He is not being exact,' Xavier said, interrupting their flow of conversation. 'They were, how you say, childhood sweets?'

'Sweethearts?' Izzy asked, not happy to learn this fact about Ed and her nemesis.

Ed drank some water. 'But that was years ago, Xav.'

His gaze connected with Izzy's and she abruptly turned away to focus on her meal. She was happier to think Ed was an employee at Catherine's father's house; discovering he was his godson made her a little uneasy. She would have to watch what she said about Catherine in future. Damn, this wasn't what she'd expected to hear at all.

Izzy was relieved when Ed's parents started speaking to him. It gave her a chance to think things through. She could hear Jess mumbling something to herself and nudged her. 'Shush, they'll hear you.'

'But I've got a few things I need to ask him,' Jess said sulkily.

'Not now. Wait until he's alone later.'

Izzy finished her pâté and waited for the plate to be collected. Their next course was a clear consommé. She didn't want to be rude so resisted asking Ed any further questions and concentrated on eating the delicious soup. The boys chatted with their parents who obviously hadn't seen Ed for quite a while. And as indignant as she was to discover his closeness and history with Catherine, she couldn't help enjoying this meal. They were obviously a close family, despite living apart.

After a course of salad, another of meatloaf, and a tarte

tatin, the girls thanked the family and suggested they leave so they'd have some time alone together.

'Go anywhere you wish,' Xav said. 'Do not worry about becoming lost, we will come and find you soon.'

They calmly left the dining room and both girls walked back the way they'd come until they reached a hallway they didn't recognize. Aware they were far enough away not to be overheard, Izzy looked over her shoulder and sighed. 'Well, that was an experience, don't you think?'

'You're not kidding.' Jess puffed out her cheeks. 'I don't know what shocked me more, discovering the guys lived here, or that Ed was their brother and used to have a thing going with bloody Catherine.'

Izzy ignored the pang in her chest. 'I know. That was a bit of a shocker, wasn't it?'

'Yep. Come on, let's get out of here,' Jess said. She looked up and down the corridor. 'Which way, do you think?'

'Um, left,' Izzy said. She'd spotted the stables as they passed one of the windows on their way to lunch and thought they were as good a place as any to go and investigate.

They wandered around trying to find their way out, eventually exiting through a back door. Hurrying away from the main building, they crossed a square surrounded on two sides by the brick stables. They stopped to have a look around. Izzy spotted an inquisitive grey mare, and walked straight up to stroke her nose.

'Why do you think he invited us when he knew the predicament Catherine's elopement had left us in?' she asked.

'No idea,' Jess replied. 'I thought he was a decent bloke. Now it's made me question why he suggested we join the group when he didn't know us.'

Izzy agreed. She was usually a decent judge of character, but maybe this time she'd been a bit overwhelmed by his presence the other night to listen to her intuition.

'I think he could be a bit of a shit,' Jess said pulling a piece of hay from a hay-net. 'Do you think he's having a laugh at our expense?'

'Why would I do that?'

Both girls jumped to hear the voice, sounding cross and very much like he'd stepped out of a British public school, as Ed entered the doorway.

'You shouldn't eavesdrop,' Izzy snapped, embarrassed to have been caught talking behind his back.

'Not even if it's about me?'

'Especially when it's about you.' Jess glared at him. 'So, are you going to tell us?'

'What?' he asked, any amusement from earlier missing from his tone.

'Are you a bit of a shit, Ed?' Izzy asked.

His mouth drew back in a smile. 'No, I'm not.'

'Because?' Jess wasn't done yet. Izzy could tell she was more upset than even she'd assumed.

He thought for a moment. 'I felt bad about what Catherine's thoughtlessness had meant to your business, so when you said you had nothing on for a few weeks I thought you might enjoy the trip.'

'You never thought to mention you were related to her though?' Jess added. 'What are you, cousins?'

He frowned, his thick, dark eyebrows giving him an angrier look than Izzy believed he meant to convey. 'My godfather spent a lot of time with my mother's family growing up and I think they hoped the pair of them would get married. However, she met my father and chose him instead. They remained friends though and when I came along they asked him to be one of my godparents.'

'You don't sound at all French.' Jess said. 'Not one bit. It's very confusing.'

'Don't I?' He walked over and stroked the grey's neck,

46

smiling when she nuzzled his chest.

Izzy watched him with the horse, wondering if it was his own. 'You don't though. I honestly would have placed money on you being British, it's weird.'

He shrugged his broad shoulders. 'Years of being educated in Jersey, I guess.'

Izzy couldn't help wondering how much her brother knew about this close friend of his. 'Have you told Alex you're a count?'

'Probably not; it's not something I talk about when I'm in Jersey and he's never been here to stay, so I doubt it's come up in conversation.' He raised an eyebrow and smiled. 'He does know I'm French though.'

'Don't think you'll get away with this by trying to be funny,' Jess pouted. 'I'm still cross.'

Izzy wished she wouldn't do that, it made Jess look like she was flirting. Then it dawned on her that maybe she was. It was her turn to frown.

The three of them stood in an awkward silence in the stables. 'Do you ride?' he asked them eventually.

'Hell no,' Jess said. 'She does, though.'

He looked at Izzy and gave her a smile. 'Would you like to come out for a ride with me?'

She pictured seeing him riding on the manor land a few weeks ago and cleared her throat at the memory. 'When?'

'Now.'

'Right now?'

'Yes, why not?' He looked at her bare legs. 'But if you've brought a pair of jeans I think you'd better change into them first.'

'I'm not sure,' she said, not wishing Jess to feel left out.

'I'm fine,' Jess assured her. 'I'll find the others and they can show me round this enormous place. Go on, Izzy. You know you'd love to. You haven't ridden for ages, not since your mum had to sell Flash when you went to uni.'

Izzy smiled. 'Great,' she said to Ed. 'I'd love to.'

Looking much happier, he nodded. 'Go and change and I'll saddle up a couple of these brutes and meet you back here in, say, fifteen minutes?'

Izzy nodded and ran back into the château.

Glad she'd travelled in her jeans, she quickly changed back into them and raced back to the stables. She only got lost once on the way, which saved time.

A few minutes later, having been kitted out in a pair of slightly too large riding boots and the stable girl's hat, she took hold of the saddle and raised her left foot behind her so Ed could give her a leg-up. She must look heavier than she actually was, she decided when he lifted her with a little too much gusto, almost throwing her over the horse's withers.

'Sorry about that,' he said, grabbing her thigh to make sure she didn't fall off the other side. 'This is Gaston, he's Roman's favourite, but he can be a little feisty so make sure you hold on.'

Great, thought Izzy, excited at the prospect of her first ride in years. She loved an unpredictable horse and was relieved Ed hadn't acted all gentlemanly and put her on a quiet thing that ambled along. She was desperate to get going. 'I'm fine, thanks.'

He checked the girth and then the length of her stirrups, shortening them slightly. 'Comfortable?'

'Perfect,' she said almost sighing with contentment. It was wonderfully familiar to be sitting on a saddle, especially a beautifully made one like this. She recognised it as a Toptani – she'd been lucky enough to own a third-hand one when she'd competed on Flash.

'I thought so.'

Izzy watched Ed take hold of the reins and mount his own horse. He's magnificent, she thought, watching Ed squeeze gently with his heels to make the black gelding walk on. 'We'll warm them up first and then I'll take you out across the meadow over there at the end of the lawn.'

They walked out of the yard in silence and Izzy began to feel mean for the way she and Jess had questioned Ed earlier. 'I'm sorry we overreacted a bit when we discovered who you really were,' she said, straightening the hat and patting her horse's neck as they broke into a trot.

'It's fine, don't worry.' He smiled. 'I forget I sound different to my brothers. I suppose it's a case of wanting to fit in with the other boarders when I was sent to school. It's not much fun being a homesick teenager, as well as having a different nationality to most of the other pupils.'

'I can imagine,' she said remembering how different she'd always felt having a slightly eccentric mother. 'My mum isn't what you'd call the norm, and to be honest I don't tell people about my family background either.'

'I'm glad you and Jess agreed to come along on this trip, Izzy. It'll give us all a chance to have a break.' They trotted along one side of the lawn, heading for the meadow. 'Xavier and Roman are typically painful brothers sometimes, but they really are great guys and I know you're going to get on well with them.'

She suspected he was right. She breathed in the warm air, scented by the pine trees they passed.

'Right, time to get these guys moving,' he said. 'They've been allowed to be lazy for far too long and Beau here loves a good gallop.'

Izzy's horse immediately copied his and they broke into a slow canter. It was bliss, with the wind in her hair and the sunshine on her bare arms. Izzy couldn't stop smiling. It was also great to be away from the others. She never really enjoyed having to make small talk.

She slowed slightly to watch Ed. He must have ridden since he was tiny, she decided; he was so natural on the back of a horse and it was wonderful to watch.

When they were further away from the château, he

looked back over his shoulder at her. 'Shall we go for it?'

She nodded, unable to hide her delight at the prospect.

'OK, first one to that copse over there chooses a forfeit for the other, agreed?'

'No problem,' she said.

Before he had a chance to start their race, Izzy squeezed her heels against her horse. He sprung into a fast canter and soon a gallop. She squealed with excitement and, eager to help him go as fast as possible, stood in her stirrups, bending her knees and leaning forward over the horse's neck. She could hear the thud of Ed's horse's hooves on the grass near to her own and turned to see how far behind her he was. Spotting him closing in on her, she shrieked with excitement and urged her horse on faster.

'Go on, you can do it, boy,' she said, sitting back in her saddle. Just when she thought she was there, Ed's horse surged in front, reaching the copse a nose before she did.

'No!' she shouted, gently pulling on her reins to slow him down. She patted the velvety neck as they cut their speed down to a slow canter. 'Good boy, good boy.'

'You're a fantastic rider,' Ed said as they slowed to a trot. 'You must have ridden for years.'

'Since I was four,' she admitted. 'My dad bought me my first pony when I was seven and my mum never forgave him for getting me into such an expensive hobby. Anyway, you're not so bad yourself.'

'Thanks.' He patted Beau's sweaty neck. 'I think we'll take these two into the copse. It's shaded and there's a small pool where they can have a drink.

'Good idea.' Now they'd stopped she realized she was hot and probably had a bright pink face from the excitement and energy she'd put into her race.

They dismounted, then, taking the reins over their horses' necks, crossed to the pond.

Izzy stopped with Gaston next to the water and stroked his neck as he bent down to drink. She bent down and pushed a hand into the cool liquid, wiping it across her face and behind her neck. 'It's hotter than I realized,' she said, aware for the first time that Ed was watching her. 'What?'

'Your forfeit,' he said, his eyes shining mischievously.

'Ahh, I'd forgotten about that.'

'Conveniently,' he teased.

She could see he was planning something. 'Go on then, what do I have to do?'

'Let me think,' he said, grinning.

Izzy held up her free hand. 'If it involves me being naked you can forget it.'

'That's a shame, now I'll have to think of something else.'

She narrowed her eyes. 'Yes, you'd better. I'm a guest here, remember? You should behave like the gentleman you're supposed to be when you're with me.'

He laughed. 'Fine, then you have to promise you'll agree to my second choice.'

'No chance, I'm not agreeing to anything unless I know what it is.'

She watched him trying not to laugh as he walked up to her. He raised his hand to her cheek and rested it there for a second before slipping his hand behind her head and lowering his head, pulling her gently to him, kissing her.

It was so unexpected, it took Izzy a few seconds to register what he was doing, but by that point the sensation of his mouth on hers and his arms around her were enough to wipe everything from her mind. She kissed him right back. Finally he released her and stepped back.

'I'm going to have to beat you in another race if this is what happens afterwards,' he teased, his dark eyes like pools of melted chocolate.

Izzy would happily have lost a thousand races right then. Boy, he was some kisser. Maybe it was true what they said about French men. She stopped her train of thought as the colour rushed to her face. 'It's hot today,' she said, reverting to talking about the weather when she couldn't think what else to say.

Ed smiled. 'It's very hot.' He stroked his horse's face and smiled when Beau nuzzled him. Izzy would have liked to do the same, but managed to restrain herself. 'I think our boat trip is going to be interesting.'

'Me too,' she said, relishing the prospect even more now.

'The others arrive tomorrow and they're all great fun, I think you'll get on well with them.' He gave her a last kiss and smiled. 'I'm so pleased you agreed to come along, even though I'm not the guy you thought I was.'

'Shut up,' Izzy laughed, punching him lightly on his bicep.

They mounted their horses and walked back to the stables, chatting about Alex. She discovered that Ed also surfed.

'Alex told me he couldn't come along because he had a surfing competition this weekend and something else on next week. How come you aren't taking part?' she asked.

Ed raked a hand through his hair, causing it to stick up in places. 'My brothers arranged this and as we don't often get the chance to spend quality time together I thought it was more important to join them on the boat trip than entering a competition I could go in for next year.'

'Or maybe you knew you couldn't beat my brother,' she teased. 'So didn't bother trying.'

He laughed a deep throaty laugh that made her giggle. 'It could have been that, I suppose.'

As they neared the stables, Izzy spotted Jess waiting for them, arms folded, a scowl on her pretty face. 'Oh dear, I think something's happened.'

'What's the matter?' Ed asked, when they reached her, dismounting and taking hold of Izzy's reins.

'Apparently two of the original party has had to pull

out of the trip because their mother has fallen ill, and you'll never bloody guess who's going to be joining us now?'

Izzy exchanged glances with Ed. She could tell he knew as well as she did that there was only one person who could infuriate Jess this much. 'Catherine?'

'Yes, bloody Catherine.'

Ed glanced in the direction of the château. 'Leave your horse with me, Izzy,' he said. 'You go with Jess. I'll sort these two out.'

'Thanks,' Izzy said, not bothering to hide her sarcasm. She would have much rather spent a bit more time with the horses, and, she admitted to herself, Ed. Listening to Jess rant about Catherine again wasn't something she relished doing. 'I'll see you later.'

'Yes, we'll meet in the room next to the tower for drinks before dinner. Six thirty suit you both?'

'Yes, see you then.' Izzy and Ed stared at each other. She couldn't help smiling and wondered if he'd enjoyed the afternoon as much as she had.

'Are you coming?' Jess shouted from across the quadrangle.

'See you then,' Izzy said quietly, before running to catch up with her friend.

Chapter Five

Ed watched her run to Jess. He suspected she was oblivious to how sexy she'd looked racing him to the copse. He was relieved she hadn't dwelt for too long on his identity. He'd learnt at a young age not to tell anyone about his family unless it was an absolute necessity. Too many women had been attracted to his older brothers for their title.

He undid Beau's girth and lifted the saddle from the horse's back, resting it on the stable door. Then, unfastening the noseband and throatlatch he carefully lifted the bridle over his ears. That kiss, Ed mused. It was as if they fitted. He knew it was one thing to be attracted to a woman, but another entirely for them to connect on that level. Kissing her was like nothing he'd ever experienced before. She looked so angelic, with her platinum blonde hair and big blue eyes, but when their lips connected he'd felt a shock through his entire body. He was in serious danger of making a fool out of himself with her.

He rubbed both horses down and leaned against the doorway, staring out at the quadrangle in the direction he'd last seen Izzy.

Izzy groaned. It had been difficult to make Jess understand that she was just as fed up with Catherine as Jess had been, but that being confined to a small boat for nearly three weeks was not the place to keep up a grudge. 'There's nothing we can do about it now,' Izzy said, checking her reflection in the mirror and smoothing down the skirt of her slightly less creased dress.

Jess mumbled something, but Izzy couldn't make it out. 'Hurry up, will you?' she said, opening the bedroom door and waiting for Jess to join her. 'We're going to be late if we're not careful.'

'The thought of having to put up with that snooty cow has given me a stinking headache,' Jess moaned as they hurried down the corridors, trying to find the rest of the guests. 'It's all bloody Catherine's fault.'

'Will you stop referring to her as "bloody Catherine". This family are very fond of her.'

'You don't know that,' Jess said, rubbing her left temple and wincing.

'The families are close, though, and don't forget her dad is Ed's godfather. So don't go on about her unless we're by ourselves somewhere, OK?'

Without waiting for an answer, Izzy knocked on the door to the room she hoped was the right one where they were all meeting for their pre-dinner drinks.

It was.

The brothers welcomed them both with kisses, as did the parents, and introduced them to a new man they hadn't met before. Stefan wasn't as tall as Ed or his brothers, but he was very blond and had a twinkle in his eye. Roman explained that Stefan would be the one in charge of the boat and would be instructing them when sailing.

'Sometimes I have to deliver boats to new owners, but this one is a friend's' he explained. 'He said he didn't mind if I made a holiday of the trip with some friends.'

'You're very lucky being able to sail as part of your job,' Jess said.

He pulled a doubtful expression in her direction. 'Not always. You will have to forgive me on the first day because I am always very seasick for the first eight hours of any trip.'

Recalling the ferry journey this morning, Izzy couldn't understand why he would want to sail if he had to go through that hell each time, and said so, making a mental note to buy seasickness medicine the first opportunity she got.

He shrugged a shoulder. 'I love the sea and sailing, and I refuse to let it get the better of me. It's not too bad and I know it will pass.'

The two other new members of the group were very slim, long-haired women. 'Nicolle and Loulou,' Roman said, as the girls smiled perfect smiles to their English counterparts. Izzy and Jess smiled at the blonde girl with the shiny hair and dark crimson lipstick. She looked so chic in her navy capri trousers and red cotton top, a red silk polka dot scarf tied around her neck.

'Ed?' the one they thought must be Nicolle asked, taking hold of his arm and leading him over to the cocktail cabinet at the end of the room. She was murmuring something to him and a pang of jealousy pierced Izzy.

'Blimey, talk about chic,' Jess whispered when they sat down next to each other, both trying not to stare at Nicolle.

'*Bonjour*,' Loulou said, coming over to speak to them with her arm linked through Roman's.

'Hi,' Izzy said, waiting for Jess to speak.

'Great to meet you,' Jess said finally. 'I think this is going to be a great trip.'

'We will have much fun, *non*?' She looked up through long black lashes at Xavier and Izzy could tell he was smitten.

'We will,' Izzy said, nudging Jess who then nodded in reluctant agreement.

Izzy could see Jess was a little out of her comfort zone, probably because she was feeling the same way. How did these girls get to be so slender, she wondered; did they survive on fresh air? She and Jess weren't exactly overweight, but they would never be as svelte as these two.

Jess rubbed her temple and grimaced. The Countess

noticed and jerked her head to Xavier. 'She is ill?'

'Jess has a headache,' Izzy explained. 'A, um, *mal a la tête.*'

She looked concerned. '*Médicament?*' She held her index and thumb two centimetres apart.

Jess didn't answer.

'Do you want a pill, Jess?' Izzy said.

Jess smiled. '*Oui, merci.*'

The Countess left the room.

'How embarrassing,' Jess said. 'I didn't mean for everyone to notice.'

They heard the Countess speaking rapidly to someone in the hallway, she soon returned holding what looked like a cross between a large pill and a small tampon and handed it to Jess.

'You will need help with the, err, pill?' she asked.

Jess shook her head. '*Non, merci.*'

The others in the group laughed. Jess and Izzy exchanged confused glances. 'What's so amusing?' Jess asked, annoyed. 'Why would I need help taking a pill?'

Ed leaned slightly towards them. 'They're amused because the pill is not one you swallow.'

'How do I take it then?' Jess asked starring at the object in the palm of her hand. The others waited a few seconds while Jess worked it out. Then, her mouth falling open, she almost dropped it. Her eyes widened. 'I have to …?'

Izzy nodded. Jess looked mortified at the prospect.

Laughing, the group turned away and began chatting about their trip.

Jess grabbed Izzy's arm. 'Iz, I'm supposed to stick this up my bum?'

Izzy nodded. 'I think it gets into your system quicker that way.'

'But the Countess offered to help me.'

Izzy giggled, unable to help herself. Jess looked horrified at this prospect.

'People in France take suppositories as a matter of course,' Ed said, not in the slightest bit embarrassed to be discussing the subject. 'They, that is we, think the Brits are a little odd for having such a problem with the concept, it really is very simple. Maman knows you might find this strange, which is why she offered to help you insert it.'

Jess frowned. 'Her offering to help me was what weirded me out,' she snapped.

'Jess, that's so rude.' Izzy glared at her.

Ed laughed. 'I think we all got that, but don't worry, you'll be fine if you just do it without over-thinking.'

Jess stared at the suppository. 'I think I've changed my mind, this headache isn't too unbearable.'

'Wuss,' Izzy teased. 'Go on, you'll be fine.'

'That's easy to say when it's not you having to do it.'

Izzy had to agree, but didn't let Jess know how she really thought. The headache had been troubling her for hours. 'Go now and do it, while everyone is chatting and won't notice you've gone.'

Jess looked unimpressed, but finished her drink and quietly slipped out of the room.

Ed walked over and sat in Jess's chair next to Izzy. 'I forget how British people react to suppositories,' he laughed. 'Poor thing, do you think she'll take it?'

Izzy shrugged. 'I hope so, if it means she shifts that headache. It was making her miserable. Would your mother really have done it for her?'

He shrugged, 'Of course. She wouldn't have been bothered in the slightest.'

Izzy could never understand how, living so close to France, with so much of the French influence throughout the history of Jersey, the locals seemed so very different to their French counterparts.

'I enjoyed our race today,' he said.

Izzy was glad he was changing the subject. 'It was great fun.'

'We'll have time to go out again in the morning, if we get up early. The grounds are beautiful just after sunrise with the mist covering the lower meadow.'

She loved the idea and said so. 'Will you wake me, just to make sure I don't oversleep?'

'Of course.' He looked up as Jess came back to join them. 'Five thirty OK for you?'

'Perfect,' Izzy replied.

He got up to let Jess take her seat. 'Everything OK?'

She beamed at him. 'If it works as well as I'm hoping, then yes.' She waited for Ed to walk away and join the others and leaned over to Izzy. 'That was actually far easier than I'd expected.'

Izzy sighed. 'Good. I suppose you'll need another drink now.'

'Hell, yes.'

Izzy didn't need to be woken by Ed in the end. She'd spent half the night dreaming that she was oversleeping, and so rose half an hour before he was due to wake her, and crept down to the bathroom to wash her face and clean her teeth. By the time he knocked quietly on her bedroom door she was dressed.

She pulled open the door. 'Hi.'

He looked surprised to see her ready to leave. 'I've saddled the horses and made us a coffee each. If you're ready,' he whispered, smiling at her, 'we can get going now.' He stood back to let her pass.

'I'll follow you,' she said. 'I still don't know my way around this place.'

He began walking. 'It is a bit of a labyrinth.'

'You must miss being here very much,' she whispered as they reached the back stairs and made their way down to the kitchen. 'Did you come back to the château in the school holidays?'

'Yes, most of the time, but my parents were very busy

trying to make this place work then. They catered for groups of people holding weddings and big parties here on the lawns or in the ballroom in winter, so occasionally they asked my uncle to keep me with him.'

Izzy nearly missed her footing on the bottom step, but Ed quickly reached out to catch her. Once she was fully upright again, she said. 'You have a ballroom?'

'I know, it does sound a bit odd, but this place is five hundred years old, and it has been refigured a few times since then. When my father was growing up his parents used to hold many parties.'

'Can you show it to me when we get back?'

'If there's time, but we're going to have to push it if we're to make breakfast at seven and we have to leave at eight to get to Marseille on time.'

Ed led them into the vast kitchen. She looked around the room, unable to see anything more modern than an old cooking range and four-ringed cooker that looked similar to the one her mother had replaced ten years before.

'It's a bit antiquated,' he said, handing her a cup of cooling coffee that was a bit strong for her taste. 'But no one apart from family usually comes down here.

She took a sip, trying not to wince. 'Those are amazing,' she said, certain her mother would covet the shiny copper pans hanging from the ceiling.

'My mother swears by them,' he said. 'although she doesn't cook very often. Come on, we'd better get a move on.'

Chapter Six

Who was this girl and why hadn't he met her before, Ed wondered as they hurried out across the quadrangle to the stables. Then again, Jersey might only be nine miles by five in size, but there were many inhabitants he had never met before. So many busy lives packed into a small island. Smiling, he took her hand and ran with her across the quadrangle lawn. 'Wait there, I'll get Gaston for you,' he said when they reached the archway to the stables.

He led her horse out of its stable and took hold of Izzy's shin to give her a leg up. This time he made sure not to almost catapult her over the horse. He didn't need to damage the poor girl with too much exuberance. Not that she wasn't tough, he mused. She was willowy and tall, with wild, blonde hair and a beautiful face, but it was her strength of character he was most attracted to. She had seemed very relaxed in front of his family, too, which was always comforting. It was a relief to meet someone who accepted his parents as they would anyone else's. He pushed away the memories of previous girlfriends, some who had wanted to be seen with him simply because of who he was.

'Are you all right?' Izzy asked, bringing him back to the present again. 'You look like you're in another world.'

'I'm probably not completely awake yet,' he fibbed. 'Come on, let's get these two devils outside.' He took his horse out of the stable and mounted. 'OK?' he asked.

She nodded, unable contain her excitement. 'This is so much fun,' she said. 'Thank you for getting up early to take me out.'

He didn't admit that it was he who should be thanking her, for it had been a joy to ride out with her the previous day and he was delighted with the unexpected bonus of spending time alone with her.

She nodded. 'I've been so excited about it that I barely slept,' she admitted.

They broke into a trot and soon they were out beyond the château lawns and cantering towards the meadow. 'You're right,' Izzy shouted, indicating the misty view ahead. 'It's magical out here at this time in the morning.'

He didn't want to go too fast yet, not until he was certain the mist was high enough for them to see exactly where they were going, so they kept to a gentle canter. He let her go slightly ahead of him to be able to give her a discreet look. She seemed so in charge.

'Hey,' Izzy shouted.

Ed looked up and noticed she was looking at him over her shoulder. She turned away to watch where she was going, not slowing down.

'You should be concentrating on where you're going, not my backside,' she teased.

Laughing, he urged his horse on to catch up with her, not bothering to admit that he'd been daydreaming. 'Sorry, I forgot myself.'

'Don't worry, I don't mind. Not this time, anyway.' She smiled at him and he was relieved to see she was amused rather than insulted.

They continued their gentle canter and he wished they had longer to stay out riding. As much as he had been looking forward to this trip, being out in the grounds of his favourite place with Izzy was more enjoyable.

'Jess is still a bit miffed about Catherine joining us on this trip,' Izzy said breaking his train of thought. 'I hope you don't take offence if she goes on about it a bit.'

'I'm not too happy she's coming either,' he said honestly. 'Don't worry about Jess's reaction though, I understand her feelings towards Catherine, especially after the way she's let you two down.' Catherine's selfish behaviour often infuriated him, and he wondered when she'd start thinking before acting. Probably never.

'It's a shame the other two who were originally supposed to join us had to pull out at the last moment,' he said, not wishing the girls to be angry with his brothers. 'I'd have been happy for the group to stay as it was, to be honest, but I think once everyone gets used to each other, they'll all get on well. Catherine might be spoilt, but she can be good fun.'

'I don't know her well enough to have seen her fun side yet,' Izzy said, waving away a bumble bee. 'A part of me feels a bit guilty for going on this trip and not staying behind to try and drum up business, but when we did try we couldn't find any bookings.'

'I really am sorry about the cancelled wedding party,' he said for his friend's part in their problems. 'I'm sure she'd be devastated to discover how badly it has affected you both.'

Izzy pulled a face. 'It's not your fault she eloped. It's our stupid fault for not making sure she signed our contract and was liable for a cancellation fee. We'll never do that again.'

'I'll do anything I can to help you, you know,' he said, wishing he could think of some way to help them resolve their financial problems. 'You only have to ask.'

'Thank you,' she said. 'but I'm sure we'll work it out somehow.'

Beau was getting fretful. He'd come this way too many times not to be aware that the meadow was the perfect place for a gallop. Ed studied the mist ahead of them, deciding that it seemed clear enough to let the horses go. Gaston, sensing Beau's excitement, began a little impatient dance, bucking and rearing.

'I think we'd better let these two get some of their

energy out of their system,' he said. 'What do you say?'

'Oh yes!'

Soothed by the joy in her face, he nodded. 'What are we waiting for then?' Without waiting for her to reply, he squeezed his heels against his horse's flanks, ready for the surge forward as it took off. He heard Izzy scream in delight behind him and laughed. She really was the most gorgeous woman he'd ever spent time with.

They loosened their reins, and Ed allowed Beau to go ahead of Gaston, relishing the warm morning air as they raced across the grass.

'I'm not kissing you if you beat me this time,' she called.

He laughed. The horses began to tire as they reached the copse, and slowed down to a canter and then to a slow trot. Ed stroked Beau's muscular neck. 'Good boy,' he soothed. He was going to miss this when he went back to Jersey. Despite there being a big riding fraternity in the island, he preferred not to compete, and in Jersey there wasn't the space to ride over fields without having to think about crossing roads, as he could here in France.

Izzy caught up to him, breathing hard, partially from exertion and party from the excitement of the gallop, he assumed. 'That was brilliant,' she said, giving him a wide grin. 'I think we should forget the sailing trip and stay here.'

He knew she was only joking, but Ed wished they really could do such a thing. 'Just you, me, and the horses.'

She sighed. 'Yes.' Then turning her head to look at him as she stroked Gaston's sweaty neck, she added. 'Wouldn't that be bliss?'

He nodded. She had no idea how much he was tempted to do just as she'd suggested. He sat in silence next to her as their horses walked lazily towards the side of the meadow.

'We haven't had any time off in the past three years,' she said eventually. 'If we haven't had a party to cater for, we've been sourcing vintage crockery and linens and publicising our business at wedding fayres. It's taken a while to build up a decent clientele and I suppose we'll just have to put this recent loss down to experience.'

'Very true.'

Ed stopped his horse and when Izzy's paused next to him he pointed out the village in the distance, with its stone spire sticking up out of the haze. 'The pool back there to the side of the lawns is where I learnt to swim,' he said changing the subject to something less likely to ruin her mood.

Izzy looked thoughtful. 'You mean the one with green water? I thought that was a large pond.'

Ed laughed. He was used to friends being surprised by their ancient stone pool when they'd come here on their first visit. 'It doesn't look much like the chlorinated pools most people have, that's true, and it's always freezing, but in the height of the summer it's perfect.'

Izzy laughed. 'I'll take your word for it,' she said.

He watched her. She was so happy despite her recent disappointment. Tired of being responsible and not acting on his instincts, Ed leaned over towards her. Come here for a moment, will you?'

'Why?' Izzy laughed, not sure what he wanted. She did as he asked, though, and brought Beau up next to Gaston's side so that her stirrup accidentally banged against Ed's ankle. She winced. 'Sorry,' she said, grimacing.

'It's fine,' he resisted the urge to rub it. She looked so concerned about him that he smiled, wanting to reassure her that he was fine.

When her knee was resting against his, he reached out and putting his hand behind her head, pulled her gently towards him and kissed her. She didn't resist. Her cool lips meeting his sent sparks through him. Ed realized that despite his usual reticence towards romance, he was in danger of falling very heavily for this girl.

Remembering the choice he was soon going to have to make, he pulled back. 'You're very lovely, Izzy,' he said, wishing life didn't have to be so complicated. 'I've really enjoyed spending time with you here.'

'Likewise,' she said, collecting her horse's reins.

He made a pretence of checking his watch. 'I think it's time we went back now.'

She nodded. He could see she was a little taken aback by his sudden change of mood. 'One last canter though,' he suggested, not wishing to upset her.

She smiled once again. 'Great, I don't know when I'll get the chance to do this again, and I can't imagine it'll ever be in such glorious surroundings.'

'Come on then,' he said. He watched her horse shoot forward and followed, struck by the sight of the woman in front of him riding with such expertise and enjoyment, her long hair flowing behind her as she almost flew towards the château. It was a vision he knew he'd never forget. His home and this woman, like two pieces in a fantasy puzzle. Unable to bear the thought a moment longer, he urged Beau on till he was alongside her. Izzy looked across at him, delight in her beautiful face as she leaned further forward in an effort to beat him. He wished he could capture this moment and hold on to it for ever.

She sat back in her saddle pulling gently on the reins to slow her horse as Ed did the same next to her. They brought their horses to a trot and then a walk. 'They're never going to cool down if we take them in now,' she said.

Much as he wanted to carry on riding out here, they really did need to get back. 'We're going to have to leave them with the stable hands unfortunately. We still have to shower and change for breakfast.' She looked so disappointed he placed a hand comfortingly on her arm. 'I can't not have breakfast with my parents today.'

'Oh, how selfish of me.'

'It's fine, I feel the same as you.'

'They must miss you very much and you've only had one night here this time.'

He nodded. 'I'll come back to see them again soon, although it won't be soon enough for my mother.'

'Look,' she pointed. 'Is that one of the staff from the stables waiting by the corner of the château?'

'It is.'

They dismounted and patted the horses. He watched Izzy giving Gaston a pat before handing him over to the stable hand. He then walked her back to her room, pausing outside her bedroom door.

'I've enjoyed our rides very much, Izzy,' he said. 'I'm glad we had some time alone to get to know each other a bit before being crammed on the boat with the others.'

'Me too,' she said, standing on tiptoe to give him a kiss.

He put his arms around her, but then a door opened and Xav whooped, making Izzy jump and Ed want to hit him for ruining the moment.

'Casanova,' Xav teased. 'Where have you been? I looked for you earlier in your room.'

'I took Izzy out for a ride,' Ed said, glaring at his brother over Izzy's head, willing him to go back into his room and leave them for these precious few minutes. 'We'll see you at breakfast.'

Xav didn't move.

Izzy stepped away from him into her room. 'I'd better get in that shower. I don't want to keep your mother waiting.'

He watched her close the door, aware that there probably wouldn't be many, if any, occasions on their trip where they could spend time alone, and wished he'd thought to say so much more to her. Although, he decided, it was probably better if he kept his thoughts to himself. He began walking to his own room at the other end of the corridor, ignoring Xavier as he passed him.

'What's the matter, little brother?' Xav laughed. 'She's very pretty, isn't she?'

Ed stopped and turned to him. 'Yes, she is, and you have a girlfriend back in Paris, no doubt, so don't play games with her, or her friend.'

'Or you, eh?'

Ed sighed heavily; he wasn't in the mood for his brother's teasing. 'I have to freshen up, Xav. Go to breakfast, one of us has to be there on time.'

Chapter Seven

Izzy was relieved not to be sitting next to Ed on the train to Marseille: his presence made her feel disconcerted, which she doubly hated because she liked to be in control. She listened as Roman told them that Catherine and her husband would be meeting them in Marseille. Stefan had left the château a couple of hours before them to get a head start and complete any paperwork, so only she, Jess, Ed, Xavier, Roman, and the two other girls were travelling together.

'Xavier, he says you make pretty weddings with plates?' Loulou said.

'Not quite,' Jess said, before going on to explain in a little more detail what exactly it was that Lapins de Lune did. 'We're event planners and we arrange weddings and large, or small, parties for clients. We hire out our collection of vintage crockery and linens and also use them in our events if they're suitable.'

'The French name, why did you choose it?' Nicolle asked.

'My last name is Le Lievre,' Izzy explained. 'Which means "the hare". I've also always had a thing about moon rabbits since my grandfather had a ceramic one in his garden that looked up at the sky.'

'Yes,' Jess continued. 'And my last name is Moon, so we came up with Lapins de Lune: the moon rabbits.'

The girls considered this information and whispered something to each other. 'That is very clever,' Loulou said eventually. 'And of course Ed he says that there are a lot of French road and house names in Jersey?'

'Yes, so having a French name for our business isn't something people find odd.' Izzy was enjoying getting to know the two girls a little better. 'So, what do you do then?' she asked them.

'I am a lawyer,' Nicolle said.

Both Izzy and Jess couldn't hide their surprise, or how impressed they were.

'Wow,' Jess said. 'You must be pretty clever to do that for a living.'

Nicolle shrugged and smiled. '*Non, pas du tout*, it is simply studying and passing exams.'

Izzy nodded. 'Yes, but years of studying and pretty difficult exams to pass. Good for you.'

Loulou held her hands out as if to show off her outfit. Izzy frowned, unable to work out what she was indicating. She couldn't possibly be a model, she was too tiny for that. She racked her brains to come up with something. 'You're a designer?'

'*Non*,' Loulou laughed. 'I would like to be one, but I work in a boutique.'

'Ahh,' Izzy pointed at Loulou's pretty summer dress. 'That's lovely, is it from the shop where you work?'

Loulou nodded. 'Yes.'

Nicolle said something to Loulou in French. Izzy was unable to catch it, but picked up that she'd mentioned Loulou's mother.

'Her mother,' Nicolle explained, 'she is a designer in Paris. She has a, how you say, row of shops?'

'Um, a chain of shops, maybe,' Jess offered.

'*Oui*, that exactly,' Nicolle nodded. 'Loulou runs one of the shops for her mother.'

'Yes,' Loulou said. 'I have two older sisters who run the other four shops between them. I like working at the shop very much.'

'Can't be bad having a mum who designs gorgeous clothes either,' Jess said enviously.

Loulou nodded. 'Yes, I like it very much.'

Xavier stopped chatting to his brothers and perched on the edge of Loulou's seat, resting his arm along the back of it. 'You ladies must stop talking about work,' he laughed. 'We are on holiday and must decide what we will be doing when we set sail on the yacht.'

'Yes,' Loulou giggled. 'We must plan some fun times.'

Nicolle joined in the chatter, giving Izzy the chance to peer over to where Ed was sitting deep in conversation with Roman. Whatever it was they were discussing looked serious and she hoped nothing had happened to cause them concern.

Once they were off the train and had made their way to the port, Izzy and Jess stopped to breathe in the warm, salty air. 'This is the start of our holiday now, Iz,' Jess said closing her eyes and turning her face up to the sun.

Izzy did the same for a few seconds, relishing the heat on her face. 'I'm already feeling a hundred per cent more relaxed than I did yesterday.'

'Me too,' Jess sighed.

They heard Roman calling them and realizing they would be left behind if they didn't get a move on. Izzy nudged Jess and pointed to the others.

'You're looking much happier today, too,' she said. 'So that issue with the suppository was OK in the end?' she whispered as they followed the others along the wide, pale stone walkways to go and find Stefan and the boat that would be their home for the next three weeks.

Jess nodded. 'I'm a convert,' she giggled. 'I'm going to buy more of them before I go back home, they're brilliant.'

'Isn't is glorious here?' Izzy asked, gazing round the huge expanse of water, so neatly surrounded on three sides by the stone promenade and road, then tall, majestic stone buildings. At the top of the port Jess and Izzy wandered along the stalls selling touristy gifts and fresh fish still being unloaded from the small fishing boats moored to the quay wall.

'Bloody hell, look at them,' Jess said, giggling.

Izzy turned to stare in amusement at two gendarmes on Segways. They stopped at the end of the promenade, checked no one was walking past, and sped off along the port. 'Now that's a unique mode of transport for a policeman,' she laughed. 'Do you think those would go down well in Jersey?'

Jess laughed. 'Probably not.'

It was so bright and clean that Izzy found it hard to imagine this place ever being the den of iniquity that her mother had described before she'd left home earlier in the week. 'So many magnificent boats here, too, Alex would love it.'

Jess pouted. 'Yes, I thought so too. Such a shame he couldn't come with us.'

Izzy didn't say anything. 'I wonder which yacht is ours?' she said.

They caught up with the others just as Roman was telling Xavier to take the group to a nearby square for coffees while he tracked down Stefan. 'I'll meet you all there soon.'

Xavier led the way, chatting to Loulou, who giggled and cheekily patted his firm bottom. 'Love's young dream,' Jess whispered.

Izzy smiled. 'It's going to be interesting when we're all crammed on a small boat together.'

Jess narrowed her eyes and smiled. 'Do I detect a hint of envy there?' she teased.

'No, you do not,' Izzy said shaking her head, aware her friend knew her too well to believe her protestations. She didn't admit that it was going to be difficult being in such close contact with Ed and on the yacht and not being able to kiss him whenever she felt the need.

'Just as well by the looks of those two,' Jess said. 'I think if there isn't already something going on, there soon will be.' Jess put an arm round Izzy's shoulders. 'I'm just worried about being with bloody Catherine and resisting the urge to push her overboard,' she added.

'Jess, I said …'

Jess laughed. 'I know. I must stop calling her that. I was only doing it to wind you up.'

'Well, it worked. And don't you dare push her off the boat.'

'As if I would,' Jess giggled.

'This place looks good,' Ed said as they arrived at a café. He pushed two tables together. 'Coffees?'

'Cappuccino for me, please,' Izzy said.

'Do you have the Wi-Fi code?' Ed asked. The waiter wrote it down on a slip of paper and handed it to him. Ed placed it on the table. 'Here you go. If anyone wants to send a message home, now's the time to do it. We won't have any Wi-Fi on the yacht.'

'What if there's an emergency?' Jess asked.

Xavier smiled. 'Don't worry, we have a radio on board.'

Izzy typed in the code for the Wi-Fi and quickly sent a message to Alex and one to her mum. She then logged on to their website to see if they'd had any emails and apart from a couple of vague queries, which she answered, there were no new bookings. Her heart sank. She didn't want to go home early, but the prospect of a July without any earnings was frightening. Bloody Catherine.

'Everything OK?' Ed asked, moving his seat closer.

The proximity of his leg to hers made her pulse race.

'Fine thanks. I was just letting Alex know we were in Marseille and about to leave.'

'Bookings?' he asked quietly.

'Nope,' she said, unable to keep concern from her voice.

75

He turned to face her. 'It'll work out somehow,' he assured her. 'Try to enjoy this time away, if you can.'

He reached out and rested his hand lightly on her back.

Izzy cleared her throat and nodded. 'I will,' she said.

They'd barely had time to start their drinks when Roman arrived in the square. Izzy spotted him looking from café to café trying to find them. 'There's Roman now,' she said to Ed.

He stood up and waved him over. 'Found him?'

'*Oui,*' then seeing the girls, said. 'Er, we must hurry back to the boat for Stefan.'

'Better drink up, you guys.' Ed picked up his tiny cup of espresso and downed it, waiting for Izzy and Jess to drink their coffees at a more sedate speed. The other girls, also having ordered espressos, were standing and waiting for them within seconds.

'Blimey, this is hot,' Jess said, blowing frantically on her drink.

Eventually, they were ready and walked with Ed and the others to the boat.

'Oh my God, look at the name,' Jess said quietly. '*Le Rêve.*'

'Yes, *The Dream.*' Izzy was looking forward to having a few long nights' dreaming, hopefully assisted by being rocked to sleep by the motion of the boat.

'No, doughnut, I meant it's our very own dreamboat.'

Izzy was struggling to work out what Jess meant. 'Sorry?'

'*The Dream* boat.'

'Er, yes?'

'Well, isn't Ed your very own dreamboat? I know Roman's mine.'

Izzy laughed and shook her head. 'I think you need to catch up on your sleep like I do, Jess.'

They stood on the quay and stared at the wooden yacht in front of them which, Izzy was shocked to discover, was only forty-six feet in length. 'Are we all going to fit on that?' she asked.

'There are three double berths,' Stefan shouted down from the deck, not bothering to hide his amusement at her shock. 'At night a two-man bed can be made up in the galley. We'll take it in turns to sleep in the berths and each night two people will sleep on deck to keep an eye on everything. We don't want to all be asleep if another ship passes by us, do we?'

'I'm not sleeping on the deck,' Jess said, grimacing at Izzy. 'I wouldn't know what to do if anything happened.'

Stefan tilted his head. 'I will teach you; it will be OK.'

Izzy wasn't certain she would want to keep watch on the deck either, but thought she'd find out exactly what it entailed before causing a fuss. Anyway, Catherine and her new husband still hadn't arrived and she hoped that maybe they might have changed their minds about joining them. Then they could all have more space.

'It's beautiful,' Izzy said, knowing nothing about boats but loving the sleek lines.

'I'm not climbing up there,' Jess said, pointing to the top of the mast.

'I can't imagine Stefan will ask you to,' Izzy laughed, hoping she was right. 'It's an impressive boat though, don't you think?'

'Certainly is.'

'Girls,' Roman called the four of them on board. 'Pass me your bags.' He took them and handed them over to Ed who was standing next to him on the deck. 'Come this way and I'll show you to your cabins.'

They followed him down the narrow wooden stairs. 'You two are on the port side,' Stefan said from the galley. When they looked confused he pointed to a door at the back of the boat on the left. 'Nicolle *et* Loulou, *à droit.*'

Izzy opened the door to where she and Jess would be sleeping and stared at the double berth that took up the majority of the small space with only a small floor area for them to stand while they changed. 'The porthole opens,' she said unscrewing two of the bolts on the sides and pushing the glass to let a bit of air in the stuffy space.

'We can store our bags under the beds, I think,' Izzy said, lifting one of the mattresses and slipping her index finger into a slot to life the wood beneath. 'Oh look, lifejackets. At least we won't drown.'

'Not funny,' Jess said, smiling. She lay back down on the mattress and turning on her side rested her head on her palm. 'This isn't too bad, quite comfortable actually.'

Izzy opened her mouth to speak when she heard a familiar voice.

'This master cabin will suit us just fine.'

'No bloody way.' Jess slammed her hand down on the mattress and sat up. She slipped on her deck shoes and wrenched open the door, peering out into the galley.

Izzy cringed and grabbed hold of the back of Jess's T-shirt. 'Hold on a sec.'

Jess pulled away. 'Hello, Catherine,' she said, sarcasm dripping from her voice. 'How lovely to see you here.'

'Jessica, hello,' Catherine's plummy tones echoed through the yacht. 'Have you met my husband, Philip Simpson? He's a hedge fund manager from London.'

There was a moment's hesitation and Izzy manoeuvred past her friend just as Jess replied. 'No, I haven't. Have you met my business partner, Isabelle Le Lievre? She's a bankrupt company director from Jersey. Some cow booked her entire stock for the busiest three weeks of the year, didn't sign the contract with a cancellation fee designed to protect the business, and then let her down without warning.'

'Hi, Catherine,' Izzy said, rather proud of her furious friend, but cringing all the same.

She saw Philip giving his new bride a puzzled look. 'I say, steady on,' he said.

'No,' Jess said, 'I will not steady bloody on. Thanks to your wife, Izzy and I have probably lost the company we've been working so hard to build up.'

'You could have said no to the booking,' Catherine said, recovered from her shock at Jess's outburst.

'I wish I bloody had. I trusted you to sign that contract.' She narrowed her eyes. 'I won't make that mistake again.'

Izzy put her arm around Jess's shoulders. 'We're still a little upset, as you can see,' she said, as Catherine was comforted by her husband who glared at Jess as if she was some sort of maniac. 'Jess, let's not ruin our trip by pointless arguments. We can't do much about it here anyway.'

'You OK?' Ed asked coming down to the galley, closely followed by Roman. They carried several bags of food. 'What's going on?'

'Where did that lot come from?' Izzy asked trying to divert everyone's attention away from Jess's outburst. 'I didn't see any food shopping before.'

'Stefan bought it all earlier,' Ed said looking from Izzy to Philip. 'Everything all right down here?'

Izzy opened her mouth to speak but Catherine, who had been standing behind Philip, noticed Ed and gave him the benefit of her gleaming smile.

'Ed, darling,' she cried, pushing past her new husband to reach Ed.

He put the bags on the small galley table. 'Why aren't you two on a proper honeymoon somewhere private? This can't have been your first choice, surely? I know I wouldn't want to be crammed on a small yacht with eight other people.'

'My thoughts entirely,' Philip agreed. 'But Catherine was determined.'

'Shut up, Philip,' she said, resting two fingers over his lips to stop him from speaking. She turned to address the others. 'Our wedding was last minute and days before we were supposed to get married we cancelled the one we'd booked. We wanted to do something more spontaneous than we'd originally planned.'

'And this was it?' Izzy couldn't help saying. Jess winked at her.

'Yes, well,' Catherine continued. 'We've known each other a long time, I think we've probably had enough holidays together not to worry about one more.'

'Not as long as you've known Ed though?' Jess asked, trying to look innocent. 'I thought you and Ed were childhood sweethearts?'

'What? Since when?' Philip looked astonished at this news. He took hold of Catherine's arm and pulled her towards him. 'Catherine, were you and,' he glared at Ed, 'him more than friends? You swore to me that there was never anything between you two.'

'I'm not discussing this with you here.' She glared at Jess and Izzy. 'Not in front of these two. Take me to my cabin.'

Jess had to admit, even if only to herself, that Catherine's denial of anything ever going on between her and Ed was a relief. However, the atmosphere already on the yacht was more than a little tense and she was going to have to watch Jess to be sure she didn't lose it with Catherine. Maybe it hadn't been the best idea for her and Jess to agree to come along.

Chapter Eight

They took the boat out for a trial sail for a few hours on the first day. Izzy and Jess stood near the front, squealing with excitement as the yacht exited the port. 'I'm so glad we decided to come on this trip, aren't you?' Izzy asked, holding on tightly to the metal railing around the deck, relieved Stefan had insisted everyone put on a lifejacket.

Jess nodded. 'Too right. This is much better than sulking in Gran's cottage back home.'

The salty wind brushed through their hair and Izzy closed her eyes, relishing the cool dampness as it hit her face. This really was bliss and it helped having Ed around in the close quarters of the yacht. She knew it was early days, but she couldn't help noticing him giving her surreptitious looks. Her stomach contracted at the memory of his firm lips on hers that first day out riding.

Jess nudged her with her elbow. 'I can tell you're thinking about someone,' she teased. 'It wouldn't be *Edouard*, would it?'

Izzy opened her eyes and put a finger to her lips. 'Shush, I don't want to talk about him here. We don't know who's listening, so no cheeky comments from you when anyone's around, OK?'

'Misery,' Jess said, giving her a meaningful wink.

'Shut up, Jess,' she said, unable to keep the smile from her face. 'I'm warning you.'

'Ooh, I'm scared.'

Izzy was about to retort, when the boat dipped alarmingly and before she could do anything a huge wave rose over the bow of the yacht, slamming into them and soaking them from head to foot. The girls screamed.

'Bloody hell!' Izzy spluttered. 'I didn't see that coming.'

Jess wrung out her hair and wiped the excess water from her face. 'Me neither.' She looked Izzy up and down and laughed. 'We're soaked.'

Izzy smiled at her drenched friend, her hair hanging limply and water dripping from her chin. 'So much for looking cool and glamorous.'

'I don't think it's going to be that sort of holiday, do you?'

'Nope, I don't.'

They heard hysterical laughter coming from behind them. 'I hate that woman,' Jess hissed, glaring at Catherine.

Izzy was beginning to feel much the same way, but wasn't going to give Catherine the satisfaction of knowing she thought about her at all. 'Stop glaring at her, she's enjoying our discomfort. Smile. Let's not give her anything to gloat about.'

Jess snorted her disapproval. 'Ooh, she's such a smug cow.'

Izzy held her arms open and turned to the others, some of whom were laughing, but not in a malicious way, others trying hard not to. 'You lot should come over here,' she said waving over to them. 'The water's lovely and refreshing.' It was. Just not in such a huge amount when you weren't expecting it to hit you.

She turned back to face the sea, giving Jess a smile. 'We're going to have fun. This is probably the last summer holiday we'll have, especially if we do find a way to salvage Lapins de Lune. We might as well enjoy it.'

'You girls OK?' Ed asked, coming to stand next to them. 'You got a bit of a drenching then.'

'A bit?' Izzy asked. 'What exactly would you term as a lot then?'

He smiled. 'It hasn't dampened your sense of humour, I'm pleased to say.'

Izzy shrugged. They might as well laugh at themselves; it must have looked pretty funny after all. 'The two English girls get a dunking,' she said.

'You might want to change into something dry,' he suggested. 'The further out from the port we get, the cooler it'll become.'

Izzy spotted Jess sneaking a peek over her right shoulder at Catherine. Before her friend had time to insist she was fine as she was, Izzy quickly said, 'You're right. Come on, Jess, let's go and change.'

'But …' Jess argued, fury on her face.

'She's right, you'll be glad you did,' Ed said putting an arm around both their shoulders. 'You're both shivering already.' He manoeuvred them gently towards the entrance of the galley. 'Go on, I won't take any arguments from you.'

Izzy wasn't sure what he could be talking about, but let him guide them towards the door and, ignoring a snide comment from Catherine, pushed Jess gently down the stairs towards their berth. Once inside, Izzy shut the door behind them. They silently unclipped their lifejackets and dropped them at their feet. She could see Jess's lips pressed together, trying not to vent about her nemesis.

Making sure the small porthole was closed, Izzy stripped off her clothes in the confined space and, grabbing a towel, dried her body and then her hair before pulling on a bikini, shorts, and T-shirt. 'She's not worth the effort,' she murmured. 'Catherine has issues, obviously, and we need to be the bigger person.'

'Persons.'

'OK, persons, and not let her nastiness affect us.'

Jess dried herself off and pulled on her dry clothes. 'That's easier said than done.'

Izzy couldn't agree more, but this yacht wasn't the

place to build resentment and certainly not the place to pick fights with people. She tried to explain her thoughts to Jess without winding her up further.

'I know you're right,' Jess said, 'but she really gets under my skin for some reason, and it's not just because of her letting us down over the wedding. There's something else I don't like about her.'

Izzy raised an eyebrow, but said nothing.

'And it's not because she's beautiful, or glamorous, it's because she's a first-class cow.'

Izzy laughed. 'Well, I feel the same way, so stop trying to persuade me how awful she is, OK?'

Jess nodded. 'Fine.'

'Now, let's go and make the most of being on holiday.'

They returned on deck and Roman explained in his broken English how Stefan had decided that the first stop on their journey would be La Ciotat, which wasn't too far along the coast and would allow them to step back onto dry land and buy more food ready for the next section of their journey at sea.

'He doesn't look very well, just like he said.' They couldn't miss how, every so often, Stefan had to lean over the side, leaving Ed to take over briefly and man the wheel on deck.

Izzy was feeling a little seasick herself and couldn't imagine putting herself through a bad bout every time she went away. 'I wonder why he doesn't get used to the motion of the boat?'

Roman shrugged. 'It is a mystery, but he loves sailing the boats, so to him it is worth this sickness.'

Nicolle called to them all. 'We will all make pairs,' she said. 'Each pair will take it in their turn to make the dinner every night we are at sea, yes?' They all nodded. 'So, who will be the pairs?' she smiled.

'I will be a team with Roman,' Loulou announced.

Roman pulled an apologetic face at her and grabbed

hold of Jess's hand, holding it up. Jess widened her eyes and glanced at Izzy. '*Non, pardon,* Loulou,' he said. '*Mais*, Jessica will be cooking with me.' He looked at Jess. 'This is right, *non*?'

'What? Oh, yes.' She raised her eyebrows and smiled at Loulou. 'Sorry, we decided this earlier.'

Izzy could see Loulou wasn't convinced, but was pleased Jess would have something to take her attention away from Catherine's nastiness. She suspected Loulou was only trying to pair up with Roman to make Xavier jealous anyway. She'd also noticed him having quiet chats with Nicolle earlier that morning.

She wondered who she'd be paired up with. She didn't know anyone but Jess well enough to make any suggestions and didn't really mind who she ended up cooking with. Whoever it was, she was bound to get to know them better and that could only be a good thing.

'Would you mind pairing up with me?' Ed asked quietly from behind her.

Izzy turned round to face him. 'Of course not, it'll be fun,' she said, happy that he'd suggested it.

'Great.' He stepped forward. 'Izzy and I will make one of the pairs.'

Izzy ignored Jess's sniggering.

'Obviously Philip and I'll be sticking together. We're still on our honeymoon,' Catherine said, reminding the girls of her elopement. Izzy braced herself for the reaction she knew would be coming from Jess.

'I can't imagine wanting to spend my honeymoon with a bunch of other people,' Jess said sweetly, looking up at Roman. 'Can you?'

He shook his head. '*Non, pas du tout.* I would want my bride all to myself for a long time.'

Jess giggled as Catherine murmured something and dragged her husband to the other end of the boat.

Izzy was going to have to find a way for this point

scoring between her friend and Catherine to stop. She hated to think of everyone's trip being tainted by something connected with their business, which was supposed to celebrate happy occasions.

'Stefan and I will make a pair,' Nicolle said. 'which leaves Xavier and Loulou.' She looked across the space at Ed. 'You will cook the first meal tonight?'

'Sure, why not?'

Izzy would rather have been able to give her night a bit of thought, or even be the one to shop for the meal she and Ed would be producing. 'Better have a look in the galley and see what we've got to work with, I suppose,' she said.

'Go on then.' They went to the galley, and bending down to open the cupboards and have a look inside, Izzy was relieved to spot a few bags of fusilli pasta, some rice, and tins of sweetcorn and tuna. 'We could make something really quick out of this lot,' she said.

'That's a relief,' laughed Ed. 'My culinary skills only go as far as basic pasta dishes and fry-ups.'

'Mine too,' Izzy admitted. 'I don't think they'll be expecting anything too clever from us, thankfully.'

He opened the fridge and pulled out a bottle of red wine, studying the label. 'I've never heard of this, but I'm sure a few glasses will dull their taste buds enough to persuade them that what we make is up to standard.'

Izzy hoped so. Then again, as much as she didn't relish being the first to cook a meal for the others on the boat, she suspected that the creations could become a little competitive as the trip went on, especially between Jess and Catherine, or maybe Nicolle and Jess. She couldn't help smiling. She was definitely going to have to look out for her friend on this trip.

'Have I missed something funny?' Ed asked, grinning.

Izzy shook her head. 'I was just thinking about Jess. I have a feeling she's somehow managed to get on the wrong side of Nicolle.'

'Catherine isn't her biggest fan either, is she?'

Izzy shook her head. 'No. Not that Jess cares about what they think.'

They stood facing each other in silence. Izzy tried to think of something to say, but when she looked up and caught him staring down at her, her words vanished. As at home as he'd been at the château, she still found it hard to connect him to the place. If she hadn't known he was a count, she never would have guessed it. He looked so, well ordinary, in a handsome, rugged, kind of way.

'Izzy?' he said eventually, breaking their silence.

'Yes?' How could such an physically prepossessing man look so unsure of himself? They stared at each other for a moment. He opened his mouth to speak then heard groans coming from the largest berth in the bow of the yacht. 'Catherine and Philip,' Izzy said, awkwardly.

'I should imagine so.' Ed held up the bottle of wine and grimaced when Catherine cried out. 'I think that's our cue to leave. We should pour everyone a glass of this. We've got a few bottles.'

She nodded, trying to ignore the heated panting coming from the closed room. 'It's only going to take twenty minutes to cook our meal,' he added. 'Let's go and enjoy a bit of our first evening on board.'

Disappointed that they'd been interrupted, but relieved to get away from the obvious sounds of Catherine and her new husband having sex, she nodded. She'd been sure he was about to say something, but what? He stepped back to let her leave the galley first.

'I'll take this,' she said grabbing hold of the corkscrew. 'Oh, and these.' She picked up four glasses.

Ed placed a bottle under each arm and picked up four more glasses. 'Good thinking. We don't want to go unprepared, do we?'

No, she thought, leading the way back to join the others.

They handed out the glasses and Ed dutifully poured everyone on deck a drink. Izzy sat down and took a sip: it was delicious. She leaned back, resting her free hand on the wooden deck, and gazed up at the sail. It was hard to take in just how huge it was. She admired Stefan's determination to keep doing the job he loved, especially when it made him so ill. She looked over at him. He seemed to have more colour in his face and she hoped his bout of sickness was behind him now.

Stefan drank a little wine and then began explaining boat health and safety. Izzy ducked along with everyone else when he demonstrated how quickly the boom swung across where they were sitting if he needed to change course at any time. They went over and over his instructions and eventually she thought that some of them had sunk in.

A little later, Catherine and Philip came up the stairs to join the rest of them, both pink-faced and looking very pleased with themselves. Catherine gave Ed a pointed look, Izzy noticed with irritation.

'Why don't you two grab a glass and pour yourselves some of this?'

'And I will repeat my instructions once again,' Stefan said, obviously unimpressed with having to do so.

'Shall we go down and start our cooking?' Ed suggested to Izzy.

'Good idea.'

It didn't take them long to prepare their meal, but working close to such a big man in such a tiny space proved a little awkward at times. Izzy was constantly stepping past him and twice he had to grab hold of her when she nearly tripped over his feet.

'Sorry, this is going to take a bit of getting used to,' he said, helping her stand upright as they waited for the water to boil for the pasta.

'It doesn't help that I'm incredibly clumsy,' she

admitted, enjoying being alone with him once again. She could hear the noisy chatter above them, and Nicolle's voice above all. 'I think Nicolle likes to be in charge.'

He nodded. 'She's very bossy.'

'Have you known the others long?' She might as well take the opportunity to get to know him a little, she decided.

'Most of my life,' he said thoughtfully. 'Nicolle and Loulou were old adversaries from when they were very little. I think one's father blamed the other's for some business transaction that went disastrously wrong in the eighties.'

'That must have been difficult for them, especially if they were friends before.'

He sighed. 'They have their moments. Both had a bit of a thing for Roman.'

'Really?' She thought of Loulou and Xavier with their hands all over each other on the way to the café. 'I assumed Xavier and Loulou were more likely to become an item.'

He nodded. 'Probably. Come to think of it, I did hear Xavier whispering to her earlier, so maybe things have changed since I was last over from Jersey.' He stepped closer to her. 'Izzy,' he studied her face. 'I really enjoyed riding out with you the other morning.'

'It was fun,' she said. 'In fact it was exhilarating.'

'I know it's too confined on this boat for us to spend any quality time together, but I like you, very much, and I was wondering if you'd like to come out to dinner with me when we both get back to Jersey?'

'I'd love that.'

His mouth drew back into a wide smile. 'Good,' he said quietly, before bending his head and kissing her lightly on the lips. He drew back and studied her face, his expression softening so that he looked less serious. 'You really are very lovely,' he said, almost to himself.

She could say the same about him, she decided, but before she could reciprocate the compliment, he took her in his arms and kissed her. She put her arms around his neck and kissed him back, relishing his lips on hers and being held against his hard chest. Yes, she definitely wanted to get to know this gorgeous man much, much better.

'Hey, the bloody pasta is boiling over,' Catherine shrieked from behind them, causing Ed and Izzy to spring apart in shock when their intimate moment was suddenly interrupted.

Ed took the pan off the ring and cleaned up the mess. 'It's only water, Catherine, you didn't have to scream like that.'

'Didn't have to spoil your moment, you mean,' she said sashaying out past them, pinching his bum, Izzy noticed, as she did so.

'This looks about ready,' Ed said, tensing slightly before pouring the pasta into a colander. He looked at Izzy and smiled. 'She really is a pain sometimes.'

Chapter Nine

Happy to see everyone enjoying their meal, Izzy placed her fork on her empty plate and rested against the low back of the deck where four of them sat. She took a sip of her wine and looked out at the horizon, feeling more contented than she had in a long time.

'That was delicious,' Jess said. The others added their compliments and Ed refilled the empty glasses. 'No idea what we'll make when it's our turn.' She nudged Roman, nearly knocking his fork out of his hand. 'Have you got any suggestions about what we can cook for everyone?'

He shook his head. 'We will make something of our choosing and if they do not like it they will not eat.'

'Fair enough,' Jess said, smiling at Izzy. 'I like that way of thinking.'

Izzy was about to agree when Stefan shouted, the boom swung round, and everyone ducked. Everyone but Jess, that was. Jess's plate dropped to the deck and she almost joined it as Roman grabbed her arm and pulled her down at the last minute, causing her to fall forward and hit her head on the deck. There was a brief stunned silence and then Roman bent to help her back to sit next to him, concern etched on his tanned face.

'Are you OK?' Izzy asked handing her empty plate to Ed and hurrying to check on her friend, but Roman had got there first. Catherine howled with laughter further along the boat.

'Bloody hell,' Jess complained, rubbing her head. 'I've only just got rid of that sodding headache. This won't be much of a holiday if I have to concentrate the entire time.'

Izzy glared at the still-laughing Catherine. 'Do shut up, you idiot,' she yelled.

'I'm the idiot?' Catherine laughed. 'Didn't you just see what happened to that dippy friend of yours?'

'Right, I've had enough of this.' Izzy stood up and went to confront Catherine, aware she'd been the one to tell Jess to rise above her derisory comments, but she didn't care.

Ed grabbed hold of her wrist and slowly pulled her back to sit next to him. 'She's really not worth it, Iz. Let her have her ridiculous amusements, she's the only one who finds them funny.'

She glared down at him, not pleased to have been held back. Thinking through what he'd just said, she took a deep breath to try and calm her temper. It worked, slightly. 'Bloody cow. Jess was right about her all along. I've had enough of her snarling. What the hell is her problem with us anyhow?' She sat back down, reluctantly doing as he suggested.

Ed stared at Catherine briefly then shook his head. 'No idea. Maybe she's jealous.'

Izzy groaned. 'I find that hard to believe.'

'Do you?'

What sort of question was that, she wondered. 'Yes. What could Jess and I possibly have that she might want?'

He bent down and whispered in her ear. 'Friendship. How many friends do you think she has?'

'Lots of them,' Izzy argued. 'Didn't you see the wedding guest list?'

He shook his head. 'I mean real friends, Iz. Like you two are to each other. The sort of friends Catherine has probably wouldn't give her the time of day if she suddenly found herself living in a small flat with no luxuries in her life.'

Izzy relaxed a little. 'That still doesn't give her an excuse to be so vindictive. Poor Jess could really have hurt herself if that boom had smacked into her head.'

He looked over at Jess. 'You OK?'

Roman put an arm around Jess and hugged her. 'She is OK. A big bum to her 'ead,' Roman said. 'It will go.'

'Not a bum, it's a bump,' Jess said. 'Bloody hurts.' She rubbed it carefully. 'I'm not sure I'm cut out for a yachting lifestyle.'

Happy to know her friend wasn't permanently damaged by her fight with the boat, Izzy laughed. 'It'll be fun, just different to what we're used to. Think how much you're going to learn.' Izzy couldn't hide her smile when Jess replied by giving her a look that would floor most people. Her 'death stare', as Alex referred to it, was legendary among their friends.

'Really?' She rubbed her head and winced. 'The only things I'm learning right now are how to put medicine in places I hadn't considered before and that nearly connecting with parts of a boat can knock you almost senseless.'

'Concentrate next time then and you'll be fine,' Izzy soothed.

After an uncomfortable night's sleep sharing a small box-sized berth with Jess, Izzy was beginning to wonder if sleeping up on the top of the yacht might not be such a dreadful idea. 'You kick like a donkey, do you know that?'

'No I don't,' Jess argued. 'Anyway, do you have any of those seasickness pills? I felt lousy yesterday.'

'I thought you'd packed a box,' Izzy said, handing her one.

'Forgot, didn't I?'

Typical, thought Izzy. Jess really needed to get more organized and stop relying on her for the boring necessities of life. 'Hopefully we'll get used to the motion before we've finished them all.'

Thankfully the weather was perfect, with the first few

days at sea warm enough for them to make the most of tanning opportunities. Stefan was friendly and although all his instructions were in French, he made sure the two girls understood what he meant. Izzy managed to keep Jess and Catherine apart, mainly because Roman and Philip worked very hard to keep each woman entertained. Slowly, Izzy began to relax. They took it in turns to cook the meals, although Izzy was sure that by the end of the trip she would have had enough tinned food to last her a lifetime.

After a meal of rice, cold meats, and salad, washed down with bottles of wine. Ed whispered to Izzy. 'Come and look at the sunset, it's gorgeous.'

Happy to be alone with him again, she moved away from the others who were deep in conversation about what they would do if they won the EuroMillions. Izzy followed him to the front of the yacht where they were hidden from view by the wooden housing.

'Beautiful, don't you think?' he asked.

'It is.'

'I'm going to miss you when you go, Izzy.'

'Me too.'

He reached out and leaning slightly forward, placed his palm against her cheek, pulling her face to him. 'You're so lovely,' he said, bending down until his lips touched hers.

Putting her plastic glass down, she put her arms around his neck, kissing him back. Breathing in the warm salty smell of his skin as they lay back on the decking, she pushed her fingers into his short hair and held his head to her. 'You're pretty wonderful yourself,' she murmured without moving her lips from his.

His right hand travelled down her back and rested at the top of her bottom as the pressure of his kiss intensified.

She couldn't wait to spend some time with him when they both returned to Jersey. Maybe then they could shut out the rest of the world and find a way to be alone for a few hours without interruption.

Izzy woke one morning to hear voices that didn't belong to her crewmates. She dressed hurriedly and went up on deck to see where they were.

'Wow, it's beautiful,' she said looking at the huge marina they were moored in with sailing boats of every kind lined up. 'Where are we again?'

'La Ciotat,' Ed said moving to let her stand closer to Stefan and the wheel of the boat.

'Port des Capucins, Port de Saint Jean,' Stefan added. 'It's one of four ports here. 'Beautiful, *non*?'

'Breathtaking.' She rubbed her eyes to try to wake up fully and leaning against the wooden rail she looked over at the row of creamy stone houses on the dock. 'I love France; I should visit more.'

'You should.'

Izzy looked up at Ed and smiled. She certainly would if he ever invited her, she decided. 'Have you been here before?'

'No, not here, but I've been to Monte Carlo and Nice a few times.'

'I 'ave been here, it is not so well known to people out of France, but it is a good place to visit,' Stefan said as he coiled ropes.

After struggling off the yacht to go and have a shower in the ablution block, they clambered back onto the boat to get ready for lunch with the others.

'Catherine hogs the bathroom on this boat so often I'm beginning to think she believes it's her own personal en-suite,' Izzy groaned.

'I hate it when they park the boat this way round. Why do they insist on tying it up with the pointed end nearest the dock?' Jess said later that evening, clamping her teeth together and determinedly hanging on to the rope at the front of the boat as her toes tried to reach the quay. 'I nearly break my neck each time I try to disembark.'

'*Attends*,' Roman called from the dock. 'I hold you.' He reached out for her, grabbing first her leg and then her hips, and pulled her in one quick movement towards him, causing them both to nearly topple over.

'Your turn now, Izzy,' Ed called, smiling. He reached forward and took her arm as she leapt forward, narrowly missing the edge. Thankfully he quickly caught her and pulled her to him.

'Oof,' she groaned as she slammed into his chest. 'Why didn't they dock it the other way round, it's so much easier to disembark that way.'

'It can't be helped sometimes,' he said. 'You OK?'

She nodded. How could she not be? They were in La Ciotat, a beautiful resort that she couldn't wait to explore and the hunkiest man she'd ever kissed had his arms around her. He let go. She looked around, seeing that the others hadn't bothered to wait for them and were already crossing over the promenade to the row of tiny restaurants.

Ed took her hand. 'Come on, you must be starving, I know I'm desperate for a solid meal after all that mushy food the others keep serving for dinner.'

Izzy laughed. He was a big guy, used to working outside, and was no doubt fed huge meals by the cook at the manor in Jersey. If she found the meals on the yacht measly, what must he make of them? 'I'm usually happy with something simple, but even I'm bored with the food we're eating. I fancy a huge steak.'

'What, only the one?'

They laughed and the sensation of being alone with him and walking in this beautiful place, with the warm setting sun still heating their skin, as the strings of the lights along the waterway slowly lit up. 'It's so beautiful here.'

'It is.' He looked at her. He seemed unsure what to say next. 'Are you enjoying it so far?'

'Yes.' In more ways than one, she resisted adding. Izzy's sole focus had been Lapins de Lune for so long that romance never entered her head. She hadn't met anyone who she'd liked enough to spend time with since David. 'I hadn't expected it to be quite like this.'

He put his arm lightly over her shoulder. 'Nor me. I'm glad you agreed to come along.'

'So am I.' She heard Jess's loud giggle and smiled. 'I think she's enjoying herself too.'

Ed laughed. 'Roman seems rather taken with your friend.' His smile disappeared and he lowered his voice. 'I'm sorry Catherine ended up joining us. She can be a bit of a brat sometimes.'

He wasn't kidding. 'Hopefully Jess will keep a lid on her temper.' Izzy smiled. 'Roman is being very attentive to her and I think she quite likes him, so that might well keep her distracted.' She wondered if Alex might be disappointed if anything did come of Jess and Roman's friendship. 'Your brothers are lovely.'

Ed raised his eyebrows. 'They can be painful, but that's because they're my older brothers and love to make me the butt of their jokes. Xavier especially.'

She thought of yesterday morning when they'd bumped into Xavier in the corridor near to her bedroom. 'I know that feeling,' she laughed. 'Alex is very protective of me because of my dad dying suddenly when I was ten.' She didn't add that his protectiveness had increased along with her mother's after her first serious boyfriend had been killed only a few years later. She cleared her throat and forced a smile. 'He's always checking up on me when we're out, but at home he's a pain and we bicker quite a lot. It drives Mum nuts. She keeps saying we should have grown out of it by now.'

'I can imagine wanting to be protective of a younger sister. I don't see my brothers that often,' Ed said, 'which is probably why we all get along reasonably well. We used to fight a lot growing up though and my mother hated it.' Ed hesitated. 'Alex did mention something about your father dying young … but maybe you don't wish to talk about it.'

'I … I don't mind you asking.' She didn't. It made a refreshing change from others avoiding the subject. She loved being able to speak about him: her brother and mother hardly ever did. 'Alex's dad was away on business a lot and Mum got very lonely. She says he was seeing other women. She met my dad at a first night of one of her exhibitions that her husband hadn't bothered attending. She was very hurt and when she and my dad were so attracted to each other he didn't fight it and they ended up having an affair.'

'Was he an artist too?'

She nodded. 'He painted abstracts,' she said thinking of the few she still had in Jess's cottage to remind herself of him. 'Mum left Alex's dad. He was heartbroken and never quite got over her. She loved my dad very much, but he died when I was ten and left her paying the mortgage by herself. '

'How sad,' he said giving her hand a gentle squeeze. 'You must miss him too.'

'I do, but thankfully I still have some of his paintings. Mum gave them to me, but ended up having to sell most of hers to raise money for my schooling and the mortgage.'

They walked in silence for a few minutes, slowing down as they neared the others who were now settling down on an outside table discussing what everyone was going to order.

'I would rather have one big love in my life than many shallow relationships,' Ed said almost to himself.

'Me, too.' Izzy usually held back from sharing anything about her dad, but somehow she wanted to tell Ed everything about her past. She could tell he'd never use it to hurt her. 'Mum says she did feel bad for Alex's dad for a bit, but when he told her he was glad when my dad died, she ended up loathing him. She never regretted giving up her luxurious lifestyle with Alex's dad and leaving him for mine. It was a true romance.'

He stared at her. 'Poor lady, losing him so young,' he said thoughtfully. 'Is she with anyone now? Your mum?'

Izzy pictured herself kissing David goodbye. She'd joked with him, telling him not to be late to collect her that evening, never imagining that a few minutes later his life would be snuffed out when his motorbike collided with a lorry. She shook her head to rid herself of the painful memory. 'She's had a few boyfriends over the years. Mum's attractive and very gregarious, but as soon as they get too serious she immediately backs off.' She wondered for the first time if she and her mother reacted to romance in similar ways. 'She mainly concentrates on her art now, making commissioned pieces and holding exhibitions of her work.'

'I'd like to meet her someday,' he said. 'She sounds fascinating.'

'I'd like that,' Izzy said. She was proud of her mum's strength of character and independent ways. 'Although she's nothing like your mother. My mum is a little unconventional and doesn't believe she has to conform to other people's notions of how she should act.'

'I like her even more for that.'

Izzy laughed. 'Good. Just so you're forewarned.'

'*Regardez ici*,' Loulou shouted. '*Le menu*.' She held two menus in the air and waved them over impatiently.

'Come on, you two,' Jess called, 'we have to hurry up and get our order in, this table is booked for another party in an hour and a half.'

'*Moules frites, s'il vous plaît*,' Izzy said to the waiter before turning to Ed. 'Did that sound OK?'

'It did,' he said, ordering a large rare steak, chips, and salad. 'Hell, I'm hungry.'

They ordered three bottles of house red and sat back to enjoy the evening. Izzy spotted Catherine sitting at the opposite end of the table to Jess and refrained from smiling when she noticed the concentration on Roman and Philip's faces as they did their best to keep the two from making any conversation.

She watched for a few minutes. 'I think they've got their work cut out for them, don't you?' she whispered to Ed.

He looked at each couple. 'Rather them than me. Your friend seems very determined and I know Catherine will be biding her time to get Jess alone for a proper row.'

'As long as they don't ruin this meal, I'll be happy,' Izzy said. She breathed in the smell of the *moules* as they were delivered to a nearby table, wishing they could relax there for the entire evening. 'That food looks delicious; I'm going to enjoy every mouthful of mine when it comes.'

'Not as much as I will,' Ed laughed picking up his knife and fork. 'I hope it's served soon, I'm ravenous.'

The following day they sailed on to Porquerolles where the water, bluer than Izzy had ever seen it, sparkled in the bright sun rays. They moored the yacht about five hundred yards from the shoreline. It was so hot on board, Izzy couldn't wait to jump into the sea to cool down.

Impatient to get into the water, she climbed down the stairs at the stern of the boat and jumped in. She swam a little way from the boat and lay back, closing her eyes and looking up towards the perfect blue sky.

'You having fun?' Ed asked, swimming up to join her.

'I am,' she sighed, relishing the coolness of the water as she moved her legs slowly back and forth. 'It's so peaceful out here.'

'It can get a bit noisy up there with the rest of them,' he said.

'Aren't you enjoying the cruise?' she asked doubtfully.

'I am, but I'm used to spending a lot of my time by

myself in a large garden, so being cooped up with so many other people in such a small space can be a bit claustrophobic sometimes. This is the perfect antidote though.'

She thought so too. Izzy closed her eyes and breathed in the warm air.

'I'd really like to get to know you better,' Ed said, interrupting her thoughts.

Izzy laughed. 'I don't think we're going to have much chance with so many of us on this yacht.' As soon as she'd finished speaking she suspected that hadn't been what he meant. She could feel her face reddening at her stupidity.

'It is a little cramped.' He cleared his throat. 'But what I meant was I'd like to start dating you.'

'Oh.' She'd expected him to say something a little less formal. She stared at him. She felt more for Ed than she had ever done for anyone, except David.

Ed turned away. 'It's fine. I understand if you're not interested in me in that way. It's just that, well, after our rides together I sort of assumed you felt the same as me.'

I do, she wanted to shout, but something stopped her. She reached out and placed her hand on his arm. 'Ed, I do like you,' she said, dipping slightly into the sea so that he had to grab hold of her to lift her up again. 'Thank you,' she said, coughing to clear her throat from the small amount of seawater she'd swallowed. 'It's just that, well, I'm going to have to think about it, if you don't mind. For personal reasons.'

He frowned and she could see he was confused by her answer. She opened her mouth to elaborate a little further when someone splashed them both and cheered.

They turned in the water to see Roman and Loulou giggling and messing about in the sea.

She shook her head and laughed. 'Maybe chat a little later?'

'No problem,' he said, going to dunk Roman.

After watching the brothers splashing each other, she and Loulou swam back to the boat.

Izzy grabbed the towel that she'd left on the deck and went to settle down on the front of the boat next to Jess. Relieved to be lying down, Izzy closed her eyes. Her cool skin dried in the hot sun and she was beginning to doze off when Jess nudged her. There were raised voices floating up from below. 'What's going on?' she whispered, looking at Jess. 'Is that Catherine and Philip in there?'

Jess giggled. 'Why do you think I wanted us to come and sunbathe here?' She pointed downwards. 'She's always so smug, but when you came out in your bikini and went to the back of the boat to get into the sea, she noticed him staring at your arse and went mad.'

Izzy usually hated the thought of someone else's boyfriend ogling another woman, but when it came to Catherine she was happy to make an exception. They dozed as the gentle sea breeze cooled their tanned bodies and Izzy held up a bottle of sun cream for Jess to take.

'Rub some into my back, will you?' Jess knelt up and did as Izzy asked. 'Do you think Roman will come and visit Jersey?'

Izzy undid her bikini top and closed her eyes. 'I should think so. Ed lives there, don't forget.'

'Good. I hate to think that this is the last time I'll see him.'

'Hmm.' She pictured Ed's sun-bleached hair, wondering how dark it would be if he didn't spend most of his time working outside. His physique wasn't as fine as his brothers', much more rugged and also much more to her taste. She groaned.

Jess giggled. 'Are you dreaming about someone? I'm sure he likes you too. Maybe you could hook up when you get home.'

Catherine's glass-splintering voice rang out. 'She's still

going on at her poor husband. She's a right little tyrant,' Izzy said, glad to be out of the way.

'Those nasty little bitches,' Izzy heard Catherine screech. The entire group must have heard her.

'I'm glad it's not her turn to do the cooking tonight,' Jess said. 'She'd probably poison us.'

They closed their eyes again and listened as Philip retaliated. He didn't have any trouble standing up for himself, Izzy noted. 'She's got her work cut out for her there,' she giggled.

'She has,' Ed said, his huge frame blocking the sun and giving them a break from the intense heat. He held two wine glasses in one hand and a can of beer for himself. 'Rosé?'

They nodded and took a glass each. 'Thanks,' Izzy said. 'I could do with this.'

'Can you hear her down there?' Jess asked, taking a sip of her drink and closing her eyes in enjoyment.

'I think everyone in a three-mile radius can hear her,' he joked. 'She's used to getting her own way, so I can't see their marriage being an easy one for either of them.'

'Come and join us,' Izzy said.

He sat down next to her and opened his mouth to speak, when Catherine shouted, 'Daddy said you were a buffoon and he wasn't wrong, Philip. You are.'

'Now you listen here …'

Before he could add anything else, they heard Xavier slamming open their door and telling them to shut up. 'If you are not able to speak like, er, adults, we will deposit you on the next port.'

The threesome laughed. 'Xav rarely loses his temper, so he must be furious,' Ed said. He drank some of his beer and rested on one elbow, facing the girls. 'I'm going to find a café with free Wi-Fi tomorrow and check my emails. If you want to come with me, let me know and I'll make sure I wake you before I leave.'

Izzy remembered that her family had asked her to keep in touch. 'I'd definitely better come with you. We've kept our mobiles off because the roaming charges are so expensive, so we'll need to check our website and any emails from home.'

'The only messages that matter to me are ones cancelling more jobs,' Jess said. 'And I don't need to see those until I get back and have no choice.'

Izzy privately agreed. She closed her eyes, trying to savour this moment on a beautiful yacht, gliding through the Mediterranean with the sun beating down, a cool glass of rosé in her hand, and a very attractive man lying next to her. She didn't want this holiday to end. Jersey and her troubles suddenly seemed so far away. She calculated the remaining days of her trip: twelve. Twelve whole days on board *Le Rêve* with Ed. Even with Catherine's determination to humiliate them at every opportunity – as well as them still having to take their turn to spend a couple of nights sleeping on deck, what could possibly beat this?

That night it was Jess and Roman's turn to cook. By the pink tinge to Jess's cheeks when she called the others to go and get their food, Izzy suspected that her friend and Roman had enjoyed a little intimacy, as she and Ed had done when it had been their turn to cook. The others ate their food in the galley, so Jess and Izzy decided to take their plates on deck. It was too hot for them downstairs, especially, Jess moaned, after spending the best part of an hour trying to cook a meal for ten people on the tiny stove.

'I hope it's not too disgusting,' she joked.

Izzy thought they were lucky to have Jess making the meal for them. She was an impressive cook, when she could be bothered. 'This risotto is delicious,' she said, eating another forkful. 'Did Roman help at all?'

'A little,' Jess replied nonchalantly, not willing to give anything away.

Voices from below stopped them from saying anything further. They rolled their eyes heavenward, waiting for Catherine to have another go at Philip. Then, hearing Philip's tones at the stern of the boat as he chatted in passable French to Loulou, they glanced at each other, wondering who could be downstairs.

'I'm so unhappy. I've made a dreadful mistake marrying that fool,' Catherine whined. Her voice floated clearly up to where Izzy and Jess sat. 'Ed, you know I've never really found anyone as perfect for me as you, don't you? I only got engaged to Phil after we split up to make you jealous.'

'What the hell?' Jess whispered, pulling a sympathetic face at Izzy. 'Oh, Iz, I'm so sorry.'

Izzy's appetite vanished. Ed and Catherine? She thought that was supposed to be nothing more than a rumour. Why hadn't he been honest with her? Then again, she mused, why should he be? They'd only ridden out together a couple of times, chatted a few more, and kissed. It wasn't as if he was her boyfriend, was it?

They strained to hear Ed's reply, but could only hear murmurs, so it was hard to work out his reaction. Jess put down her plate and stood up.

'Where are you going?' Izzy asked.

'To see what they're doing in that cabin.'

Izzy watched her friend creep over and bend down silently, peering into the cabin below through a porthole. Jess's expression changed and she glanced over at Izzy, shock registering across her face. Unable to help herself, Izzy went to join her friend, pushing her out of the way so she could have a look. She stared into the cabin just in time to see Catherine stand on tiptoes and kiss Ed. Izzy gazed down at the man she was falling for, unable to look away as Catherine's hands began undoing the top of his shorts.

'What's going on?' Jess asked, frantic to know.

Izzy couldn't speak. She saw Ed's hands go down to Catherine's, just before Jess pulled her away. 'What's happening, Iz?'

Izzy let her see and moved back on shaky legs to sit back down. Jess hurried behind her. 'Oh, Iz, I'm so sorry. I really thought he liked you.'

Chapter Ten

Ed held Catherine's wrists tightly, pulling them away from his flies. 'What the hell do you think you're doing?'

'You don't want me,' she said, bursting into tears. 'Bastard.' She flung herself down on the bed and cried.

Ed stared after her. He'd never seen her so distraught. He wanted to comfort her, but didn't dare give her the wrong impression, so pushed his hands deep into his pockets and waited for her to calm down. It didn't take long.

'Right, are you going to tell me what this is all about?'

She wiped under her eyes and sniffed. 'I'm sorry. I shouldn't have done that.'

'No, you shouldn't have.' He leaned against the cabin wall. 'What would Philip have thought if he'd come in and seen you?'

'I know, I know, shut up.'

'Catherine, you know I see you as my cousin, not …'

'A woman?'

He could see she was still angry with him. 'I don't think I've given you the wrong idea.'

She exhaled sharply and pushed her hands through her usually immaculate hair. 'You haven't.'

He wanted to be on deck, making the most of being with Izzy, but couldn't leave the situation unresolved. 'Tell me what's upset you. I can see something is wrong and I know it's got nothing to do with me.'

'It's my father,' she said sniffing again.

'Go on.'

She pulled at the duvet cover on the bed next to her. 'I

overheard him speaking to you about money before I got married.'

Ed closed his eyes. 'You weren't supposed to know,' he said.

Catherine looked up at him, her eyes filled with unshed tears. 'Is he going bankrupt, Ed? Will he have to sell our home?'

Ed, unable to see her so devastated and frightened, sat down next to her and took her hands in his. 'No, we're going to do everything we can to make sure it doesn't have to come to that.'

She looked down at her hands in his. 'How, though?'

He didn't know that yet. 'We're going to have to come up with some ideas, and if you want to help,' he squeezed her hands gently, 'which I'm sure you do, then you can maybe go and ask your clever husband to help you come up with a few ways to help your father out of this financial mess.'

'Just don't tell those girls,' she whispered.

Ed thought that was rich coming from the person who'd seriously damaged their business, and said as much to her. Catherine snatched her hands away from him.

Ed studied her; she was acting so out of character, it didn't make sense, even after what she'd told him. Then it dawned on him. 'That's why you eloped, isn't it?'

She nodded, still staring at the floor. 'I couldn't let him pay for a wedding if he didn't have the money,' she said.

So there it was. The reason why she'd run off without anyone having a clue it was about to happen. 'I'm helping your dad and I need you to go and apologise to Jess and Izzy for letting them down.'

'I didn't mean for it to ruin them.'

He nudged her shoulder with his own. 'I believe you, but they don't know that. I'm sure they'll feel much better if they know that you never intended to hurt them. You don't have to tell them why you eloped, just say that you didn't think of the consequences.'

He looked down at the top of her head while she considered his suggestion. 'Well?' he asked, now desperate to return to the deck and see Izzy again.

'Fine, I'll apologise.'

Ed came out on deck about a few minutes later looking a little harassed, but didn't mention anything of what had happened in the cabin. He sat down beside Izzy and Jess and stared out at the horizon. 'You two looking forward to docking in Le Lavandou tomorrow?'

'Yes,' Izzy replied, determined not to let him know how devastated she was. 'After the café Jess and I thought we'd go and explore the town, see if we can find a few bits to take home with us.'

'We did?' Jess frowned. Izzy glared at her. 'Oh, yes we did.'

'Mind if I tag along with you?' he asked giving her a smile that earlier would have sent excited shocks pinging through her body, but now only added to her heartache.

'Not this time,' she said, not caring that he seemed hurt by her, no doubt unexpected, reply. 'We're having a girly day together.'

'Yeah, that's right,' Jess said, not bothering to hide her distaste of him. 'I'm sure you'll find other companions to spend the day with.'

Ed frowned. 'Have I done something to upset you two?'

Izzy shook her head.

'Just because we'd prefer to spend the day together,' Jess said, 'it doesn't mean you've done anything wrong. Or maybe you've got a guilty conscience about something. Have you, Ed?'

He gave them a quizzical look then turned to Izzy. 'I didn't think I had. Izzy, is there something I've done to upset you?'

'Yes, there is.' She glanced at Jess. 'For once Jess was trying to be subtle, but I'm past caring about niceties,' she said. 'I want to know …'

'Edouard de Lys,' Philip shouted from the galley as he marched up the stairs to join them. 'You and I need a chat.'

'Shit,' Izzy said. 'Why can't we ever have a proper conversation on this bloody boat?' She narrowed her eyes at Jess.

'I was looking forward to you giving him hell,' Jess murmured as Philip marched up to join them.

Ed groaned. 'What could we possibly have to discuss, Philip?'

'I think you know.' Philip smiled at both girls. 'Sorry to interrupt your cosy little chat, but this,' he pointed to Ed. 'well, I was going to say gentleman, but he is no gentleman in my books. He and I need a few minutes alone if you don't mind me taking him from you, girls?'

'Take him for as long as you like,' Jess said, turning away.

Ed shrugged. 'What the hell is wrong with you all tonight?' He stood up and, giving Izzy one last confused look, followed Philip down into the galley.

'Shall we go and have a listen?' Jess asked.

'No thanks,' Izzy said. She'd had enough of snooping to last her a lifetime. 'Catherine and Ed might enjoy all this intrigue, but I don't like playing games. I was stupid to think he might be different, but maybe they're more similar than I'd assumed.'

'More involved too, going by what we saw earlier.' Jess sneered. 'Rotten shit.'

After a restless night's sleep, Izzy woke Jess at 7 a.m. so that they could wash and dress, ready for docking. 'We can find breakfast in the town,' she suggested.

They disembarked quietly and wandered around Le

Lavandou for about an hour, window-shopping. The town was gorgeous, with colourful flowers and palm trees along the promenade and a white-sand beach along from the quay.

'Gran came to the Côte d'Azur in the fifties,' Jess said as they licked ice-creams. 'She said it was a place I should be sure to visit.'

Izzy looked out at the deep blue sea nearby. 'She was right and I'll bet this area didn't look too different back then either.'

Unsure which café to choose, they settled on the first one they came to that advertised free Wi-Fi.

A waiter came over and asked them what they would like, so Jess and Izzy ordered croissants and coffees and set about checking if anyone had replied to their advert for bookings. 'Nope, nothing,' Izzy said miserably when she saw that the only messages on their website were a couple about Christmas parties and one query about a wedding for the following summer.

Jess sighed heavily. 'It's all my fault. We're going to end up having spent years building up a business for nothing.'

'Shut up, Jess,' Izzy said, sick of hearing her friend blaming herself for something they could do nothing about. 'Something will turn up, we just have to be patient.' She logged into her email and straight away saw at least nine or ten messages from Alex or her mum, and several from unknown addresses. 'Oh, hell.'

'What's the matter?'

Izzy sighed nervously and told Jess about the emails as she clicked the first one open. 'I hope everything's OK at home.'

The waiter placed their croissants and coffees down on the table. They thanked him and Izzy began opening each message. Three emails in and her heart was pounding.

'Girls,' Ed was calling from the street. He held up his

hand. 'It's OK, I'm not stopping. I know you're spending the day by yourselves. But I brought some of these for the others on the boat and thought you might want some too.'

'What are they?' Jess asked, taking the brown bag and opening it. 'We already have croissants here.' She pointed to their plates.

'So I see.'

Izzy was still focused on her phone.

'What is it?' Ed asked, sitting down opposite her and placing the bag on the table.

'Iz?' Jess tore off a bit of her pastry and popped it in her mouth. 'What's the matter, hun?'

'There's been a fire at the Encore Hotel in Jersey and they're desperate to relocate a wedding party by next weekend.'

'Isn't that the hotel run by that actress and her singer husband? Used to be called "The Bombshell"?' Jess asked. 'I loved her in those horror movie re-runs.'

Izzy shook her head. 'No, her mum was the Jersey Bombshell, but she was in those horror movies. She's a friend of my mum's. They saw each other in the market yesterday and she told Mum all about the wedding disaster. Mum apparently said that Lapins de Lune will be able to find another location and set up a marquee with all the trimmings.' She bit the skin around the edge of her thumb trying to work out exactly how she was supposed to do this from the south of France.

'That's great news, isn't it?' Ed said. 'And it's next weekend?'

Her heart sank. This was the news she'd dreamt of receiving, but if they accepted this opportunity, and they really had no choice but to do it, then she would have to cut short this trip. She looked up at Ed. Maybe that might be a good idea though after what she'd seen yesterday. To stay on the boat with the thought of clandestine meetings between Ed and Catherine wasn't something she relished.

112

'Next weekend.'

'That's pretty short notice,' he said.

'Well *obviously*,' Jess said.

'Where will you hold the reception?'

'That's the problem,' Izzy said, not wishing to be as blatantly rude as Jess. 'I've no idea. There won't be any available hotels or places able to hold something like this, not mid-summer.'

They were silent for a few moments. Ed cleared his throat. 'Timing is always a sod, isn't it?'

'Yup,' she said wondering if he'd realized what she and Jess might have seen. She read the email to him. 'How does she expect me to find a location this close to the wedding? We've only got a tiny patch of lawn at the back of Jess's cottage and Mum's garden certainly isn't big enough.'

'But you can do everything else that's needed?' he asked, rubbing his unshaven chin,

'Of course, that's no problem. It would just be hard work setting it all up, but we're not afraid of hard work.'

'She says you've got to let her know within twenty-four hours, otherwise Francesca from the hotel will ask around and go with whoever can accept the work first.'

It wasn't long. Izzy racked her brain to think of suitable locations, or friends with large enough gardens who wouldn't mind strangers tramping over their lawn for an afternoon and evening.

'When was the email sent?' Ed asked.

Horror shot through Izzy; she could already be too late to accept the business. She scanned the emails and checked the date and time. 'Yesterday lunchtime, damn it.'

He frowned. 'We're an hour ahead of Jersey time, so that gives you about two hours to come up with something.'

Izzy did her best to be positive at all times, but even she knew that to find a location back home in two meagre hours, when she wasn't there herself, was almost impossible. 'I'll email Mum so they know I've seen it, and ask them to go back to Francesca and say I'm trying to sort something.'

She typed frantically, pleading with her mother to try and get more time for her and Jess to work things out. She didn't want to end her trip so early, but the thought of pulling this off excited her. 'I really didn't expect something to come up, not at this late stage.'

'We don't have any choice, though,' Jess said, looking very relieved. 'But where are we going to hold the reception? We don't have anywhere we can use, do we?'

Izzy cringed. 'Not really.' She took a sip of her coffee, trying to quell the rising panic that they might miss this unexpected opportunity. 'We really have to pull this off, Jess.'

'Maybe I can help you?' Ed said thoughtfully.

'How?' She gave it some thought. 'The only problem I have is finding a suitable location. It has to be pretty with a large lawn area for the marquee and hopefully a decent amount of parking nearby.'

He frowned thoughtfully. 'I could ask my godfather to let you use the manor grounds?'

'Catherine's dad?' She glared at him as she said the girl's name, unable to help picturing Catherine's hands fumbling with his shorts.

'If you'd rather not, I understand, but I think she owes you girls, don't you?'

She did, but Izzy suspected he didn't realize quite how much they felt Catherine owed them. Explanations for her nastiness would have been one thing. She pushed away the thought of him and Catherine and what might have been between them. This was about the business, and that was about Jess as much as her.

'If she's willing to help us, that would be wonderful.'

She motioned for Ed to take a seat and he sat down in

the vacant chair next to her and began drafting a message.

'Izzy,' Jess snapped. 'Think about what you're saying.'

Izzy stared at her. 'I know exactly what I'm saying, Jess.'

Ed shook his head. 'What is going on with you two?'

'Nothing that concerns you,' Izzy said. 'If you can contact the Seigneur and ask him, I'll let Mum and Alex know we can take on this job.'

Ed studied her for a few seconds. 'Fine,' he said, sitting down and immediately emailing his godfather, while Jess went to order another round of coffees for them both as they waited for a reply.

'I'm sorry you have to cut your trip short,' he said pressing send, sounding, Izzy thought, as if he truly meant it.

'We didn't think we'd have to go home so soon.' Home, she hadn't thought how they'd get back yet. She chewed her lower lip. 'Bugger, I'm going to need to book our trip home.'

'Would you like me to book something for you?'

She shook her head. He'd done enough. She didn't want to be beholden to him for anything else. 'No, it's fine thanks. I can do it.'

She contacted her brother to ask him just that. It didn't matter that they hadn't yet received a reply from Ed's godfather; she would find somewhere to hold this wedding reception, somehow. The most important thing now was to get home. Her message sent, she looked back up at him. He hadn't had to help them out like this, she thought.

'Thanks for your help, Ed, it's good of you, especially as we're bailing on everyone so early.'

He stared at his phone and then looked at her. 'I'd still like to see you when we're both back in Jersey, if that's OK.'

She liked him, very much, but she wasn't about to spend time with a man who was so casual when it came to

115

the opposite sex. 'I don't think so,' she said.

He reached out and took her hand in his. 'What have I done to upset you, Iz?' He glanced over her shoulder then focused his attention back to her. 'I know something's happened, but I can't think what.'

She shrugged and went to pull her hand from his, but he squeezed it lightly before letting it go. His eyes widened and she could see that he'd realized what must have happened. 'Shit, you saw Catherine and me in the cabin yesterday, didn't you? How?'

'Bloody right we did,' Jess said arriving back at the table and sitting down. 'We thought you were a decent bloke, Edouard de Lys, but you're nothing more than a cheap shit.'

'Jess, that's enough,' Izzy said, shocked at her friend's outburst. 'To be fair, we shouldn't have been looking in the first place.' She turned to Ed. 'But you're right, we did see you two together.'

He looked angry then hurt. 'What exactly did you think you saw?' His phone buzzed, but he ignored it.

'Aren't you going to check your phone?' Izzy asked, frustrated by the turn in the conversation.

'Yes, when you've answered my question.'

Irritated that he was forcing her to reply to him, she said, 'We saw her kiss you, and …'

'And what?'

'She undid your shorts.'

'Yes,' Jess said, sitting down opposite him. 'And don't deny it because we saw you helping her get them off.'

He closed his eyes and rubbed his face wearily with his hands. 'You must have stopped looking at that point, I presume?'

'Yes, I think we'd seen enough, don't you?' Izzy was mortified for having to admit she'd been spying and furious with him for bringing back the memory so vividly.

He turned to her, resting his arm on the back of her

chair. 'If you'd have looked a few seconds longer you would have seen me take hold of her hands and push them away.'

'So you're trying to tell us *now*,' Jess said, her voice low and threatening. 'Don't listen to him, Iz.'

'I can make my own mind up, thanks, Jess,' she said before focusing her attention to him. 'Well?'

'I promise you nothing happened.'

'Ha,' Jess glared at him. 'You would say that though, wouldn't you?'

He looked at both of them, resting his gaze on Izzy. 'I admit she came into my cabin and tried to kiss me.'

'She did bloody kiss you, we saw it,' Jess said, tearing at her croissant.

'Yes, she did,' he conceded. 'But Izzy, if you'd kept watching you would have seen that when she went to undo my trousers I stopped her.'

Was that what he was doing when he lowered his hands to cover Catherine's, Izzy wondered. She wished she'd kept looking.

'We had a row, then I came straight up on deck to join you both, remember?'

'Bollocks,' Jess said. 'You didn't come up for a while. We all know what can happen in that time, don't we?'

'That's a matter of opinion,' he snapped. Softening his gaze, he looked at Izzy, appealing for her to believe him. 'I promise you nothing happened. Catherine and I are history, we have been for years. Though to be honest it never was a great romance, just some teenage fumbling.'

'Fumbling?' Jess sneered. He ignored her comment.

'I've answered your question, now can you look at your phone?' Izzy said, desperate to reply to her mum. 'Maybe it was your godfather.'

'You do believe me, Izzy?'

She nodded, not wishing to continue the conversation and desperate to discover what his godfather had said.

117

He picked up his phone and checked, nodding. 'It is. He agrees that Catherine owes you two and has said you can hold the reception at the manor on Saturday.'

Izzy clasped her hands together and beamed at Jess.

'Brilliant,' she said to Ed. 'Please thank him for us and say I'll pop round as soon as I can to make any arrangements.'

He typed his message and pressed send. 'I'm relieved everything is going to work itself out for Lapins de Lune; you two deserve to make your business a success.'

Izzy nodded. 'Thanks for coming to our rescue with the manor gardens, we really appreciate it.'

'I'm glad to be of some use. I just wish we weren't parting on bad terms and that you'd believe me about yesterday's incident.'

Izzy felt the same way, but it couldn't be helped. She had enough on her hands making this business work.

'I'm sorry too, Ed. Maybe you are telling the truth, but whatever really went on between you and Catherine isn't any of my business. Life is going to be really hectic when I get back, so I probably couldn't make any definite plans anyway.' She quickly sent a message to her mum and brother telling them that everything was sorted.

Ed stood up to go, picking up their bill.

'No need to do that,' Jess said. 'We can pay for ourselves.'

He placed it back down on the table. 'I'll leave you both to enjoy your day then. Have fun.'

They watched him go. 'I really liked him,' Izzy admitted miserably as she watched the broad-shouldered, blond man walking away.

'I wonder how soon Alex can get those flights for us?' Jess asked impatiently. 'I don't want to have to deal with any lengthy goodbyes from Roman. I can't imagine he'll be as accommodating as Ed when he hears that we're leaving so soon.'

Izzy didn't have to wait long for Alex to contact her. There were no flights available at this short notice, but Alex had booked tickets for the ferry from St Malo for the next day, and they needed to leave as soon as possible if they were to get there on time.

'How will we get there by tomorrow lunchtime?'

Izzy typed a search into her phone. 'It says we need to get to Le Lavandou *gare*, then take a train to Toulon, then Chevaleret, wherever that is, then one from there to Montparnasse in Paris and then to Rennes and on to St Malo.' She sighed.

Jess frowned. 'Why does it have to be so complicated?'

'Because we need to get home as soon as possible, so have to take the earliest connections.' She checked the details again. 'It's going to take us, without the waits in between the trains about, um,' she calculated the travelling time, 'about eight and a half hours, and the one from Le Lavandou only goes twice a day, so we need to get back to the boat, pack, and hurry to the station.'

Jess groaned and finished her coffee. 'Better move it then, hadn't we?'

They hurried back to the yacht and broke the news to Nicolle and Xavier, who were the only ones on board.

'That is sad,' Xavier said, giving both girls a bear hug. 'Maybe you will be able to come and stay with us at the château sometime?'

'Maybe,' Jess said, her eyes filled with unshed tears. 'We can't even stay on the boat tonight because we've got to get to the station now.'

Despite her feelings towards Ed, Izzy was sorry not to be able to see him one last time before leaving. 'We need to get going as soon as possible to make our connection home,' she said, zipping up her rucksack and hoping she hadn't forgotten anything in her rush to get ready.

'Roman will be very disappointed you haven't wished him *au revoir*,' Xavier said.

Jess sniffed. 'I know. Please let him know that I would have liked to see him again, but it can't be helped, I'm afraid.'

Izzy picked up her rucksack and put it over one shoulder. 'We've had a great time getting to know you all, though,' she said. 'Thank you so much for asking us to come along.'

'It has been a pleasure. *Mais* Edouard, he will be very sad you have left us, I think.'

Izzy smiled. 'He knows why we're going, so it won't be such a surprise for him. He understands.'

They hugged Nicolle, who also seemed genuinely sad that they were cutting their trip short, and disembarked.

'I'm glad Catherine wasn't there to smirk,' Jess said as they rushed along the pavement. 'I might have lost all resolve and finally slapped her smug face. Mind you, we could have wiped it off her face if we'd told her that her dad's saved our business.'

Izzy laughed. It felt good to do so. 'Good point.' She put her arm around Jess's shoulders and gave her a squeeze. 'It's been fun though, I'm glad we came, even if we did only manage to see a couple of places. Maybe we'll come back here again someday?'

'I hope so,' Jess said miserably.

They turned a corner and only just managed not to crash into Catherine and Philip.

'So it's true then,' Catherine said, pushing her oversized sunglasses back into place on her nose. 'You're going back to Jersey already.'

'We are,' Izzy said, not wishing to elaborate.

'I'm told that you're going to be doing a wedding reception at the manor.'

Izzy noticed she didn't look very pleased at the prospect. 'What of it?' Jess said.

'Ed said I owed you both an apology for letting you down.' She shrugged. 'I do feel guilty, although I'm aware you probably won't believe me. I'm sorry I've put you both through all this trouble. If I hadn't eloped, you wouldn't be in this mess.'

Izzy hauled her rucksack back onto her left shoulder. She wasn't going to give Catherine the satisfaction of pretending she was sorry they were going home. 'Yes, but if you hadn't eloped then we would never have come to France at all. So, if you think about it, you've done us a favour in the long run.'

'Yes,' Jess said eagerly, picking up on Izzy's train of thought just as she knew she would. 'And it's not as if we've lost out completely, is it? We still get to hold the wedding reception we'd imagined at the manor. So, everyone's happy.'

Izzy smiled at Jess. 'Exactly.'

Catherine cleared her throat. 'Um, I'm glad. I didn't like to think I'd ruined your business, which is what Ed accused me of the other day.' She took one of both Jess and Izzy's hands in her own and gave them a sickly sweet smile that didn't look remotely genuine. 'I'm pleased that's settled and we can all be friends again.'

Again? Izzy hadn't thought they'd ever really been anything more than acquaintances, but nodded anyway.

'No hard feelings,' Jess said.

Catherine walked off, linking arms with Philip.

'He didn't say very much, did he?' Izzy said as she checked her watch and began jogging towards the station.

'Too busy looking at my boobs,' Jess said. 'Sleazebag. Oh God, I hope we make the train.'

They ran in silence for a few seconds.

'I wonder when Ed gave her an earful?' Jess asked, almost tripping on a loose stone at the edge of the pavement.

'No idea,' Izzy said, not really wanting to think about Ed at the moment, although the thought that he had told Catherine off about leaving them both in the lurch did soothe her fury at him a little. 'Does she have to have someone to fight with all the time?' she asked as they reached the entrance to the station. She couldn't help wondering why Catherine, who had everything anyone could ask for, never seemed to be truly content.

'Seems like it,' Jess said. 'Spoilt cow.'

Thankfully the train was on time and they didn't have to wait very long. They bought their tickets and a couple of cheese baguettes for the journey and sat down to wait.

'I wonder how much Alex had to pay for our fares,' Jess asked dreamily. 'It's typical of him to take charge.'

Izzy laughed. 'He's my brother, Jess. Do you seriously think Mum would let him get away with not organising this, especially as she's the one who instigated the new booking for us?'

'Probably not. She's a bit scary, your mum, isn't she?'

The girls laughed at the thought of Cherry. Both of them had experienced her wrath as they were growing up and she hadn't differentiated between them if they'd misbehaved in her home. 'She is a bit of a tyrant at times.'

'She is,' Jess agreed. 'Now, we have to stop dwelling on what might have been and focus on what we're going to do with this wedding.'

She was right. Izzy pictured the beautiful landscape at the manor. 'We shouldn't have to do too much preparation really,' she said. 'It'll probably be very like Catherine's wedding.'

'Yes, but I think this will be a smaller affair. Maybe we need to sort through our stock to have some sort of theme. We can ask the bride what colours she's using and match the crockery to it.'

'Good idea,' Izzy said and went quiet for a moment. 'Poor Francesca and Rick, having a fire at their hotel. Mum was saying that Rick would rather spend his time entertaining at night than running the business properly, and Fran's not much better.'

Chapter Eleven

'It's weird to be waking up here in the cottage and not on the boat, don't you think?' Jess asked, landing heavily on Izzy's bed the next morning. 'I suppose we need to get up to the Encore and find out more about this couple.'

Izzy rubbed her eyes, looked at her watch, and groaned. 'We should get a move on, I suppose. Mum has given me their contact details, but I want to chat to Francesca at the hotel to see what they had planned to have when ...' she struggled to remember the bride's name '... Lacey was holding the reception there. We'll need to get the linens and crockery back out, but must check on final numbers. They were hoping for seventy-five, but there could be a few more or less by now.'

Jess walked over to the window and pulled open the curtains. 'The weather's holding, thankfully, and I've checked the forecast and it's giving twenty-four degrees and clear skies for Saturday, so that's a plus.'

'You're excited, aren't you?' Izzy asked, swinging her legs over the side of the bed. It cheered her to see Jess raring to go once again.

'Relief, more than anything, although I am a little sad I couldn't spend more time with Roman. I was getting to like him quite a bit.'

Izzy brushed her hair and clipped it up. 'More than my brother?' she teased, used to Jess changing her mind every few minutes. She walked out of the room and made for the kitchen. She needed her first coffee of the day if she was to get her brain working at a decent level and there was no time to waste if they were to pull this last-minute wedding reception off successfully.

Jess followed her in and leaned against the work surface next to her. 'I'm not sure. They're so different.' She held up her hands, palms upwards as if weighing out the differences in the men. 'Roman, a dark French count, and Alex, a blond surfer dude. Both fun, both bloody sexy, but only one of them has ever kissed me or shown much interest in me.'

'So, Roman then,' Izzy teased, pushing away the vision of Roman's younger brother. She sighed and pressed the switch on the kettle.

Jess nudged her. 'Maybe. I'm not sure yet.'

Instead of bothering to cook a breakfast, they treated themselves to bacon rolls on Rozel Pier, before driving out to the Encore. Izzy drove the van slowly up the steep hotel drive, marvelling at the thirties splendour of the white Art Deco hotel.

'This is like something out of *Poirot*,' Jess said staring open mouthed out of the side window. 'Oh my God, I want my house to be like this when I make my fortune.'

'We'll have to rake in a few more bookings then,' Izzy laughed, silently agreeing with her friend's assessment.

'Yeah, I guess so,' Jess said. She pointed to the side of the building. 'Better park out of the way there, I don't think this van fits into the style of this place.'

'Darlings,' Francesca shouted, arms outstretched as she floated out to greet them in a long velvety ensemble that fitted well with her surroundings.

'I didn't know you knew her that well,' Jess whispered out of the side of her mouth.

'I don't,' Izzy giggled. 'Come on, let's go and say hi. Mum said she's lovely, if a little eccentric.'

'The words kettle, pot, and black spring to my mind.'

'Shut up and get out,' Izzy said, trying not to look too amused. 'Hi, I'm Isabelle and this is my business partner and friend, Jess.'

Francesca took one of their hands in each of hers and squeezed. 'Lovely to meet you both. Cherry said you were beauties and she wasn't joking.' She glanced over her shoulder and lowered her voice. 'The bride and groom are in the bar area waiting. They're very young and I can't tell you how grateful I was when your mum said you could take over their wedding reception for me. I would have hated to let them down.'

'We're happy to have the opportunity to help them,' Izzy said honestly. 'I was sorry to hear about your fire.' She looked up at the magnificent building, imagining the loss to the heritage of the island if something this magnificent had burnt down.

Francesca shivered theatrically. 'We were very lucky, it was in the orangerie at the back. It was an eighties add-on, so not part of the original building, which is good, but we still don't really know what happened.'

'Something to do with the electrics,' a handsome older man said, coming to stand next to Francesca and resting his arm around her shoulders. 'But we're not fretting about that now, are we, Frankie?'

She smiled at him and rested her head on his chest momentarily. Izzy realized how frightening it must have been for them potentially to lose their home and business.

'I'm Rick,' he said, shaking their hands when Francesca let go of them, 'Frankie's husband. We're very grateful to you girls for cutting short your holiday to come back here and rescue us.'

'It wasn't completely selfless,' Izzy admitted. 'We were also glad of the business.'

'Cherry said about that spoilt little brat, Catherine de St Croix.'

'It's fine now,' Izzy said, not wishing to get into a bitch-fest about Catherine.

'Come. Let's go and meet Lacey and Jack,' Rick said, taking Francesca by the hand and leading the way inside.

Izzy leaned into the car, took out her notepad and biro, and followed them in with Jess.

'We've done this many times before,' Jess assured the bride and groom who sat opposite them looking anxious. 'You leave everything to us.'

'So, your caterers are aware that the food now needs to be delivered to the manor?'

'Yes,' Lacey said. 'We spoke to them as soon as Francesca told us that you'd be taking over our reception.'

'We've worked with them before,' Jess said. 'So we'll give them a call and talk everything through to make sure everything works smoothly.'

The bride confirmed the numbers and told them she wanted as much pink as possible.

'I'm not sure what we're going to do about the floral arrangements though,' Lacey said. 'Francesca and Rick are going to give us cuttings from the garden here.'

'That's great, but in case they're unable to supply us with as much as we'd like, we'll need to find another source to ensure we have enough for the wedding,' Izzy said. 'Maybe we can ask the Seigneur if we can take a few cuttings from his gardens?'

'We want the arrangements to look as rustic as possible. I can't bear ones that look too contrived.' Lacey turned to her fiancé looking close to tears. 'I can't have my wedding without the flowers being perfect, Jack,' she said.

He hugged her. 'I'm sure it'll be fine, babe. Isabelle and Jess know what to do.'

'Yes, we do,' Izzy said, wondering if she could ask if they could cut some from the manor and picturing how many she could cut from the cottage and her mum's place before the tiny gardens were bare. 'Don't worry about a thing. Leave the planning to us.'

Izzy gave the couple her most comforting smile. 'Your wedding day is going to be perfect.' She looked at her pad and the few notes she'd made. 'Our linens are basically all white, although some have colourful embroidery,' she explained. 'The crockery is all different colours though and we'll ensure that the main colour being accented is pink. The bunting in the marquee will be floral, mixed with stripes and spots. It's retro, it's fun, and most of all I think it's going to work very well with the rest of your plans. You'll see, your day is going to be perfect.'

They waved goodbye to the couple who looked much happier than they had when Jess and Izzy had arrived. Relieved to be back doing what she enjoyed most, Izzy's nerves began to subside as they drove back to the cottage to start rearranging their stock.

'This really does have to be perfect,' Izzy said a couple of hours later. 'We can't leave any chance for error here.'

Jess handed her several napkins to place on top of one of their piles. 'Did she say her dad worked for the local gazette?'

Izzy nodded. 'She did, and that they've invited a journalist and photographer from *The Jersey Scene* to cover the reception.'

'Wow,' Jess gasped. 'They only cover the top weddings each year. This is either going to be the best publicity we've ever had, or the worst, if anything goes wrong.'

Izzy sighed heavily. 'Yes, Jess, and that's why we absolutely have to make sure that we double check everything.'

Jess nodded. 'Thank heavens Catherine is going to be away for another two weeks. She'd love to mess this up for us.'

Izzy had been thinking the same thing. Despite Catherine's protestations that she wanted them to be friends, she was sure it was only because they were near the yacht and others could possibly be within earshot. 'Yes, well, she can't do anything from the Mediterranean, can she?'

'Ha. No, she can't.'

Izzy didn't dare let Jess know how relieved she was. Catherine might be dizzy and flippant about most things, but one thing had dawned on her, which was that Catherine would do anything to get what she wanted. Seeing her go for Ed in the cabin that night made her realize he was the one thing Catherine didn't have, which was probably why she was so determined to get him.

She suppressed a shudder. She never really fought with other people, but Izzy wasn't about to let this nasty woman get in her way when it came to her business – and, yes, if she decided she wanted to be with Ed, then she wasn't about to let Catherine ruin things for her with him either.

Ed. She sighed. Whatever she'd been telling herself about having too many things to focus on in her life to waste time thinking about him, Izzy still couldn't help imagining what might have been between the two of them. He was an amazing rider, and even if he was a bit too upper-class for her usual tastes, he was also tall, rugged, and outdoorsy, as well as kind and supportive. She gritted her teeth.

'What's the matter?' Jess asked. 'We haven't forgotten anything, have we?'

Izzy shook her head. 'No. I was wondering why Ed did what he did with Catherine.'

Jess put an arm around her. 'I know; it stinks. She is gorgeous, though, and they did have some sort of history together, so maybe he didn't think it was as slimy as it looked.'

Izzy nodded. 'I just wish I hadn't seen her undoing his shorts. Bloody man.'

Jess went to argue, but Izzy held up her hand. 'It's no use, I know what I saw.' She'd seen how girls had thrown themselves at Alex and how he'd responded, and as much as she liked to think that Ed had slightly better morals than her brother, realistically she didn't hold out much hope.

Taking a deep breath, she pushed aside her thoughts of Ed and picked up her pencil. 'Enough wallowing,' she said. 'Time to get on with this wedding.'

'It's a shame the marquee is a bit too large for their numbers,' Jess said. 'I suppose they were lucky to get one at all this late.'

Izzy agreed. 'I've been thinking about that and maybe we could extend the dance floor and put in an extra table for drinks.'

'And perhaps we could put together an extra arrangement for that table. Smaller, because we'll need to incorporate it into our budget.'

Izzy nodded. 'I was thinking about asking Ed, but he'll still be away. We're going to have to ransack our families' gardens and do our best.'

They worked on their plans until they were interrupted by Izzy's phone vibrating on the desk. 'It's Mum,' she said, answering. 'Hiya.'

Before she'd even finished asking the flower question, Cherry was screeching down the phone, 'Please tell me you're on your way?'

Confused, Izzy asked. 'Where to?'

'The manor, of course. Where do you think?'

'We're not due there until later this afternoon.' She glanced at her watch. It was only one thirty and she was sure her mother had said three o'clock for them to meet the Seigneur.

'You were supposed to meet Toby de St Croix at one o'clock, I told you this the other day. He's just rung to ask where you've got to.'

Izzy shrugged when Jess mouthed what was wrong.

'Isabel, I distinctly remember telling you one o'clock.'

Izzy suppressed a sigh. 'Mum are you getting your twenty-four hour clock muddled again?'

She could hear Cherry mumbling to herself. 'Oh hell, what did I tell you?'

'You said three o'clock.'

'Shit. He told me thirteen hundred hours and I must have thought that was three. He's just been bellowing at me about another appointment he can't miss in town. How soon can you be there?'

Bearing in mind their cottage was at one end of the island and the manor house was practically on the opposite side, Izzy figured out it would take about twenty minutes, and said so. 'But we'll leave straight away. Call him back, please Mum. Tell him there was a mix-up with the times and we're on our way.'

She waved for Jess to follow her and grabbing her notepad, pen, and car keys ran outside explaining as they hurried up the lane towards the hill where their car was parked. 'Bloody Mum,' Izzy said. 'She's hopeless with any sort of timing. Typical artist, my dad used to say.'

They arrived in a shorter time than they'd expected thanks to the roads being fairly clear for once. Drawing up through the impressive crested entrance with its tiny cottages on each side, the girls stopped talking as they slowed down, seeing the Seigneur standing, arms crossed, on the edge of the large lawn area near to the parking space.

'You're late,' he said, rudely tapping his watch as if they misunderstood what his curt words had meant.

'I know,' Izzy said, as they both hurriedly got out of the car and went to join him. 'I'm terribly sorry, but …'

'When my groundsman turns up I'll explain things, to save me doing it twice.' He indicated over his shoulder towards the manor house where neither of them could see anyone waiting for them. 'He'll show you where I've agreed for the marquee to be erected, as well as the only places anyone will be allowed to park. Do you understand?'

'Yes,' Izzy said, only just refraining from telling him she wasn't stupid.

Before they had a chance to thank him, he marched off towards a shiny black Mercedes and mouthed something at the driver who was waiting for him.

'He's a scary bloke.' Jess said, grimacing, 'No wonder Catherine is like she is, she obviously takes after her father.'

'I'm not surprised he's cross,' Izzy said. 'I think he's been pretty much coerced into this by Ed, my mother, and Francesca.' Izzy leaned closer to Jess and whispered. 'I've heard rumours that Francesca and he had a bit of a thing back in the seventies.'

Jess laughed and linked arms with Izzy. 'He sounds like he was a bit of a lad in his time.' She giggled. 'Hey, he said the groundsman was going to show us around. I thought that …'

'Yes, me too,' Izzy said, the same thought dawning on her at that moment. 'But Ed's still cruising with the others …'

'No he isn't,' said a deep voice from behind them.

Chapter Twelve

'What are you doing back here?' Jess asked, squeezing Izzy's elbow so hard she was sure it would bruise.

Izzy couldn't think of a single thing to say. 'When did you get back?' she eventually asked.

He shrugged, one of those slow, lazy, French shrugs that made Izzy's stomach contract. 'You don't seriously think I'd let you two sort out a wedding at this place without any help, do you?'

The girls exchanged surprised glances. 'Um, yes, actually,' Izzy said. 'We thought you …'

'… and Catherine.' Jess said, stopping suddenly and grimacing at Izzy.

He frowned. 'Me and Catherine, what?'

'Um,' Jess pulled a face. 'Well, you and she seemed very, um …'

'What? I've told the two of you that there's nothing between us. Why won't you believe me?' His cheerful mood seemed to have dissipated rather rapidly, Izzy thought.

'I think what Jess is trying to say,' Izzy turned to face Jess, 'badly,' then addressed Ed once again, 'is that we just assumed you'd both be with the others on holiday still.'

'I see.' He shook his head and glared at Jess.

Damn, thought Izzy, he wasn't going to let this rest. She pulled Jess away and they began walking towards the manor house. 'We have so much to do, Ed,' she said over her shoulder. 'but we'd be grateful for any help you can give us.' She spotted the Seigneur coming out of the front door and glaring at his watch. 'Now you're here your godfather can explain his thoughts about the wedding arrangements.'

Ed's long legs made quick work of beating them to the front steps. He folded his arms and glared down at Izzy. Izzy couldn't help thinking how much his stance resembled the Seigneur's as she looked from one to the other. By the look on Ed's face he wasn't going to let them pass until they'd answered his question.

'You're late,' his godfather said.

'Sorry, Uncle,' Ed said. 'There's something I need to clear up with these two.' He focused back on Izzy and Jess. 'Can we have a quick chat?'

'For pity's sake,' his godfather scowled. 'Hurry up.'

'Thank you.' Ed motioned for Jess and Izzy to follow him away from the house where they could speak without being overheard.

Izzy swallowed. 'Jess was saying how close you were and, well ...' Izzy hesitated, not sure what to say next.

'I thought we went through this the other day?' he said keeping his voice low. He reached out, resting a hand on Izzy's shoulder. She hated to see him look so hurt. 'You obviously don't believe me.'

'I know what you said, Ed,' Izzy whispered, clearing her throat and willing Jess not to interrupt. 'But you must agree it did look a little odd.'

'Do hurry up, Ed,' the Seigneur called impatiently.

Izzy tensed and gave Jess a pointed shut-the-hell-up look. She didn't need Jess being overheard by Catherine's father talking about what they'd seen his daughter doing. She forced a smile.

'Firstly,' Ed said, looking, Izzy thought, more furious than she would have expected – it was disconcerting to see someone so enraged, especially when the rage was directed at her, 'I don't know where you two were when that happened, but you didn't see what you thought you saw.'

'What on earth is going on here?' his godfather asked, walking over to them impatiently.

Izzy stared at Ed. Surely he wasn't going to admit what Catherine had tried to do to him?

'Nothing exciting, I can assure you. This is Isabelle Le Lievre and Jessica Moon, the two girls I was telling you about with the events planning business, Lapins de Lune.'

'We met a little earlier,' he stared at Izzy. 'Interesting name. You have a look of your mother about you,' he said. 'She's a forceful lady.'

Izzy took that as a compliment, and refrained from saying that Cherry would probably say something similar about him. 'She is.'

He took the pipe out of his mouth and stared at it for a few seconds before placing it back into his pocket. 'I've been outnumbered by Cherry, and of course Ed here.' For the first time Izzy saw softness in his face, it made him appear far more attractive. 'They insisted I allow you to hold this wedding reception in my grounds.'

'And we are very grateful,' Izzy said when he hesitated. She could see he wasn't convinced it was such a good idea. 'We'll be on hand to make sure no one wanders off into the gardens and that every scrap of refuse is removed by the following afternoon.'

'Good. Good.' He kicked a stray leaf with the toe of his shiny brogue, and nodded. 'Ed, I'll leave it up to you to show these young women where everything should go and my expectations of the event.' He looked over their heads at the grounds. 'Yes, well, it can't be helped.'

Izzy didn't like to assume what he must mean so stood silently, not daring to catch Jess's eye.

'Thank you, Uncle.'

'Drink at six thirty sharp,' he said without waiting for Ed to reply before turning on his heels and returning back inside his home. The invitation was directed solely at Ed and Izzy was more than happy not to have been included in the summons.

Ed watched his godfather close the heavy wooden door behind him and then looked at Izzy, his expression changing to one of sadness. 'I like you, Izzy, I thought you knew that. I'm not about to mess about with one girl when I like another.'

'I …' He looked so disappointed in her that for a second she forgot how it had felt to be the one to witness them together.

'I hoped you'd worked that out about me.'

Izzy cringed inwardly. 'We're only telling you what we saw.'

'Yes, but you believed what you thought you saw, didn't you?' Ed continued.

She couldn't lie to him. 'Yes.'

'Oh come on,' Jess said. 'It wasn't as if we knew you well, was it? How was she to know that you and,' she looked towards the closed front door, 'Catherine weren't secretly getting it on?'

Ed stared at Izzy, not taking his eyes from hers. 'Because I thought she knew me a little bit better than that, Jess. Don't you trust your instincts, Izzy?'

He sounded so convincing she desperately wanted to believe him. 'Most of the time.'

'And what did they tell you when you saw me with her?'

Izzy thought back. 'I couldn't believe what I was seeing. It was a shock,' she admitted.

'You see, you've just said you didn't believe it.'

She was getting confused and it annoyed her. 'No, I said I *couldn't* believe what I was seeing, there's a marked difference in the two.' She sighed. 'I did think there was something between us, but whether you like it or not, I don't know you all that well and so, when I saw you and her together, I didn't really know what to think.'

'Then I'm very sorry,' he hesitated. 'For both of us.'

He turned away and began walking. 'Come on, we'd better get a move on. You've only got a couple of days to get this wedding set up. We don't have any time to waste.

'Ed, I …' Izzy started, not sure what she was going to say next.

He turned around to face her. 'It's fine. These things happen. I'm just sad it happened between the two of us, that's all.' He started to walk off.

So was she. She stood silently wishing things had been different.

'I wish I'd never suggested snooping on them now,' Jess murmured.

'I didn't have to look,' Izzy said. 'Come on, we'd better follow him.'

Without referring to the matter further, Ed showed them a room next to the kitchen where he explained they could store their linens before the wedding. 'My godfather has also agreed to give the bride and her party one of the spare bedrooms with an en-suite,' he said, showing them to a pretty floral-pink room and bathroom at the top of the stairs. 'The housekeeper has been asked to make sure that a few cool drinks are provided for them on a tray.'

Izzy could see it was going to be spectacular, maybe even bigger than Catherine's wedding. They'd planned many weddings but none on such a grand scale as this one. 'Thanks, Ed. This is going to be perfect. I'm sure the wedding party will be ecstatic when they realize how beautiful it's going to be.'

He smiled, but she noticed it didn't reach his eyes. She would have given anything to take back what she and Jess had told him.

'I'll be here until the wedding is over to help you put everything together,' he said, his tone matter-of-fact. 'The assistant gardeners will help carry anything you need to be moved. When do the furniture and marquee arrive?'

'The marquee will get here on Wednesday,' Jess said,

'and you shouldn't be needed to help erect it, but if you're around to make sure that it's put up in exactly the right place that would be brilliant.'

'He nodded. 'Of course.'

'The chairs and tables, including a smaller one where the wedding cake is going to be displayed, will arrive on Thursday,' Izzy added. 'and we'll come here and place everything where we want it to be on Friday.'

He walked over to the bedroom window and pointed to the lawn. 'The marquee can go in the middle, and the parking will be to the left side of the manor house, but I'll make sure there are a few signs put up there.'

Jess gazed out at the grounds. 'We'll get the linens and crockery in the cupboard over the next few days, so that the day before the wedding we can come and dress the tables and chairs and make sure the floral arrangements and chandeliers are where they are supposed to be.'

'Right,' Ed said, leading the way over to the door. 'If you don't need me for anything else, I'll get on,' He glanced at Izzy then out through the door as he turned to leave. 'If you need me for anything and can't find me, just ask the housekeeper, Marie. She's pretty good at tracking me down.'

'I'll bet she is,' Jess teased, coming back to stand next to Izzy, only to be greeted by a sullen glance from Ed and an elbow in the ribs.

'What did you say that for?' Izzy asked as Ed disappeared into the manor house. 'He already thinks we've got him down as some sort of man-whore.'

Jess grimaced. 'I don't know why he's so bothered what we think.'

'I do.'

'Sorry, I'm feeling a bit bad about the spying stuff.'

Izzy sighed, glad to have the wedding to focus on now that she'd messed up everything with Ed. 'No, me and my big, insecure imagination. If it wasn't for me peeking in that cabin and then assuming the worst, we wouldn't have fallen out with him.'

'At least you'll get to see him here,' Jess whispered as they walked back to the van. 'Maybe you'll get a chance to sort out your differences.'

Izzy doubted it very much. 'You think so?' she asked.

Jess thought for a moment. 'Maybe. You'll have the opportunity if we're not too rushed.'

Later, when they'd spoken to Lacey about her new venue, she was over the moon. 'You're both so clever,' she said when they arrived back at the manor later that day to show her around. 'I was so scared that our day would be a disaster when the Encore couldn't cater for us after their fire.'

Izzy and Jess barely managed to hide their relief as they talked her through the settings for the marquee and the large pond and wooded area where she could have her photos taken. Izzy left Jess to carry on while she went to find the kitchen and ask the housekeeper if they could quickly show Lacey upstairs.

She walked through to the kitchen and was greeted by a gorgeous woman in a grey uniform, polishing a silver salver. She had an air about her that made Izzy think that she should be giving the orders rather than carrying them out. Izzy could see she had an enviable figure even though she was wearing an unflattering outfit. She looked up at Izzy, her dark, almost black eyes framed by the longest lashes Izzy thought she'd ever seen on anyone.

'Hi, you must be Izzy or Jess,' she said. 'I'm Marie. Ed told me to expect you.' She laughed at Izzy's shocked silence. 'You were expecting someone a little older perhaps, dowdy maybe?'

Izzy realized she'd been gawping, and blushed. 'I'm so sorry, I, well, yes, I was,' she admitted. 'I'm Izzy, by the way.'

'I was surprised the Seigneur agreed for a wedding to be held here: he's usually incredibly private.'

'We were so pleased he said yes.' Izzy looked around the vast old-fashioned kitchen. Even this was full of character and beautiful in its own way.

'Come, let's go and find the bride, I'd love to meet her,' Marie said.

Izzy felt as if she'd known her from somewhere before. Marie seemed so familiar somehow, but she couldn't think why.

'Ed tells me you and your partner were on the cruise in the south of France,' she held a baize-covered door open for Izzy.

Izzy nodded her thanks and walked ahead. 'Yes, we were sad to cut our trip short.'

'This is Marie, the housekeeper,' Izzy announced as she and Marie joined the others. 'She's going to show us the room that you and your party can use before the reception.'

'The most important thing,' Lacey told them as they walked up the grand, oak staircase with its carved bannister, 'is that no one apart from those invited finds out where our wedding reception is to be held.'

Izzy waited for Marie to open the door to the room and then walked in behind Lacey. 'We never divulge any information about our clients,' she assured the girl.

'It's Jack's ex, you see,' Lacey said going over to the window and looking out at the view. 'He and Kate were engaged and she never got over him leaving her for me. She's always promised to ruin our wedding if she ever discovered where and when it would be held.' She turned to face them. 'I wouldn't be surprised if she'd had something to do with the fire at the Encore.'

Jack's face reddened. 'She's worried, that's all,' he said. 'I keep telling Lacey that she's over-reacting.'

'No, I'm not,' she said, glaring at him.

140

He stroked Lacey's arm. 'Lace, you know as well as I do that she only said that to upset you. We both know she's full of crap and always coming out with ridiculous things. Has she ever carried out any of her threats before?'

Lacey stared at him thoughtfully.

Marie laughed. 'I doubt she'd go to those lengths,' she narrowed her eyes. 'Don't you?'

Lacey shrugged. 'Probably not.' She tilted her head to one side and pointed to the en-suite bathroom. Marie nodded for her to go inside and have a look. 'I'll be glad when we're married and it's all over,' Lacey said, as she went in, widening her eyes for emphasis.

'I hope there isn't going to be any drama here on Saturday,' Marie said quietly when Lacey was in the bathroom. 'This is a respectable place and it will be the first and last wedding the Seigneur holds here if there's any chaos.'

'No,' Jack said. 'Please don't worry. My family are aware of Kate's threats, she was just upset when she discovered we were getting married, that's all. She'll stay well away.'

'Good,' Jess said as Lacey came back, no doubt relieved to hear that this was probably a case of Lacey getting pre-wedding nerves.

They all walked back downstairs, Izzy and Marie following behind at a slight distance.

'And what did you think of Ed's parents' château?' Before Izzy had a chance to answer her, Marie added. 'It's beautiful, isn't it?'

'Oh,' she said, surprised Marie knew about her and Jess visiting the place, 'yes it's magnificent.' She giggled. 'Jess and I kept getting lost, it's so big.' She grinned at the memory. 'And so many corridors.'

Marie laughed. 'I know. I got very disorientated when I stayed there, but it helped me get used to finding my way round this place.'

Izzy blinked, unsure what to make of the conversation as they walked out through the double-width front door and out into the strong sunlight. 'Oh, you stayed there too? How was it?' She hesitated. 'Have you worked here long?'

'Nearly ten years now. I came straight here the day I arrived in Jersey. Roman arranged this job for me with the Seigneur,' Marie said just before they reached the edge of the lawn, to join Lacey and Jess. 'I guess I never meant to stay here for so long, but I just fell in love with the island.'

'Roman?' Izzy was intrigued. 'So, you lived in France before coming here?'

'Yes,' she laughed. 'Didn't Ed tell you? We used to be married.'

Chapter Thirteen

Izzy barely registered that Jess was saying something. Her mind whirled with this startling information. Marie and Ed were once married? She hadn't seen that coming. They stopped in front of Jess and Lacey. She could see Jess giving her a quizzical look, but now wasn't the time to pass on this new-found information. After all, she still needed it to settle in her own brain first. Married! Ed? And to Marie ...

'It was good to meet you,' Marie said, shaking hands with Lacey. 'I'm almost as excited as you lot,' she said winking at Izzy. 'We haven't had a wedding here for years, not since the Seigneur broke up with his wife.'

'Well,' Lacey said, her wide blue eyes shining emotionally. 'When we planned our big day, Jack and I never envisioned it being this posh. We never would have tried to book anywhere this special, even if we had thought we could afford it.'

Marie laughed. 'The only posh one here is the Seigneur, and he's really friendly when you get to know him. Mind you, he can seem a bit imperious at times.'

Izzy watched Marie's mouth move but couldn't hear any more of what she was saying. Marie was very beautiful, down to earth, and friendly, and she could see what Ed would have seen in her, but it was like a physical slap in the face to discover he'd been married. What was wrong with her, she mused. And she'd been stupid enough to worry about his feelings for Catherine. This was another level entirely.

It wasn't as if she knew him that well, so why did it

143

shock her so much to discover he had a past? Because she loved him, that was why. And there was no doubt about it, she was bloody jealous.

'You OK?' Jess was asking.

Izzy glanced from her friend and realized the other two were also waiting for her to answer.

'Everything all right?' Marie asked. 'You're really pale.' She took Izzy's arm. 'Come on, let's get out of this heat and go inside for a cool drink.

She let Marie lead her back to the kitchen. They had just sat down when Ed walked in.

He stopped abruptly when he spotted them. 'I didn't expect to see you all in here.'

'Come in, Ed,' Marie said waving him in to the room. 'This is Lacey, Saturday's bride.'

'Lacey, pleased to meet you.'

Lacey beamed up at him. 'Jack and I are so excited. He's taken time off work to come with me today.' Izzy could feel the excitement emanating from the pretty girl. 'We really are massively grateful to you all.'

'It should be a good day, if the weather holds,' Ed said.

'Weather?' Lacey asked. 'I thought the forecast was good.'

He shook his head. 'I don't think we've seen the last of this heat, but there is a threat of fog.' He looked over at Lacey. 'I hope you don't have any last-minute guests flying into the island, they might have a problem getting here if the fog does come down.'

Lacey laughed. 'The only reason I wouldn't want fog is because we wouldn't be able to have our photos taken with these brilliant views of the garden.' She giggled. 'The only person who could miss our wedding would be Jack's nasty auntie. She's caused all sorts of problems with his family so no one would miss her if she didn't get here.'

Izzy glanced at Ed when the others laughed. He was watching her intently. 'I thought you'd left,' he said moving to stand next to her.

'They came back to show Lacey around,' Marie said. 'Then Izzy had a bit of a turn so we all came in here where it's cooler.'

Concern washed across his face. 'You're OK though?' he asked.

Izzy, comforted by his obvious concern, smiled at him. 'We've been racing around trying to do too much, probably,' she said, hoping to lighten the mood.

'You know I'm around if you need me, don't you?'

She nodded. 'Yes, we do.'

Marie took five glasses from a shelf and held up a jug. 'I can offer you all fresh orange juice, or there's tea if you'd prefer.'

'Orange juice,' they replied in unison.

'My mum is going to be so full of herself at work after Saturday,' Lacey said taking the glass of juice from Marie. 'Dad's always saying she's never satisfied, but this will please her no end. She'll be boasting about my wedding day for ever now.' She giggled. 'Imagine if I told her I'd changed my mind and didn't want it here.'

Jess choked on her drink, and Lacey shook her head frantically. 'Sorry, I was joking. I'd never let you lot down.' She put her glass down on the table. 'This is more than I could ever have wished for.'

'Phew,' Marie said. 'That's a relief. I think you nearly gave these two girls a heart attack at the thought of pulling out, especially after all the planning they've done for your wedding and cutting their holiday short to hold it for you.'

'You were on holiday?' Lacey asked, frowning.

'We were,' Jess said, still furious at the unfunny joke. 'But we were happy to cut short our trip to come back and do this for you.'

Izzy, could tell Jess was doing her best not to react badly to Lacey's teasing. She was desperate to calm the situation down before matters got out of hand. 'Yes, we were,' she turned to Lacey who was now looking a little unsure of herself, 'we were happy to. This wedding will be the biggest one we've done to date, so we're as excited as you for Saturday.'

Lacey took hold of Jack's hand. 'Phew, that's a relief. I would have hated for you to have missed out on your holiday just because of us.'

'We didn't entirely. So don't worry about it.'

'I don't mean to sound grumpy,' Jess said, taking another sip, 'but we've put a lot of emotion, time, and effort into making your wedding perfect,' she looked at Ed. 'We all have. So, please, keep the jokes about something less serious.'

Lacey smiled. 'Will do. Sorry. Jack's always telling me off for saying the wrong thing.'

'I know someone else a bit like that,' Izzy teased, widening her eyes pointedly at Jess.

'Who? Oh you mean me, thanks.'

'Don't forget, though, that Dad works for *The Jersey Scene* and they'll be doing a piece on my reception.'

'Yes,' said Jess sounding, Izzy thought, far friendlier at this reminder. 'We're very excited to be featured.'

'About the food,' Lacey said. 'Francesca said you'd be able to make suggestions about what we should serve everyone.'

Izzy nodded. 'We'll have caterers to make the food and we thought you could have the usual afternoon tea served with extras such as elderflower and prosecco jellies, and leafy salads with pumpkin, sunflower, and poppy seeds, topped with nasturtiums picked in the manor grounds.' She was relieved to see Lacey's smile widen.

'Yes,' Jess added, 'and of course there'll be Jersey new potatoes and plates of sandwiches like egg and cress, cucumber, fresh Jersey chancre crab. There'll be tiny fancies, scones with jam and cream, and strawberry tartlets on our cake stands placed on each of the tables.'

Lacey clasped her hands together. 'It sounds perfect.'

'Yes,' Izzy said, enjoying Lacey's delighted smile. 'It's not your typical wedding feast, it's based on a tea party theme, but these seem to go down very well, we're pleased to say.'

Ed, who'd been leaning against the wooden work surface by the sink in silence, put down his empty glass and stood up. 'Right, I'd better get on.' He walked to the back door. 'I'll see you around.' He waved to Jess, Izzy, and Lacey. 'I hope your day goes well.'

'I'm sure it will with these two in charge,' Lacey said, giving him a cheeky wink.

Ed laughed, which made Izzy's insides contract. Why did she want him so much, especially now?

'I'm sure it will too,' he said. He smiled at Jess and Izzy and then left.

'Hey, hang on a minute,' Marie shouted.

Ed popped his head around the doorframe seconds later. 'What time shall I pick you up tomorrow?' he asked Marie.

'No later than seven,' she said. 'Now bugger off.'

He walked away, raising his hand to wave.

'He's so dreamy,' Lacey sighed. 'Not as gorgeous as my Jack, of course.' She gave him a peck on the lips. 'but if I was single I'd have to make a play for him.'

'He's a great guy,' Marie said, collecting their empty glasses and carrying them over to the sink.

Izzy stood up. 'Come along, you two,' she said forcing a smile at Jess and Lacey, who was still staring out towards the empty doorway after Ed. 'We've got a lot to do.'

'Yes and I can't wait to get home and call Mum,' Lacey said, 'she's going to be beside herself when I tell her about this. Thanks, Marie, that juice was delicious.'

Jess and Izzy thanked her too and left the house with Lacey. Izzy was struggling to understand why Marie and

Ed had divorced. Had she sensed a frisson of attraction between them? She hoped not. They seemed perfectly friendly and obviously still got along well and she couldn't help wondering what had made them split up?

She pushed away the pangs of jealousy she couldn't help feeling. She needed all her focus to be kept on the matter in hand and this wedding was, if nothing else, the occasion they'd been waiting for to secure their business's finances, at least for a month or so.

The following day, making coffee, Izzy was feeling much better. She slowly pressed down on the handle of the cafetière. 'Coffee's nearly ready.'

'I've done a recount and we're definitely down two sets of crockery,' Jess shouted from the living room. 'But the new stuff is gorgeous,' she added.

They rarely turned down the offer of vintage crockery and it had been quite a surprise when had Cherry offered them her favourite fifties set earlier that morning.

Happy to be busy preparing for work, Izzy had begun to recover from the shock of her discovery the previous day. Ed was obviously still involved with Marie at some level. She would be a fool not to take this knowledge seriously. Since Marie had let her know about her history with Ed, Izzy was determined to keep any connection with him purely businesslike from now on.

'I can't believe she's given this to us, can you?' Jess asked, holding a red and green patterned cup in one hand and a small matching milk jug in the other. 'It's to die for.'

Izzy agreed as she carried through the tray of coffee. 'My gran gave her that set,' Izzy said looking up once she'd placed the tray down on the old Cunard trunk that served as their coffee table. 'I never imagined she'd part with it.'

'Glad she has though, aren't you?'

Izzy wasn't sure. It wasn't like Cherry to be

sentimental about belongings, so it was even more surprising that she'd made a point of passing one of her few treasures away, even if it was to them. 'It makes me a little sad for some reason.'

'Izzy, shut up and sort out those linens, will you?' Jess said. 'You've been in an odd mood since yesterday and I've no idea what's happened to make you so quiet. I thought you'd be happy now that Saturday looks like it's going to be a success.'

'We don't know that yet,' Izzy said, folding the last of the tablecloths and putting them away. 'But it should be.'

Jess went out to the tiny kitchen and Izzy could hear her wrapping Cherry's cup and jug. 'I'm trying to work out why you're acting so oddly,' she called out.

'I'm not,' Izzy lied, making a promise to herself to buck up and put on a more convincing happy face. Jess knew her too well to be fobbed off with her insistence that everything was fine.

Jess came back into the room empty-handed and sat on the arm of her grandmother's chintz armchair. 'Well? Spill. I'm not doing any more packing until you tell me what's wrong with you. Go on, I'll bet it's got something to do with Marie. She said something to you about Ed and Catherine, didn't she?'

'No, she didn't actually.'

Jess tucked a stray strand of her hair behind one ear and narrowed her eyes. 'Well, something bloody well happened between you. You seemed very pally and I wouldn't put it past you to have hidden something from me so that I didn't kick off. Am I right?'

Uncanny, Izzy thought. 'No, you're not, so shut up.' She poured coffee into one of the mugs for Jess and handed it to her. 'Drink this and please stop going on. I'm tired, that's all,' she hesitated. 'And not a little stressed about Lacey's wedding. Let's stop chatting and get organised.'

Jess pulled a face, but carried on packing.

Later, Izzy had just finished sorting out the linens and bunting, when the phone rang, disturbing her counting process.

'Bugger,' she groaned, picking up their landline. 'Hello, Lapins de Lune, Izzy speaking.'

Jess came back into the room and pointed at the laptop and mouthed, 'Booking?'

Izzy shrugged and waved her away.

'Izzy, is that you?' someone sounding very much like Lacey asked.

'Yes. Lacey? Is everything all right?'

Lacey laughed. 'Yes, of course. I was phoning to ask if you and Jess wanted to come along to our barbecue on Bonne Nuit beach tonight? We're having a pre-wedding get-together for the family and close friends and I'd love you and Jess to join us and get to know everyone before Saturday.'

Relieved, Izzy said, 'Yes, we'd love to.'

Chapter Fourteen

Izzy and Jess stepped off the bus. Despite the warm evening Izzy was glad she'd thought to tie her denim jacket around her waist. The sun would soon go down and it would be cold on the beach.

'I wonder how many people they've invited,' Jess asked, her sandals slapping against the cobbled slipway as they walked.

'No idea. This really is such a pretty beach,' Izzy said dreamily.

They reached the sand and could hear the laughter and chatter before they saw Lacey and Jack.

'We're over here,' Lacey waved, stepping around the granite wall.

Jess and Izzy waved back and hurried to join them.

'Thanks so much for inviting us,' Jess said.

'No problem. Come and meet everyone,' Lacey linked arms with both girls and led them to the noisy group.

'Mum, Dad, this is Jess and Izzy, who've taken over planning our wedding.'

They smiled at Lacey's friendly parents and said hello. Izzy was pleased to notice that Lacey's dad was busy with the barbecue. In fact, he had two going and was already cooking meat on both. 'That looks delicious,' she said.

'I thought I'd get you all fed before you consume too much of the good stuff,' he joked. He nodded in Lacey's direction. 'I think she's had a couple already and I don't want her exhausting herself before Saturday comes. She's got a lot going on this week.'

Izzy sensed he was looking forward to Sunday when

the entire wedding was over and done with. Most of the fathers she'd come in contact with since they'd started Lapins de Lune seemed to find it all a bit much, especially when their daughters were as excitable as Lacey.

'This time next week, you'll be able to relax and wait for the wedding photos to arrive,' she teased.

'Don't remind me,' he laughed. 'Her mother is already fretting about how many we should order and then there are the ones that will need framing.' He began turning the chicken over. 'I don't recall our wedding being so much effort. It lasted one day and then we went on honeymoon.'

Izzy nodded and took the glass of rosé Jack had brought over and was holding out in her direction. She suspected that Lacey's dad had probably only had to worry about his stag party and turning up on time at the church with the best man and the rings.

'And you know Jess and Izzy,' she heard Lacey saying to someone. Intrigued to see which member of Lacey's party she already knew, Izzy turned round with a smile on her face and was stunned to see Ed staring back at her, a beer in his hand.

He looked as surprised to see her. 'Izzy? I didn't realize you'd be here too.'

'Lacey wanted us to meet her family; you?'

'I'm here as a thank you for sorting out the manor for the reception.'

'And I'm here,' Marie said from over his shoulder, 'as a thank you for arranging cool drinks yesterday.' She came towards Izzy and leaned forward to give her a hug. 'I think they're just very grateful the wedding is still going ahead. It's good to see you again. How's everything going for Saturday?'

So this was why Ed had to be ready to collect Marie no later than seven o'clock, Izzy thought. She smiled, not wishing to appear rude. 'We always make sure everything is spotlessly laundered, ironed, and packed away in tissue paper after each event, so it never takes too long to get our stock ready. The main thing we have to check is that all the crockery is still perfect and that we have enough with a hint of the colour the host has requested.'

Izzy couldn't help staring at Marie. As envious as she felt about her connection with Ed, she couldn't help but like the woman; she'd been so helpful at the manor.

'Izzy?'

She realized Marie was saying something. 'Sorry, I was miles away.'

'It's OK, you've got a lot on your mind. I was only saying not to hesitate to call me if you need anything. Lacey is so sweet and I'd love to help make sure her day is as perfect as possible.'

'That's very kind of you, thanks.'

'That goes for me too,' Ed added, looking, Izzy thought, a little uncomfortable.

'Thank you.' Unsure what to say next, Izzy changed the subject. 'Have you heard from any of the others how the trip is going on the yacht?'

Ed shook his head. 'No. I should think they're having far too much fun to worry about any of us.' He took a sip from his can. 'It must be a relief to have more room now the three of us have left.'

'True. It was a bit of a squash for ten people.'

Marie sighed. 'What a shame you had to cut your trip short. Ed was relieved though that you were able to take on this other wedding to make up for Catherine's. It was typical of her to cancel without a thought for anyone else.'

'Yes,' agreed Izzy. 'She caused us quite a lot of worry over that. But Lacey's wedding will go some way to recovering the costs we would otherwise have lost.'

'It won't make up for it completely though, will it?' Marie asked.

'Leave it, Marie,' Ed said.

Izzy shook her head. 'No, Ed, she's right. It won't

153

make up for it, but we're hoping that the beautiful setting at the manor will be good publicity for us and might help us get bookings for future events.' She looked from Marie to Ed. 'Do you think the Seigneur could be persuaded to take further bookings, or is he still only willing to allow this wedding to take place up there?'

Ed moved from one foot to the other. 'I'm not sure. I'd like him to reconsider and agree to make the most of the manor, but he's stubborn.'

'It's a shame,' said Marie. 'I'd love it. It can get a little boring working at the manor sometimes and I'd love to maybe do some of the catering.' She looked up at Ed, giving him some sort of message Izzy wasn't party to. 'After all, that's what I'm trained to do, isn't it?'

Izzy wasn't sure why this information surprised her, but for some reason she'd simply thought that Marie's job entailed looking after the house in some way. 'You're a chef?'

Marie nodded. 'Trained in Paris. It's how we met.'

Izzy could feel her eyes widening and was unable to hide her surprise. 'Oh, I hadn't realized.' She looked up at Ed. He shifted his weight onto the other foot. Why was he so uncomfortable discussing this, she wondered?

'Yes, I was staying with Roman in Paris and he persuaded me to go out with him and his then girlfriend and Marie.' He looked down at Marie and smiled at the memory. 'He thought we would get along well because we were both fluent in English.'

Marie laughed. 'I can speak French, though, and was there to learn the language more thoroughly as well as training to become a chef.'

'So, how long were you together?' Izzy asked. There, she'd said it. Now he had to talk about it whether he liked it or not.

Ed stared at her for a moment before speaking. 'Two or three years, wasn't it Marie?'

'Yes, not too long, but it was fun while it lasted.'

They both laughed at the in-joke.

Izzy frowned. She opened her mouth to speak. 'But …' she began, tempted to ask him why they'd split up if they'd had so much fun together.

'Izzy,' bellowed Jess from a few yards away. 'Come here, quickly.' She waved her over frantically. 'Hurry up.'

Izzy groaned. She looked up at Ed and could see an unmistakeable twinkle in his eye at this reprieve. She wished she'd discovered more, but when Jess shouted for her again, she rolled her eyes heavenward and went to move away. 'I suppose I'd better get over there and see what she wants.'

Marie smiled. 'We'll catch up with you later.'

Izzy hurried as fast as the soft golden sand would let her to Jess's side. 'What did you do that for?' she asked, irritated with her noisy friend.

'What's the matter with you? I thought you'd want to hear this.'

'Go on then,' Izzy said, trying to hide her annoyance. She hoped she'd get another chance to speak to Ed, but glancing over her shoulder in his direction, noticed that Lacey, her mum, and a few aunts had circled him, looking very determined, and it didn't seem as if they had any intention of leaving him for a bit.

'This is Jack's brother,' Jess said.

Izzy held out her hand and shook the tanned one being proffered to her.

'I'm Dan,' he said.

'Good to meet you, Dan,' Izzy said, still not sure why Jess had dragged her away from Ed to introduce her to this handsome man. 'Are you the best man?'

He nodded. 'Yes and I'm terrified as hell. I still haven't worked out what to say for my speech and Jess thought you might be able to give me some pointers.'

'Me?' She glared at Jess who seemed very pleased with

herself for some reason. 'I'm not sure how though.'

Jess nudged her. 'Why not? You're great at knowing what to say and the poor guy needs help. She's being modest.' She smiled at Dan. 'She's very good at speeches, and if she can't come up with the goods I don't know who else can.'

'Great,' Dan beamed at Izzy. 'Can we maybe meet up for a coffee tomorrow and go through what I've drafted so far?'

'Well, I …' This was a blatant lie; she'd never written a speech in her life, and Jess was clearly trying to set her up with him. She was about to say no when Dan spoke again.

'Please,' he said. 'I'm desperate.' He looked over at Lacey laughing loudly at something Ed had said. 'She'll kill me if I don't come up with something. When I asked Jack for help, he said he had too many other things to do.'

Izzy couldn't help feeling sorry for him. She could only imagine how much of a nightmare it had been for them all since the fire at the Encore had put paid to their original plans. 'OK, I'll do it,' she said. 'But I really don't have any experience, whatever Jess might have insinuated.'

'Maybe not, but you've done enough weddings, so you must have heard loads of speeches.'

Put like that, how could she refuse? 'I've got a busy few days, so shall we say nine at St Catherine's tomorrow? I'll have a think tonight and see what I can come up with.' She tried to recollect what she'd heard other best men saying in their speeches. 'You'll need some anecdotes.' She raised her eyebrows. 'Clean ones, mind.'

'Great stuff.' He gave her a hug. 'I really appreciate this, Izzy. We'll have breakfast, on me.'

'No problem,' she said, not looking in Jess's direction, but aware her friend was amused by this scenario. 'It'll have to be a quick breakfast though because I really have a lot on this week.'

'You're brilliant. Thanks, girls.'

They watched him go and as soon as he was out of earshot, Izzy glared at Jess. 'What did you go and do that for?'

Jess looked nonplussed. 'I thought you'd like him. He's hot, don't you think?'

Was she serious? Didn't she realize how much work they had on over the next few days? 'I honestly didn't notice, Jess.'

Jess looked bemused. 'Listen, whether you admit it or not, I can see you've got the hots for Ed and by the looks of things he's got the hots for that housekeeper woman, Marie. So, there's no harm is showing him what he's missing and spending a little time with the best man, now is there?' She winked slowly at Izzy. 'Especially as he's tasty. Hey, imagine how delicious he's going to look dressed in a morning suit.'

Izzy barely managed to refrain from telling her friend exactly what she thought and if they hadn't been in public and surrounded by clients then she would have done so, in no uncertain terms. 'You can be so bloody irritating sometimes, do you know that?' she said quietly through gritted teeth. 'Just don't do it again, OK?'

'Fine, I won't.' Jess sniggered. 'Unless you don't get a move on and stop wasting your time mooning over the count.'

'Food's ready,' Lacey's dad shouted, saving Jess from an earful.

Lacey's dad waved his metal tongs in the air, looking very proud of himself. 'Grab a plate and then line up for some of the best nosh this side of France.'

Izzy and Jess picked up a plate each and stood in line. The food did look mouth-wateringly good and she was looking forward to tasting it. Lacey's mum pointed to a picnic table with salads, baguettes, and cheese on it. They waited their turn and were treated to a delicious-looking chicken breast each.

'Come on, let's go and sit over here,' Jess suggested, making her way over to several rugs that had been placed in a semi-circle on the outskirts of the barbecuing area. 'This family knows how to organize a beach party, don't they?'

Izzy popped a cherry tomato into her mouth and nodded. It was delicious. She sat down next to Jess and kicked off her flip-flops.

'That was pretty insensitive when you tried to set me up with Dan just then,' she said, unable to mask her irritation with her friend any longer.

Jess frowned, her hand stopping mid-air on its way to lifting a small Jersey Royal into her mouth. 'Sorry, I just thought it would be a good idea if you tried seeing someone else,' she said, biting off one half of the tiny potato and eating it. 'You need to forget about Ed and meet someone who you can feel as much for as you did David. But I didn't meant to upset you.'

Izzy believed her. After all, hadn't Jess been the one who'd pushed her to do all the things that had eventually culminated in her coming to terms with David's loss? 'I know,' she said, 'but please don't do it again.'

Jess stared at her briefly. 'I won't,' she said eating the rest of her potato.

Izzy closed her eyes. Just like all their arguments over the years, as soon as the issue had been dealt with, they moved on. This was just what they needed, she decided, forgetting her annoyance as her toes wriggled in the warm, soft sand. They were halfway through their plates of food when Ed and Marie came over.

'Hi, ladies, mind if we join you?' Marie asked sitting down before they had a chance to reply.

Izzy looked up and saw Ed looking uncertainly at the sand where they were sitting, and then at his laden plate. 'Let me take that for you,' she suggested, reaching out for it. 'We don't want you dropping that lovely steak.'

'No, we don't,' he laughed.

For someone who rode a horse with such lightness and grace, he really could be quite cumbersome, Izzy thought with amusement as he struggled to sit down. It was good to know that Ed wasn't perfect at everything.

'Thanks,' he said, when he was finally down. 'I'm starving.'

Marie shook her head. 'There's nothing graceful about you, Ed,' she teased. 'Do you know that?'

Izzy laughed to hear Marie echoing her own thoughts.

'He's too big to be light-footed,' Jess said, trying to spear a bit of sweetcorn with the prongs of her plastic fork.

'Er, he *is* right here,' Ed said, 'and if you must know, he can be light on his feet when he needs to be.'

Izzy laughed. 'Poor you, do you feel outnumbered?'

'Never.' He smiled at her cheekily.

Ed shook his head and took a mouthful of steak, eating quietly as Marie chatted about the beach party and how it had been too long since she'd last been to one.

They were interrupted by a loud cheer as a couple Izzy vaguely recognised walked over.

'You came,' Lacey shouted, running over to greet them. 'Look, Jack, it's Bea and Luke.'

Jack ran over, beer in hand, to put his arm around Lacey. 'Where did you park? It's packed up there.'

'We came in Luke's boat,' Bea said. 'We've been making the most of this glorious weather and sailing round the island.'

'Which is why we're a bit late,' Luke laughed. He held up a bag for Jack. 'Here are a few mackerel, caught about an hour ago.'

'Brilliant,' said Jack looking delighted. He took the bag, peeked inside to inspect the contents and nodded. 'I'll take these over to her dad, he'll be stoked to have them.'

Ed got up and headed over to the new arrivals. 'Hey, guys, I didn't expect you two to be here. Good to see you.'

Izzy watched the tall men. They both had wavy hair and powerful physiques, but Ed was clean-shaven, unlike Luke, who still looked like he'd rather spend time fishing than battling with a razor. 'Remember how nervous we were when we took on the planning for Luke and Bea's wedding,' Jess said.

'Ah, yes, of course,' Izzy said, remembering how grateful they'd been to Bea and Luke for letting them arrange the reception for their wedding, 'our first professional wedding.' She recalled the chaos of the mislaid linen and their disorganisation. 'We learnt a lot from that day.'

Bea laughed. 'I'll bet you did.'

'Blimey, he's still as tasty as ever,' Jess whispered when Bea walked off to speak to the others.

Izzy had to agree. Luke was lovely to look at, certainly, but judging by his long glances at Bea whenever she spoke he was still very much besotted with her. She was pleased. She'd love for someone to look at her in that way. An image of Ed doing just that popped into her mind.

'Are you daydreaming about him, Izzy?' Marie teased.

'What? Of course not. I was ...' She stopped herself just in time from admitting what she'd been thinking about. She needed to stop this nonsense. She and Jess had far too much at stake to waste time dreaming about unattainable men. 'Nothing.'

Marie frowned thoughtfully. 'I'm not sure.' She thought for a moment. 'If you weren't thinking about Luke, then you must have been thinking about –' she hesitated and raised her eyebrows, 'Ed?'

'Don't be ridiculous,' Izzy said, forcing a laugh and deciding it was time to go and get a refill. 'Anyone want a drink?'

Jess held out her empty glass and Marie shook her head slowly. 'Izzy?'

'Stop it, Marie. You're completely wrong,' she said

taking her plate and scrunching it into a bin bag.

She walked over to the makeshift bar area, and while waiting her turn to pour some drinks, looked over at Marie and saw the way she was watching Ed. She's a strong woman, Izzy mused. She could see, even if Ed couldn't, that Marie still loved him very much. Yet they were no longer married. It didn't make sense.

She refilled their plastic tumblers and turned to go back and join Marie and Jess, but became distracted by Luke's beautiful, blue and white yacht, moored just outside the harbour wall. She couldn't help picturing herself and Ed on it, off on a long, lonely sailing trip, just the two of them.

'Somewhere nice?' a deep voice asked behind her.

Izzy jumped, spilling the rosé. 'Shit. Will you stop doing that to me?' She gathered herself, embarrassed to have been caught out. 'Sailing off into the sunset, if you must know,' she said , laughing.

Ed looked over at Luke's boat and shrugged. 'It's beautiful, isn't it? It would be my ideal boat, but he'd never part with it. He lived on it for a while before he and Bea got together.'

She didn't explain that she hadn't meant Luke's boat, but the sailing off bit.

'For pity's sake,' Jess groaned, reaching the pair of them and taking two glasses from Izzy's hands. 'We're dying of thirst waiting for you to come back with these.' She walked off back to the rug.

Ed stared at Izzy for a few seconds as if he was trying to make up his mind about something. 'Do you fancy a bit of a walk to work off all this food?'

'That would be lovely.'

They began walking down towards the wetter sand near the waves, away from the others. 'It's good to see you again, one-to-one,' he said eventually. 'I think we need to clear the air.'

'I think that would be nice,' she said honestly.

He looked down at her as they walked, slowing his step. 'I'm not sure, but I feel like something has been said.'

'About you and Marie?'

'Ahh, that. Yes, she told you then?'

'Yes, she told me that you were married,' Izzy said, determined to keep any hurt from seeping into her voice. She stopped walking, scrunching her toes up in the wet sand. 'I have to admit it came as a bit of a shock, Ed.'

He pushed his hands into his shorts pockets. 'I can imagine. I know how this must seem, but it's not what you might think.'

'Go on, then.'

She knew she was being curt, but she was fed up with not knowing the score.

He looked out across the bay. 'Marie and I are very close, that much must be obvious,' he admitted quietly. 'And yes, we were married.' He began walking again, almost as if he'd forgotten she was next to him.

Intrigued and needing to discover just how close Marie and Ed still were, Izzy followed.

'She told you we met in Paris. Roman's girlfriend thought we'd get along.'

'Yes,' she said, 'and did you?'

'Yes. We spent a couple of weeks together. I showed her the city and all the places I loved best.' He looked down at Izzy. 'It was a strange time in my life,' he said, without adding any further explanation as to why.

'So you fell in love.'

He hesitated before nodding. 'Yes.' He thought for a moment. 'I'm nearly ten years younger than she is. She was much more mature than I was then.'

'Go on.'

'Marie showed me life was for living and that it was wrong not to make the most of each day. I just ...' he

162

hesitated, 'Well, I did, I fell in love with her.'

His honest words pinched at Izzy's heart, but she needed to know more about this man and the woman he'd loved enough to marry.

He took a deep breath and exhaled sharply. 'It didn't take long to discover that I wasn't the man she wanted to spend the rest of her life with.' He smiled down at Izzy to soften his words. 'Don't get me wrong, I was devastated when she sat me down after a couple of years and told me she needed her freedom. She insisted I go off and live the life I should be living, rather than settling down. I really wasn't ready for that then.'

She could still see how deeply this must have hurt him, and without thinking she reached out and took his hand.

'You must have been heartbroken when she did that?'

He nodded. 'I was. She was my first love, I suppose.' He smiled at her and gave her hand a gentle squeeze. 'It's fine, though, I'm over it now. I'm used to having Marie as a close friend rather than as a wife.'

Izzy wanted to believe him. She liked the comfort of having her hand in his, but not wishing to impose herself on him, pulled away. She looked over to the others and, surprised to see they'd walked so far, said. 'Are you sure she isn't still in love with you?'

He laughed. 'Hell, no, and if you asked her she'd tell you straight. We just work together now.'

Maybe she'd imagined the meaning behind the looks Marie had given Ed when she thought he wasn't looking. It was a relief. She didn't often like being proved wrong, but this time she was glad of it. 'I suppose we'd better get back,' she said. 'We don't want everyone to think we're ignoring them.'

She turned and had only taken one step when Ed took hold of her hand once again, pulling her gently back. 'Izzy, wait a second.'

She stopped and looked up at him. She didn't really

want to hear any more.

'It's fine,' she lied. 'You've explained it all to me now; I don't need to hear any more.'

'No, but I …'

She snatched her hand from his, regretting her hasty reaction almost instantly when she saw how hurt he was by her actions.

'Really. It's none of my business, Ed.' She laughed to soften her words. 'After all, it's not as if anything much actually happened between us.' She walked on and after a brief hesitation he followed her. 'We kissed, that's it. I shouldn't have over-reacted earlier. It's nothing to do with me what you've done in the past.'

She forced a smile to try and convince him that she was telling the truth. 'Come. Let's go back to the others now. I'm parched and we don't want to let the others drink everything before we get back.'

He caught up with her and they walked in silence for a bit.

'I let you think I liked you, Iz, because I do,' Ed said. 'Very much.'

Izzy mulled over his words. She would be ecstatic to hear him say this if she hadn't known about him and Marie being together. Even if they weren't right now, there was still very obviously a close connection between the two of them and she couldn't help suspecting that Marie would still like there to be more.

'Thank you?' she said eventually, feeling awkward and not certain how she should react to this. She spotted Bea waving at them.

'You're missing the puddings,' she shouted, pointing at a table filled with colourful cupcakes. 'Hurry up.'

'We're on our way,' Izzy called.

'Izzy, wait, please,' Ed said.

She stopped, not wishing them to continue the conversation near the others.

'Ed, really, I have no problem with you and Marie, I promise. And, I'm very grateful for you persuading your godfather to let us hold the reception at the manor: it's probably going to save our business. So, let's forget about this and go and have fun with the others.'

It was a relief to be back among the noise and laughter. She sensed Ed's presence over her shoulder and tried not to look at him, but forgetting, glanced at him a few minutes later, relieved to see he was laughing with Luke. Happy that things were back on a happier setting, she took the cupcake Lacey held out to her.

She licked her lips after taking the first bite. 'This is delicious, Lacey,' she said. 'You should consider having a display of these at the reception.'

'Don't even go there,' Jack laughed. 'She's driving everyone nuts with the arrangements we have agreed on. We don't need to come up with anything else for her to fret over.'

'Shut up, Jack,' Lacey said giving him a playful slap on the chest. 'I'm not that bad.'

'No?' he shook his head. 'I can't imagine what we ever spoke about before we got engaged.' He pulled a frightened face at Lacey. 'What will we have to talk about after it's all over?'

She slapped him again, harder this time. 'Shut up, you fool. I'm just excited …' she hesitated, 'and a bit worried about his ex.'

Jack shook his head. 'Kate hasn't bothered us for weeks, Lacey, so stop stressing about her.'

She kissed him on the cheek. 'OK, bossy boots.'

Izzy shook her head and smiled. They were so very much in love and it was heart-warming to see them together. 'I think you'll have more than enough to think about by the sounds of things,' she said. She spotted Jess and Bea giggling to one side of the group and went to join them.

'What am I missing?' she asked, their amusement infectious.

'Did you ever discover what was behind that locked door?' Bea asked.

Jess shook her head and gave Izzy a puzzled look. 'No, actually, we didn't. Iz, why haven't we got round to getting a locksmith to unlock that door?'

Izzy shrugged. 'I don't know. It was your gran's house, not mine.' She'd often wondered what was kept in the room they'd discovered by accident months after Jess's gran had died.

Bea shook her head. 'You two are useless sometimes. How can you spend years visiting a place, then move into it and miss a room?'

'To be fair,' Izzy said, 'there was always a wardrobe in front of it and we only found the door when Jess decided to repaper the spare bedroom and moved it.'

'What about that extra window? How did you manage to miss that?'

'A few weeks after we'd found the door to the room a neighbour was helping us prune the apple tree, and that's when we found the window hidden behind the branches, and realized the cupboard must be a room.'

'Well, if you like I could pop round one evening,' Luke offered, 'see if I can do anything with it. I can't promise anything, but it might save you getting a locksmith.'

'Fantastic!' Jess said. 'We badly need the space. We really should have got round to this before, but we're always so busy.'

'I'll come over tomorrow just after supper time if that suits you both?'

'We'll make sure it does,' Jess joked. 'Although can you imagine if it's just a room full of spiders and dust, we'll be well disappointed.'

Chapter Fifteen

Izzy and Jess arrived home an hour later, tired but happy.

'I think this is going to be our best wedding yet,' Izzy pronounced. 'I can feel it.'

'Bugger the wedding,' Jess said, slumping down in her favourite armchair. 'What about you and Ed?'

'What about us?'

'What were you talking about? Your conversation looked pretty intense.'

'Not that you were watching us, or anything,' Izzy teased.

'Well, it did.' She narrowed her eyes. 'He likes you, Iz, I'm sure of it.'

'I think you're imagining things, Jess.'

Jess went to argue and Izzy held up her hand. 'Stop right there, I don't want to go over and over the same thing,' Izzy said. 'Especially when it's obviously pointless.'

'What makes you think it's pointless?'

Izzy sighed. 'I just do. Tea?' she asked, determined to distract Jess.

'Go on, then, misery guts.'

Izzy filled the kettle and put it on, then headed back to the living room. 'It was kind of Luke to offer to open that door for us, wasn't it?'

'Yes, very. I hope he manages to, although I don't want him to damage the door, it's very old, my grandmother said two centuries.'

'Was it your gran or her mum who closed off the room?' Izzy asked as the kettle finished boiling. She went to make their drinks, relishing the thought of a cup of tea despite the heat of the evening, and carried them through to the small living room.

Jess took her cup and leaned back in the chair, yawning. 'Your mum said she'd look into it. She seemed to think there was some sort of intrigue about Great-gran. She died before I was born, but Gran gave me the impression that she was very sad for some reason.'

Izzy couldn't wait to find out more. 'I'll phone Mum tomorrow, try and chase her up a bit.'

'Hell, it was hot today,' Jess moaned. 'I hope this weather cools a bit by Saturday, otherwise those poor guests are going to melt in their fascinators.'

They were just finishing their drinks when there was a knock on the door. The girls had barely had time to give each other questioning glances when Alex walked in.

'You could have waited to be let in,' Izzy teased.

Jess's face reddened and she made an excuse to go and finish sorting non-existent washing.

'To what do we owe this honour?' Izzy asked motioning for him to take a seat.

'I caught Luke down at Bonne Nuit earlier. He said you and Ed seemed to be arguing about something, and I thought you should know a bit more about him.'

'And?'

'Did he tell you he was once married to Marie?'

'Yes,' she said.

He looked satisfied with her answer. 'I didn't know you and he were getting close.'

She sighed. 'We're not. Thanks, but I know more than enough.'

'But ...'

'No,' she said standing up. 'I appreciate you're looking out for me, but I'm not interested in Ed in any way other than as a friend.'

He didn't look convinced. 'Sit down. I don't want to

argue with you about this. I just want to speak to you.'

It dawned on her what must have happened. 'Mum asked you to come, didn't she?'

He shook his head.

'Rubbish, I know she did. Well, you can tell her I'm fine. I'm also twenty-four and not an idiot. I can figure out for myself whether or not the guy I'm interested in is a nutter or not.'

'You said …'

'I know, and I'm not interested in him. So, as I'm standing now, do you want a beer or something else, or not?'

He laughed. 'I'll take a beer.' He peered through to the kitchen. 'Where's Jess gone?'

Izzy went to fetch a beer from the fridge. 'No idea. She'll be back in a bit though, I should think. Why?'

'No reason.'

Now here was something, Izzy thought. Maybe Alex had finally realized that Jess liked him. Izzy only just resisted smiling at the thought of how switched off her brother could be at times. And how he had seemed oblivious to Jess's infatuation with him.

'I'll go and find her,' she said.

'Great, it'll be good to see her again,' he said, opening the can and settling back down in the chair.

Izzy bent down to whisper to him, 'Don't mention anything about Ed and Marie being married once, I haven't told her.'

His mouth dropped open. 'So now who's keeping secrets?'

'Leave it, Alex. I will tell her, just not yet.'

'Fine, whatever.'

Satisfied that he would keep quiet, Izzy went through to the tiny hallway and called up the stairs for Jess. 'Come and say hi to Alex,' she called. 'He's wondering where you've got to.'

Jess stomped to the top of the stairs and peered down. 'Why? He's never asked to speak to me before,' she said.

Izzy smiled. 'He just wants to say hi. Come down when you've finished whatever you're doing up there.'

Jess didn't reply, but went back to her room. Izzy headed to the living room again. 'She's coming in a minute. Why are you so interested in where Jess is anyway?'

It was his turn to look uncomfortable. 'No reason,' he said not meeting her gaze. 'You're together most of the time, so I just assumed she'd be here now.'

'That's rubbish, and you know it,' she teased.

He glanced at the door, presumably checking that Jess wasn't in hearing distance and leaned closer to Izzy. 'I'm not sure what's got in to me, Iz, but for some reason I can't stop thinking about her.'

Izzy stared at him, and his tanned face reddened.

'Stop staring at me like that.' He puffed out his cheeks then rubbed his unshaven chin roughly. 'I don't know why. It's not like me at all. I think it was when Roman rang me the other day and he was going on about her.'

'Roman called? What did he want?' Izzy knew she was changing the subject, but didn't want to continue this conversation when Jess could walk in the room at any moment.

'Don't think I don't know what you're doing, Iz,' Alex said, raising an eyebrow, 'but if you really want to know why Roman called, it was because he wanted to know how things were with you two and if Catherine was causing trouble yet.'

'Catherine?' A heavy sense of foreboding crept up through her body like a virus. Izzy dreaded Alex's next words.

'I thought you might not have seen her.' He took a few gulps of his beer.

'Seen her?'

'Look, um …' he stood up as if he'd changed his mind about being there.

'Go on, tell me,' she said.

'Tell you what?' Jess asked from the doorway, her arms filled with linens.

Alex leapt up and went to take them from her. 'Where do you want these putting?' he asked.

Jess glanced at Izzy. She looked stunned by this uncharacteristic gentlemanliness. 'Um, on that table will be fine, thanks.'

Izzy pointed to the armchair Alex had just vacated. 'I think you're going to need to sit down for what's coming next.' Jess sat and Izzy looked back at her brother. 'Alex, tell us.'

'Catherine was so cross when Ed left the cruise that she had a row with that drippy husband of hers and caught the next ferry home.'

Jess groaned. 'So her husband is still on the dreamboat with the others?'

Alex nodded. 'Wouldn't you be? I should think he's pleased to see the back of her.'

Jess looked at Izzy. 'Ed must have seen her, surely? He could have said something to us about her being back at the manor.'

Izzy couldn't agree more. There was too much riding on the success of this wedding for her to want to chance any hiccups with Catherine.

'It'll be fine,' Izzy said, trying to reassure her friend. 'Maybe she'll want to make amends like she said before we left France. You never know.'

'Really?' Jess stood, hands on hips. 'You really think that Miss Higher-Than-Mighty Bloody Runaway is even going to be aware how much damage she could potentially do to us?'

Izzy couldn't argue with what she was saying and Jess knew her far too well to be fobbed off with lies. 'Of course

171

not, but we know what she's capable of.'

'And Ed will be there to keep an eye open for her doing anything she shouldn't,' Alex said.

Both girls glared at him. 'You would think so, wouldn't you?' Izzy said. It was her turn to be furious and the mention of Ed's name was the flame that lit her emotional fuse.

'He's a good bloke, Sis,' Alex said frowning. 'He wouldn't let her do anything to harm your business.'

Jess laughed. 'I hope not, but anyway, Izzy is having breakfast with the gorgeous-looking best man tomorrow morning, so I think she's probably had enough of Ed for the time being.'

'What are you going on about?' Izzy asked. 'He asked me to help with his speech.'

Alex finished his beer, swallowing the last few mouthfuls and carrying his can out to the waste bin. 'Before you two start bickering, I'll get going,' he said.

He popped his head around the doorframe. 'Next time, I'll make sure someone else breaks bad news to you two.' He laughed. 'You're both pretty scary, do you know that?'

'Rubbish,' Izzy said, standing up to give him a hug. 'Thanks for coming to see us. We do appreciate it, even if we hide it well.'

Chapter Sixteen

The following morning Izzy was woken by her mobile making a racket next to her head. At first she thought it was the alarm, then she realized someone was calling. She picked it up. 'Mum, are you OK?' she asked, her voice hoarse.

'Of course I am, darling. Why are you still in bed, it's seven o'clock. Surely you should be up and dressed by now?'

'I'm not, though.'

'No need to sound rude, Isabelle. My damn van has packed up and I'm in a hurry to get to Devil's Hole to deliver to a client.'

'Devil's Hole?'

'Well, near there,' she explained. 'It's her husband's birthday today and she wants it ready for when he flies back to the island. He's been away on business and …'

'Mum, please, enough,' Izzy said. 'Can't you ask Alex to help?'

'I have, Isabelle, but he doesn't have a van. I need *your* van, now. Are you going to come and help me or not?'

Not willing to spend the next decade listening to her mother ranting about her lack of support in times of crisis, Izzy sat up and said. 'Fine, I'll be there as soon as possible.'

Her mother rang off and Izzy struggled to think how to contact Dan to cancel their breakfast. Eventually, having phoned Lacey, who gave her Jack's number, who gave her Dan's number, she got hold of him and arranged to chat to him later over the phone. 'So sorry to do this to you, Dan, she said, 'but I have to help my mother deliver a sculpture this morning.'

He was very sweet and even offered to help. 'No, it's fine, thanks,' she said. 'My brother will be there.'

Soon she was pulling into her mother's small driveway.

'Where have you been? I've tried to call you several times.' Cherry's hair was sticking out at all angles from under a lime green silk scarf wrapped roughly around her head.

'I came as quickly as humanly possible,' Izzy said, trying not to snap. Her mother was obviously stressed.

'Right, you open the back of the van and I'll help Alex lift it inside.'

'Have you any idea how heavy these creations of mine are?'

'Heavy, then?'

'Very.'

'So how are we going to carry it?' she asked looking around for something to help them move it to the van.

'The boys are sorting it out right now,' Cherry said, looking at Izzy as if she was completely stupid as she opened the van's back doors. 'Here they are.'

'Shit, Ma,' Alex puffed, red in the face from exertion. 'This monster weighs a bloody ton.'

'He's not a monster,' Cherry said loudly. 'The sculpture is called *The Man*.'

'Yeah, whatever.' Alex puffed out his cheeks. He was carrying one end backwards out of the cottage. Izzy barely had time to wonder who could be at the other end when Ed stepped forward, not quite so red in the face as her brother, but still struggling a bit under the enormous weight.

'We'll tie it with these old sheets,' Cherry said, inspecting it for damage once it was in the van. 'I want this to reach the client in perfect condition.

Alex rubbed his hands against his jeans and looked across at Izzy. She could tell he was trying not to be rude about the likeness of the unattractive man their mother had spent hours perfecting.

'Right,' Cherry said, locking the front door. 'You boys hop in the back with *The Man* and I'll sit with Izzy in the front. Come on, darling,' she said patting Izzy on the shoulder. 'We'll be late if we don't get a move on.'

After a short drive, they came to the client's house and Izzy waited by the van while Alex and Ed carried the sculpture inside. She realized they were near to the Priory Inn where they'd find Devil's Hole. This was a large pond with a creepy statue of the devil rising out of it. She hadn't been there for years, and wondered if Ed would be interested in going to see the statue and taking the walk past it to the large blowhole eroded from the cliffs that so many tourists had enjoyed visiting over the decades.

'Mum's having coffee and discussing figures,' Alex said as he and Ed came back outside. 'I hope she isn't too long, I've got a new student coming to the beach for a surfing lesson in an hour.'

Ed spoke to her for the first time. 'I'm surprised to see you here so early, I thought ...' He stopped suddenly as if something had occurred to him.

'What did you think?' she asked, intrigued.

He looked away from her.

'What?' she asked.

'No, it was nothing really,' he said.

She was beginning to think he'd gone a little mad when she spotted Alex chewing the side of his thumbnail. 'What have you said to him?'

He looked aghast. 'Me? Why would you think I've said anything?'

She narrowed her eyes. 'Because I know when you're being shifty, now spill. What have you said to Ed?'

Alex couldn't catch her eye. 'I might have told Ed about you having breakfast with the best man this morning.'

Izzy's heart sank. She was fully aware that her brother would have hinted that the breakfast could have involved far more than a fry up. She focused her attention on Ed. 'And did he happen to insinuate that this breakfast possibly followed a lengthy night of the athletic-in-the-bedroom kind?'

Ed laughed. 'He might have.'

'Bloody hell, Ed, shut it.' Alex threw Ed a thunderous look.

Izzy punched her brother hard in his right shoulder. 'That's for being a little shit-stirrer and meddling.'

He scowled at her, rubbing his shoulder. 'That hurt.'

'Good. I want to know why you felt the need to tell him that.'

'I thought he should know.'

'Why?'

'Because,' he scowled at her.

'But that's not how it was, Alex.' She was sick of the way Ed made her feel. One minute she was sure he liked her, the next she suspected him of still having feelings for Marie.

She pointed at the pathway leading to Devil's Hole. 'Right, you come with me,' she said to Ed, then looking at her brother, added. 'You stay here with the van and wait for Mum. When she comes back, give me a call.'

She turned away and began walking. Ed immediately fell into step next to her.

They reached the green pond where the metal statue of the devil stood, rising out of the middle of the water.

'I've always hated that thing,' she said. 'Look at his hairy legs, and those horns.' She shivered. 'Alex used to say he'd come to get me in the middle of the night if I didn't share my sweets with him.'

'That wasn't very nice of him,' Ed said, amused. 'My brothers used to terrorize me with similar things. I think he's impressive,' he said, stopping to look at the menacing

176

statue before walking on. 'Where did he come from, do you think?'

Izzy recalled her dad telling her something when she was small. 'I think the original devil was washed up about a hundred and fifty years ago after a shipwreck. Dad said that the figurehead was dumped by the sea in the actual hole in the cliffs,' she pointed along the pathway. 'Down there where we're going now. He said the hole was a hundred feet across and almost two hundred feet deep, but I'm not sure if it is that big because I've never looked down properly.'

'Sounds interesting,' he said quickening his step. 'We'd better hurry if we want to get there and back before your mum finishes her chat.'

Izzy walked faster to keep up with him. 'It's too dangerous to go to the bottom of the blow hole, but we can look down from a viewing platform the National Trust for Jersey have set up. They've done a lot of work down here in the past few years,' she said.

'So is it called Devil's Hole after the hole or the figurehead shaped like the devil that was washed up?'

'I suppose it's after the figurehead. I'm not sure, but I think it was carved into the shape of a devil.'

Ed whistled, impressed. 'So, why is it now standing in the pond?'

Izzy liked being able to tell him something he didn't already know. Ed seemed to be so knowledgeable and this made a nice change. 'The one in the pond is a metal replica. I think there've been a few over the years.'

Ed laughed.

'I have to admit to being jealous of this best man,' he said eventually. 'I hated to think of you spending the night with another man.'

'Oh.' She didn't know what else to say, and didn't look at him, but began walking again so that he couldn't see the ridiculously wide smile on her face. For once she was actually pleased with her brother's meddling. 'Come on,' she said, breaking into a run. 'We need to hurry up and see the hole before Alex calls us back to the van.'

The pathway went on around the cliff face for far longer than she remembered. 'I can't believe you've never been here before.'

'Neither can I, especially now that I've been here and seen what a lovely spot this is.' He stopped walking and stared out to the channel. 'It's going to be another glorious day, don't you think?'

'Yes,' she said stopping next to him and following his gaze. 'We're lucky living here.'

He was silent.

Izzy looked up at him to try and gauge what he was thinking. 'Is something wrong?'

He turned and taking both her hands in his, said. 'Izzy, I meant what I said before. I hated thinking of you with anyone else.' He shrugged. 'I know I've got no right to say that, but it's true.'

'So, what's wrong with that?' she asked, confused.

He took a deep breath. 'I'd like nothing more than to spend time with you, properly getting to know each other.'

She liked the idea too, very much. 'And that's a problem because?'

'I have to return to France. To the château. My father is soon to have major surgery on his back and my brothers have their work commitments in Paris. I need to go and run the château for my mother.'

'Oh,' she said, clearing her throat and forcing a smile onto her face. 'You have to be there for your family, I understand that.' She might understand it, she thought, but she didn't have to like the idea.

He bent down to kiss her, slowly at first, but as soon as she reacted to his kiss, he took her in his arms. The thought of not kissing him again like this hit her like a punch to the stomach. Eventually he pulled away. 'I really like you, Izzy. I wanted you to know that but, at the same time, thought I should tell you I'd be leaving soon.'

She took hold of his hand and they began walking. They really wouldn't have much time to see the cavern if they didn't keep going. 'It's fine,' she lied. 'I understand and I'm glad you told me.'

They walked the rest of the way in silence. Izzy's mind whirled and she wondered what Ed was thinking. She knew he loved his family home, but he did seem genuinely upset to be leaving Jersey.

'Do you know how long you'll be gone for?' she asked.

'No. I suppose for as long as it takes my father to recover from his surgery.' They reached the railings at the top of the cavernous space. 'There's a risk that he could be paralysed, so it could be for good.'

She looked up at him and touching his right cheek with her palm stood on tiptoes and kissed him. 'I'm sorry. You must be very worried about him.'

'We are,' he said, exhaling sharply. 'Now. We must make the most of this.' He bent forward to try and see as far down past the grassy, craggy sides into the deep crevasse as possible. 'That is deep.'

She stepped back. 'I hate heights, she said turning away from the deep hole eroded into the ground in front of them and focusing on the sea views behind her. 'I'm not going to look into there.'

Her phone tinkled, and Izzy took her hand from the warmth of Ed's and answered. 'Oh, fine. We're on our way.'

Chapter Seventeen

Having dropped her mother and the men off at Cherry's cottage, Izzy raced home to wake Jess. While her friend was in the shower she cleaned out the inside of the van and then began loading the hampers of linens and crockery.

They drove up to the manor and noticed Ed sitting on a ride-on mower, leaving perfect lines on the vast lawned area in front of the manor where the marquee was going to be erected.

Izzy checked her watch. 'The marquee guys should be here in the next few minutes.'

They stood and watched Ed for a bit. 'I can see why you're attracted to him,' Jess said. 'Roman is a darker, shorter version, isn't he?'

Izzy agreed.

'Hey, girls,' Marie shouted from the front door. 'This way.' She waved them over. 'If you want to start bringing in your linen and crockery, I can help you. I thought we could store it in the old butler's pantry until you need to set everything out.'

'Brilliant, thanks,' Izzy said, as they opened the back doors to the van. 'We have everything we should need, so we'll just traipse these hampers inside.'

The three of them made short work of the trips into the house and soon all the boxes were stored neatly.

They'd only just finished when the sound of a lorry hooting outside caught their attention.

'That's probably the marquee guys now,' Jess said. 'We'll see you later, Marie, thanks for your help.'

'No worries,' she said, giving them a smile.

They walked outside to see Ed chatting to three men. He was pointing out exactly where the marquee needed to go and laughing with them about something. 'Here they are now, Jess, Izzy?'

'Hello again,' Izzy said. 'I can see you know where Ed wants everything; do you need us too?'

'Can you let us know where you'll want the entrance?' he said. 'I presume you want if facing that way, with the windowed side overlooking the lake?'

Izzy nodded. 'Perfect. Would you like something to drink?'

They all asked for coffees and Jess and Izzy watched them start unloading the lorry.

'I'll soon be finished, then I'll come inside and join you,' Ed said.

'Great,' Izzy replied. She helped Marie take drinks outside for the men and noticed Ed wasn't anywhere to be seen. He must be putting the mower away. She followed the housekeeper back along the cool hallway to the kitchen and heard his deep laugh with Jess joining him.

'Ahh, there they are,' Jess said as they came in. 'Ed thinks this is going to be the start of something positive for the manor.'

'What's that?' Marie asked.

'Weddings, parties, the sort of events Lapins de Lune put on. I think it's just what this place needs, don't you?'

Marie thought for a moment and smiled. 'Yes, I think it's a brilliant idea.' She turned to the girls. 'This place is wasted most of the time. It's a shame not to make the most of it.'

'But I thought the Seigneur was very private,' Jess said.

'He is,' Ed said, 'but sometimes you have to think about the future and adapt to make sure it fits in with your lifestyle. He might be grateful for these events if he'd only think about it and give you the chance of putting them on.'

Izzy felt mean about the way she'd doubted Ed to her

brother the day before. 'We would certainly welcome being able to cover the events here: it's magnificent, both inside and out.'

'Yes, it's like something out of a fairy-tale,' Jess said dreamily. 'Although it's not quite as dreamy as your parents' château,' she added.

Ed leaned back against the worktop and crossed one ankle over the other. 'They're very different to each other.'

'But both are very beautiful,' Marie said. 'I love the château,' she said to Jess. 'We had many happy months there before coming here.'

'We loved it too,' Jess said, honestly. 'Neither of us had ever been to anywhere like it, let alone stayed there for a few days. It was wonderful.'

'We were lucky to go on the trip at all,' Izzy said. 'If Catherine …' She heard the unmistakeable sound of heels clipping down the tiled hallway and stopped talking.

'If Catherine what?' the lady herself asked, arms outstretched as if to announce her arrival.

'If you hadn't buggered off and left us in the lurch, we wouldn't have been invited on to the yacht,' Jess sneered.

Catherine acted as if Jess hadn't spoken. She spotted the jug on the table and opening one of the nearby cupboards, took out a tall glass, and poured herself some juice. 'Mmm, this is delicious.'

'Thank you,' Marie said. 'It's from a batch I made last year.'

Catherine stood still, her glass half-lowered as she gave Marie a withering look that Izzy was sure would flatten most people. 'So you're still here then?' she said as if she'd only just noticed Marie sitting at the head of the table.

'Don't start,' Ed said a distinct threat in his tone.

Catherine glanced at him. 'I see you're still hovering around her, Ed. Didn't learn from being burned the first time then?'

Ed slammed down his glass on the side so hard, Izzy was stunned it didn't break. She and Jess swapped glances and waited for him to retaliate.

'You never know when to mind your own business, do you? As usual you're making assumptions about Marie and me. If you're going to be here for the foreseeable future, I think you should at least try to get along with everyone.'

Catherine placed her glass gently down on the table, making an obvious point, and said, 'This is my home, Ed, not yours. I'll act how I see fit here and,' she looked at Marie, 'if you don't like it, you can leave.' She raised her hands and smiled. 'Marie, my father will be returning home this afternoon and I'll be dining with him, so maybe you should think about what you're going to prepare for us to eat later, say, eight o'clock?'

Without waiting for Marie to reply, Catherine turned on her skyscraper heels and walked out of the kitchen, leaving them all open-mouthed at her attitude.

'Well,' Jess said. 'She doesn't change, does she? Still a snooty cow.'

Izzy couldn't agree more. 'We only left her a couple of days ago, Jess, she's not going to have gone through some sort of miraculous change of personality in that time.'

Jess looked at Marie. 'Why does she hate you so much?'

Marie shrugged. She looked as if she couldn't have cared less what Catherine thought of her. 'Jealousy, I think.'

Jess laughed. 'Why would she be jealous of you?'

Izzy, horrified at Jess's words, nudged her sharply in the ribs. 'That sounded dreadful!'

Jess mulled over what Izzy had said and her eyes widened. 'Sorry! What I meant was, when she has everything anyone could want, why would she have such a problem with you? It doesn't make sense.'

Marie nodded. 'You're right, it doesn't. I'm sure she's always had a soft spot for Ed – I've seen it while they've been here together.'

Izzy could understand Catherine feeling that way, although most people would surely try to hide their feelings.

Ed moved to leave. 'I'd better get on. There's still a lot to oversee in the grounds if you want everything to be perfect for Lacey's day.'

Izzy looked at her watch, horrified to think they were wasting so much time when there was still a lot of preparation to do. 'Come on, Jess. We need to unpack all the linens.' She looked at Marie. 'They get creased very easily and look messy if we're not careful.'

Marie collected their glasses and carried them over to the sink. 'No problem. Call me if you need anything.'

Jess followed Izzy to the butler's pantry and once they were inside, closed the door quietly behind them. 'Marie is lovely, isn't she?'

Izzy opened the first box. 'Yes, she's ever so nice.'

'I couldn't bear to work here with Catherine lording it over me, could you?'

Izzy shook her head. 'We do have difficult people to deal with at some of our events, though,' she reasoned.

'Too right we do,' Jess agreed, opening another box and carefully lifting out the linens to place them on a tissue-covered table. 'I hope we don't have any of those annoying guests this weekend.'

Izzy laughed. 'Me too, although I'm more concerned about this ex of the groom. She sounds like a right nutter.'

'I know, I've been worried about her making an appearance too.'

Izzy finished emptying a box and pushed it under the table. 'Hey, I wonder when they last had a butler working here?'

'Maybe Marie will know.' Izzy unbuckled the worn

leather straps on the top of the hamper and, raising the lid, carefully lifted out the first item of crockery. She unwrapped it from its paper covering and held up one of the chintzy vintage cups. 'This is so pretty,' she said. 'I'd love to have more of this set at my wedding if I ever get married.'

'Oh, Izzy,' Jess frowned. 'You'll find someone you want to be with one day.'

'I'm not so sure about that.' She placed the cup down and unpacked the rest of the box. It wasn't that she didn't believe in marriage, more that she didn't believe she could find anyone else she could imagine spending the rest of her life with. A vision of Ed wormed into her mind and she pushed it away.

'We're going to need to ask Marie for some trays to carry these out to the marquee when we've got the trestle tables up in the correct places.'

'I'll go and ask her for some. We'll save time if we place them in colour-coded groups in here, then we can set the tables quicker once we're ready for them.'

'Good idea,' Izzy agreed. 'Even one will do for starters.'

She never minded packing and unpacking their stock, it was all so beautiful. Jess's gran must have spent decades collecting her prized crockery, Izzy mused yet again. She wondered if it was to help make up for the loss of her darling husband, Pierre. It always gave Izzy a lump in her throat whenever Jess's gran had spoken about him and how his dying so suddenly of a heart attack, a month before Jess's birth, had nearly finished her off.

Izzy recalled afternoons sitting in front of Mrs Moon's living room fire, drinking mugs of hot chocolate and listening to her tales. Mrs Moon had spent the Occupation in Jersey with her mother and father, meeting Pierre several years later when he'd come over from France looking for work at a neighbouring farm.

Izzy heard Jess coming back into the room and cleared her throat to push away the constriction her tears were causing. She turned away from the door and hurriedly rubbed her eyes. 'Did she give you one?'

'Excuse me?'

Ed's shocked reply surprised her and she spun round, the saucer she was holding slipping from her hand and crashing onto the cream-tiled floor.

'Shit.' Izzy bent down to collect the shattered pieces, nicking the palm of her hand in the process. 'Ouch.'

Ed hurried over, looking anxious. 'Here, let me.' He placed the shards on the table, lifting her hand to check the damage. 'That's quite deep. You're going to have to put a dressing on it, otherwise you're going to spoil your linen.'

'That's all I need.'

'Sorry.' He took a clean cotton hankie from his trouser pocket, shook it out, and placed it over her bleeding hand, tying it hurriedly. 'I shouldn't have burst in here like that.'

Izzy shook her head. It was so unusual to see someone carrying a linen handkerchief these days. She couldn't help being charmed to discover this about him. 'It's not your fault,' she said, forcing a smile onto her face. He lowered her hand and blood dripped onto the tiled floor.

'You're going to have to hold that up for a bit until it stops bleeding so much. I'll call Marie: I'm sure she's got some paper stitches somewhere.'

Izzy raised her eyebrows. 'Blimey, she's organized.'

He smiled, looking slightly less stricken. 'She trained to be a veterinary nurse, but ended up not working as one for very long when she discovered she was better suited to cooking for people rather than looking after sick animals.' He left her in the pantry and went out to the kitchen. 'I'll give her a call and get something to mop that up with.'

Izzy wondered if there was anything Marie couldn't do. If she hadn't been quite so friendly and helpful to her and Jess, Iz was sure she'd have a hard time not being jealous of the woman. It was an odd feeling. She rarely felt envy, believing that everyone had their own problems to cope with and that somehow balanced out people's lives. She couldn't imagine what Marie's downside must be. She'd even chosen to dump Ed. She looked up and noticed him standing at the doorway studying her.

'You OK?' He looked so concerned.

She nodded, wondering how anyone could choose not to be with someone as gorgeous as him. She mentally slapped herself. She had to focus on the wedding, and this was a heck of a setback.

'Keep that hand up,' Ed said, taking hold of her wrist and raising it.

'You're very bossy.'

Ed smiled.

'You can talk,' Jess said, walking in and stopping dead when she took in the scene. 'What the hell have you been doing? I've only been gone five minutes.'

Ed roared with laughter. 'I've missed you two, you know. You're both a little crazy and it really wasn't the same when you left the boat.'

'Is that why you raced back after us?' Jess asked, winking slyly at Izzy. 'We wondered why you appeared back in Jersey so soon.'

He turned to face Jess. 'Maybe.'

She walked over to Izzy and took hold of her hand, carefully lifting the handkerchief to inspect the damage. 'Is it very deep?'

'Deep enough,' Ed said.

Izzy watched them, wondering if they were aware she could answer for herself, but enjoying their chatter. She hoped Marie would hurry up so she could get back to unpacking the stock.

'I've finally found them,' Marie said, holding up a small red tin. 'You OK, Izzy?'

'I'm fine, thanks. She untied Ed's tight knot with her

free hand.

Marie waved Ed out of the way. 'This room is too small for all of us and I'm sure you must have jobs to be getting on with,' she said in a jovial way. 'Anyway, it's a while since I've done this and I don't need an audience.'

Ed walked over to the door. 'No problem.' He smiled at Izzy. 'I'm sure Marie will do a sterling job sticking your hand back together.'

'I'm sure she will. Thanks for patching me up, Ed. I'll wash your handkerchief and get it back to you in the next day or so.'

He shrugged. 'No rush.'

Marie placed her tin onto the worktop and pulled up a stool. 'This must sting,' she said, inspecting Izzy's hand. 'I'll be as quick as I can.'

Jess grimaced. 'I'll get on with the unpacking and leave you two to it.'

'So, you wanted to become a vet, Ed tells me?' Izzy asked, wondering why Marie hadn't pursued her dream.

'Yes, but it wasn't to be, unfortunately.'

In a couple of minutes she'd stuck the paper stitches in a neat little row along the cut.

'I thought I should stick on too many rather than too few,' Marie said, wrapping a bandage around Izzy's hand. 'The skin should start to knit together very soon, but I would wear a latex glove over the bandage for the time being, just to help keep it clean and dry. I'll find some for you.'

Izzy looked at Marie's handiwork and nodded. 'Thank you, that's brilliant.'

'So tell me,' Marie said as she packed her first aid tin. 'Has Catherine been bugging you at all since earlier?'

'No, thankfully,' Jess said, re-entering the room. 'Maybe she's found someone else to annoy.'

'Let's hope so,' Marie said, and left.

It didn't take long to finish the unpacking. They joined

Marie for another drink in the kitchen while the marquee was erected and Ed called on the other two gardeners to come and help put up the trestle tables where Jess and Izzy wanted to place them.

'I'll just take a picture for Lacey,' Izzy said, holding up her camera. 'We don't want her changing her mind about the room layout after we've done the tables.'

They didn't have to wait long for Lacey's reply. She phoned back almost immediately. 'It's perfect,' she squealed into Izzy's ear, making her wince. 'I can't wait to see what you've done when everything is laid out in all its finery.'

Neither could they. 'She's happy,' Izzy said to Jess, relieved. 'We can start putting out the tablecloths now.'

Izzy's phone rang and seeing Alex's name on her screen she answered it. 'Hi, how was your new student?'

'Fine thanks, although I was a few minutes late thanks to you and Romeo taking so long to get back to the van from looking down cliff faces.'

'Yes, sorry about that.'

'Is Jess with you?'

'Yes.'

'Could I speak to her?'

'Sure.' Izzy held her mobile out towards her friend. 'Jess, it's Alex, he'd like a word.'

Jess frowned. 'With me? Why?'

'No idea.'

She watched Ed and the other gardeners straighten out the tables. She liked that he looked like a perfectionist too.

'Well, that was odd,' Jess said a few moments later, handing Izzy back her phone. 'He's asked me if I'll go surfing with him.'

Forgetting about Ed for a moment, Izzy stared at Jess. 'But you can't surf, not really.'

'I know, that's what I told him,' she said, her cheeks reddening. 'But I've pestered him a bit about giving me surfing lessons and he's had a student dropping out this afternoon and wanted to know if I can take his place.'

'What, now?'

'Yes. You don't mind, do you?'

Izzy shook her head. 'Of course not, we've done as much as we can here today.'

Jess pulled a face. 'I meant about me going surfing with your brother. I need to go right away, so you'll need to find another way home.'

'Hang on a sec ...' Before she had a chance to finish Jess had run to the van and jumped in. Izzy sighed as she watched her friend racing off down the gravel driveway. 'Bloody hell.'

'What's the matter?' Ed asked, walking up to the marquee entrance. 'Everything OK with Jess?'

Izzy watched the dust cloud rising along the driveway behind her retreating van and shook her head. 'Yes, it's fine.'

'An emergency?'

'Only if you call Jess racing off to have her first surfing lesson with my brother an emergency.'

Chapter Eighteen

'Jess has left you stranded then?' Ed asked.

Izzy nodded. 'She thought you might be able to give me a lift to the cottage.' It had dawned on her that maybe Jess had left her behind deliberately.

'I've finished here for the day, too,' he said. 'I was going to go kayaking this afternoon. Would you like to join me? Or maybe you should keep that cut dry.'

Izzy had always planned to go on one of the kayaking courses she'd heard people talking about on the island, but had never got round to doing anything about it. 'I've never done it before though.' She glanced at her throbbing hand. 'I don't think it really needed the paper stitches, and the seawater will probably do the cut some good.'

'No problem. I have a double kayak. You won't need to do anything except sit back and enjoy the view. I'll do all the paddling.'

'I think I can manage that,' she said, smiling.

'Fine,' he said after giving her comment some thought. 'We can always turn back if your hand hurts too much though. I have a lifejacket and helmet you can borrow, if you don't mind getting your outfit wet.'

Izzy shook her head. 'I'll just go and fetch my bag. I'll be right back.'

She ran inside and snatched up her bag, then headed to the kitchen to find Marie.

'Looking for me?' she heard her ask from one of the rooms off the hallway.

'Yes, I'm about to shoot off now, but Jess and I will be back tomorrow morning,' she said. 'I just wanted to thank you for all your help today, and for this.' Izzy held up her hand. 'You did a great job.'

'You off home?'

Izzy shook her head and smiled. 'No.' She told Marie about Jess racing off and that Ed had invited her to go kayaking with him.

'He's brilliant at that,' Marie said. 'You'll have great fun, though I'd keep the glove on.'

'I'll see you tomorrow.' She ran back outside to Ed's Land Rover, and climbed in.

Ed waved at Marie, who was watching from a window, and started the ignition. 'She'll be questioning me tomorrow, making sure I remembered my manners and wanting to know that I dropped you off safely tonight.'

'Why?'

Ed shrugged. 'Not sure, but Marie is a worrier and I think she still feels a bit responsible for me.' He slowed down as they reached a junction. 'She acts like an older sister sometimes, bossing me about.'

'It's nice having someone looking out for you,' she said, thinking of Alex and how he was the first one to sort out anybody who had been horrible to her.

They drove along the busy roads until Ed slowed down at some traffic lights along the end of the Esplanade.

'Look at that,' he said indicating the silvery reflection of the bright sunrays on the almost still sea of the bay. 'It's a perfect day for kayaking. I think you're going to like it. Who knows, you might even want to come out with me again sometime.'

She hoped so. This really was an experience she was looking forward to putting into practice.

Ed drove through the tunnel to Green Street and through Georgetown to St Clements.

'Where are we going?' Izzy asked.

'Just out towards Longueville. To my lock-up, where I keep my boards and kayaks,' he said. 'We're nearly there.'

They turned off the road down a lane and came to a small farmstead. 'This place is lived in by a friend of mine when he's on the island. I rent one of the smaller barns for any equipment that doesn't fit into my cottage at the manor.'

Izzy couldn't help wondering how pretty this place must have been before the town had reached this far and how lovely it was for the farm to have retained the few fields around it in such an unexpected place.

They picked up the kayak, oars, helmets, and lifejackets and headed for the bay again.

'I thought we could go out at St Catherine's,' he said as they rounded the corner just after Archirondel Bay.

'Sounds great,' Izzy agreed.

It didn't take long for them to get organized and set off. Ed took her through the basics and was relieved she took to it quickly. 'Well, I wouldn't expect anything less from an islander,' he said. 'Especially from one who has the island's premier surfer as her older brother.'

They paddled next to the mile-long breakwater and around to the left towards the pretty bay of Flicquet. Izzy listened to Ed talking about the first time he'd come this way.

'I discovered little coves and bays that are usually impossible to see from the roads,' he said. 'It really was magical.'

She couldn't believe how peaceful it was. Summer was always so busy on the island, with holidaymakers and families making the most of the good weather, but out here the only sounds were made by seagulls, water sloshing over shallow rocks and their oars gliding through the water, pushing the kayak ever forward. 'Everyone should be made to do this,' she said, unable to believe how pretty everything looked from her current perspective.

Ed laughed. 'I agree, but I don't think you'd get away with decreeing something like that.'

As they rounded the next bay Izzy gasped. 'Dolphins,' she whispered excitedly.

Ed nodded. 'I was hoping we'd spot these guys. I saw them the other day when I was out here for a few hours. They're gorgeous, aren't they?'

'Lovely,' Izzy sighed. She'd been lucky enough to see a pod of dolphins once when her mum had driven her and Alex down to St Ouens for breakfast a few years before. But this was the closest she'd ever been to them and it was magical.

Ed stopped paddling and they sat silently watching the graceful creatures playing in the warm sea of the bay, undisturbed by anyone else. 'They're enchanting, don't you think?'

'I do,' she whispered.

Ed watched for a few more minutes before turning his torso around towards Izzy. 'They're not the only enchanting creatures here today,' he said, his voice deep and melodious.

Izzy almost held her breath as he leaned in and kissed her. She had to bend forward so that their lips could connect fully, but wasn't going to miss the perfect opportunity to kiss this gorgeous man once again.

Ed eventually moved away. 'I'm not as agile as I'd like to be, it seems,' he joked. 'Maybe you should sit in the front next time.'

'I'm happy to do that,' she said truthfully. 'Oh, look.' She pointed out to the dolphins, as one leapt high into the air. 'How can people keep these lovely animals in aquariums?'

'It should be illegal,' he said. 'I hate to think of them restrained.'

They watched the dolphins playing for a while longer.

'We should have come out earlier,' Ed said. 'The sun's going down and we don't want to be out here when it's dark.'

Izzy wished they'd come out earlier too; she wasn't ready to go back, but knew he was right.

Ed turned the kayak around in a large circle and they began their paddle back to the breakwater. 'I'm glad you've enjoyed this afternoon,' he said. 'We'll have to make a date to come out here again.'

'I'd like that very much. When do you think we should next come out?'

'You make a suggestion and I'll fit in around you. My calendar isn't as restricted as yours. As long as I carry out the work I need to do at the manor.'

She thought quickly. 'How about Tuesday morning?' 'We need the Sunday to pack up after a wedding and the Monday to clean everything up. Tuesdays are best for me.'

'Tuesday it is then.'

He sounded pleased, she thought. Then his stomach rumbled, making her laugh.

'Sorry about that. I haven't eaten much today, so maybe a visit to the café for supper would be good.'

Izzy was pretty hungry too. She'd eaten meals at the café many times and always enjoyed the food.

Ed paddled to the slipway and stepped out of the kayak, holding it steady and pulling it higher so that the water was shallower for Izzy to then get out. She helped him carry it up to his Land Rover and load it onto the roof rack.

Ed unlocked the vehicle and reached in to grab a towel for Izzy. 'Here, you can use this to dry off.'

She unclipped her helmet and lifejacket and handed them to him, drying off her legs and arms and retying her ponytail. When they were both dry they walked up to the café.

'Yes, please,' Izzy said when the waitress told them about the specials they had on offer and came to the lobster, telling them it was the last one and that if they liked they could prepare a basic *fruits de mer* for them to share. 'Would that suit you too, Ed?'

'*Bien sûr*,' he said, for once forgetting to reply in English.

'Ahh,' the waitress said, waving her pencil in the air, '*Vous êtes Français, non*?'

'*Oui*,' he replied, and chattered away to her in his native language for a while.

Izzy smiled. She liked the sound of him speaking French. He seemed so very English most of the time.

He glanced at Izzy. 'Sorry, I'm being rude.'

She shook her head. 'No, it's lovely to hear you speaking French and I could work out some of what you were saying. Carry on.'

But he didn't. The moment had passed.

'Are you enjoying living in Jersey?' he asked the waitress, who, going by Izzy's less-than-fluent French skills, had just told him that she'd only been on the island for the summer, but was loving it so far.

'Very much, it is a pretty place and I can be in St Malo in just over one hour. My family lives two hours by train after that, but still very close to travel home if I wish to. Will you both have the *fruits de mer* then?'

'Please.'

The waitress bent down slightly, lowering her voice. 'For a fellow countryman I will ensure you have the very best seafood we 'ave to offer.'

Izzy wouldn't argue with such a promising offer. 'I look forward to sampling it,' she said.

Ed nodded. '*Et moi aussi*.'

The waitress looked much happier as she moved on to the next table.

Izzy always enjoyed visiting the comfortable café, with its view of St Catherine's wide bay and the long, wide granite breakwater that her great-great-grandfather had come over to Jersey from Ireland to help build back in the mid-1880s. To some locals whose families went back centuries, she still wasn't considered a local. It made her wonder how long her family would have to live here before she was truly considered so.

She realized Ed was talking to her and leaned forward to hear him better over the building chatter of the other diners, resting her forearms on the cool granite table. 'Sorry, I was miles away.'

'It's fine, don't worry.' He took her hand and gave it a gentle squeeze. 'I've really enjoyed myself today, Izzy. I know you said you're happy to come out with me kayaking on Tuesday, but do you think we could go out on a proper date one evening?'

'Are you sure?' It seemed a bit of an about-turn after their conversation earlier in the day.

'I don't see why not, Izzy. I only told you about me going so that you knew and neither of us allowed our feelings for the other to get too deep.'

'Well, OK then.' She was happy to see him again, and if her heart got a little crumpled in the process then it was her own lookout. 'I'll look forward to it.'

'I'd love to invite you to the cottage to cook a meal for you, but now that Catherine has come back to the manor I wouldn't want her finding an excuse to interrupt our evening. I know she apologised to you girls, but I still don't completely trust her to behave properly towards you.'

Neither did Izzy. 'That's fine,' she said. 'I would offer to cook for you, but I'm a pretty lousy chef.' She laughed. 'And knowing Jess, if she thought someone was making a delicious meal she'd find a way to invite herself to join in.'

He frowned. 'Our living arrangements aren't perfect, are they?'

Izzy didn't want him to think that she resented Jess in any way, so said, 'Not at all, I love living at the cottage, it's comfy and in a perfect location. Jess is a great housemate too. Well, she's my landlady really, I suppose. But, no, it's not the most private place.'

'I didn't mean to insult Jess,' he said. 'She's lovely and you obviously get on very well.'

'I know,' Izzy said. 'I didn't want you to think I was moaning about her, she's fabulous.'

'She is. You said she was out with Alex this afternoon?'

'Yes. I hope he remembered she's a novice surfer. He can be a little overbearing when he wants someone to do well.'

'Do you surf?'

She nodded. 'Not for years, but when I was about eight Alex decided that I needed to learn and took me down to the beach every day for the entire summer holidays.'

Ed whistled, impressed. 'You must be very good then?'

She shrugged. 'You would think so, but I'm only OK. I'd need to put in some serious practice before I could call myself any good now, much to Alex's disgust.'

Ed laughed. 'I like your brother. We had a lot of fun when we were at school together, although we did get up to a few things that almost got me expelled.'

'No! What?' She was intrigued to know what they could have done that was so bad.

Ed sighed. 'Well, let's just say we were fourteen and too young to be sneaking lager and cigarettes into the school.'

She thought for a moment. 'I think I remember that,' she stared at him. 'Weren't you caught trying to sell them to the other boys?'

He nodded. 'Yes, to my shame. My godfather was furious and threatened to send me back to France.'

The waitress stopped by their table with the food. Ed let go of Izzy's hand and they sat back to give her space to lower a cradle of locally caught delights.

'Wow, this looks amazing,' Izzy said, staring at the display of king prawns, moules, oysters, whelks, and a lobster and dressed crab sitting on a bed of crispy lettuce.

'Enjoy,' she said smiling at them both. She seemed unsure whether to say something further and then added, 'This is your first date?'

Izzy shook her head. 'No. We're not on a date,' she laughed.

Ed stared at the waitress pointedly, smiled, and asked, 'Why do you think we're on a first date?'

The waitress hesitated, then said. 'You, er, look a little shy, but both very happy to be with each other.'

Izzy hated the thought that her shyness was so obvious. It hadn't occurred to her that Ed ever looked remotely shy or awkward.

'No, we're just friends out for a meal.'

The waitress looked at him and smiled. 'Of course, I am mistaken. Please, forget me and enjoy your food.'

She walked away and Izzy stared after her before turning her attention back to Ed. 'Do you really think we look uncomfortable with each other?'

'No,' he soothed. 'She probably noticed me looking a little less sure of myself than I usually do.'

Izzy was taken aback by his comment. 'I didn't realize you two had met before.'

'Not to talk to, but I have been here a few times with my godfather and I think even with Alex once or twice, so she probably notices a difference in my behaviour.' He laughed. 'Then again, I'm bound to be a little different when I'm with a lady to when I'm having dinner with those two.'

Izzy smiled. 'Yes, you're probably right.' She looked at the sumptuous plate of seafood. 'Tuck in,' she said, 'I'm still deciding what to have first.'

'I think we should both have some of this,' he said, lifting half a lobster onto her plate with his fork and a knife and then the other half onto his own. 'It looks so fresh.'

She watched him and sensed the waitress watching

them. Looking over at her, Izzy smiled. She didn't blame the woman for watching Ed over the summer – after all, she'd been doing the same thing for the past couple of weeks.

The meal was delicious and getting to know Ed a little better was interesting. 'I can't believe you spent time working on a ranch in Arizona,' she said after he'd paid the tab and was walking with her back to the Land Rover.

'I was seventeen, and I suspect my parents thought I was too young to be getting serious with Marie and needed to be sent somewhere where I'd be exhausted each day and unable to get into trouble at night.' He held the door open for Izzy, helped her inside and got into the driver's seat.

'They meant business sending you that far away,' she joked.

'You're not kidding.' He put the key in the ignition, started the engine and drove off. 'The ranch was about fifty miles away from the nearest town.'

'Sounds tough.'

He nodded. 'Yes, but I did end up enjoying myself. I loved the scenery and was able to go out each evening with Angel, one of the guys who worked on the ranch. He was a fascinating character and taught me how to lasso cattle.'

Izzy pictured a young Ed out riding in the sunshine. 'Wow. The most exciting job I had was a Saturday job working at a newsagents.'

'That doesn't sound too bad,' he said as they reached the top of the hill before turning down towards Rozel Bay and the cottage.

'It wasn't. I read all the magazines for free. It saved me a fortune.'

Ed laughed. They continued in companionable silence for a while, till he broke it.

'So, when can we do this again?'

'I'm free most evenings,' she said, wishing she

sounded a little less available. 'I mean, we're so busy in the daytime that I tend not to do much at night.'

'That's good to hear.'

'That I'm unpopular?' she joked.

'No, that now you've told me your diary is fairly free, so you can't refuse to come out with me.'

'I can always refuse,' she said giggling.

'True, but I'm hoping you won't.'

He had to park up the road from the cottage in the nearest available parking space. 'How do you two cope when you need to bring the van closer to the cottage to load it in the summer?'

She opened the door to get out. 'We park outside the cottage. Our neighbours know we won't be stopping there for long so we don't usually have a problem.'

He walked with her down to the cottage. 'I've enjoyed today very much,' he said.

'Me too.'

They reached the front door and seeing the lights were still off, Izzy dug around in her small bag for her front door key. She located it and turned to him. 'Would you like to come in for a coffee?' she asked, looking over her shoulder.

'Yes, that would be lovely.'

Izzy couldn't help wondering if Jess was back yet. She unlocked the door and walked in. 'Take a seat in the living room and I'll put the kettle on.' She went to the kitchen and took two mugs from the cupboard. 'I'm afraid we've only got instant left,' she shouted, aware that he was probably used to proper coffee.

'That's great.'

She made the coffees and carried a mug each into the living room. 'Sugar?'

'No thanks.'

She sat down in the chair next to the sofa where he was sitting. 'So, when are we going out?'

He laughed. 'You tell me. I'm pretty flexible.'

'How about next Friday?' she suggested.

Ed frowned. 'That's over a week away. How about Sunday? If you're not too shattered after Lacey's wedding celebrations.'

'OK, great.' She was glad he'd brought the date forward. She didn't want to be the one to seem too eager.

'Now we're alone, Iz,' he said, 'I wanted to speak to you about France and what you think you saw with Catherine and me in that cabin.'

Izzy lifted up her mug of coffee and blew on it. 'I believed you when you explained about it before. I know she's determined and difficult,' she hesitated. 'I have to admit discovering you and Catherine had some sort of history together was a bit of a shock.'

'It was nothing, really.'

He shrugged, believing him. 'And finding you were married to the woman you still live near and work with was a little harder.'

'Ahh, I can see how that must look.' He rubbed his unshaven chin. 'My relationship with Marie is completely different now to how it used to be and I admit that for a while I found that difficult.' He stared at her to gauge her reaction. 'I promise you, Iz, that we really are finished and have been for a long time. She's a good friend of mine now. I wouldn't be able to live at the manor with her there if I didn't think she saw me the same way.'

Reassured, Izzy smiled. 'I believe you.'

'Good, I'm relieved.'

'We've all got a past, Ed,' she said thinking about David, the man she'd thought she would be married to by now. 'We've all been disappointed at some point too and I think it shows strength of character that you and Marie have been able to move forward with your relationship and remain friends.'

'It does make life a lot easier,' he said. 'I can't imagine

my godfather would have us both living there if he thought there would be problems. He's a private man who doesn't like dramatic shows of hysteria.'

It must be hard for him having a daughter like Catherine then, Izzy thought, but held back from voicing her feelings.

Ed laughed.

'What?' She couldn't understand what he found so funny.

'You were thinking about Catherine, weren't you?'

'No,' she fibbed. Then seeing his expression and that he obviously wasn't convinced, smiled. 'OK, I was. How can she be so unlike him?'

'I think she takes after her mother rather than him. She was very …' he considered his next words. 'Shall we say, exuberant? I think she nearly sent him insane when they divorced and she made such a fuss of the settlement he intended giving to her. It was fairly rough for him for a couple of years.'

His voice trailed off and he reached out, taking her mug from her hands and placing it on the table. Then he took hold of Izzy's hands and lifted them to his lips.

Her stomach contracted at his touch and her heart began to pound more rapidly. She looked into his blue eyes and yearned for him to kiss her.

'I want us to forget about both our pasts and everyone else and get to know each other, at least for the time I have left on the island.'

'So do I.'

He pulled her gently to her feet, took her in his arms, and kissed her. The pressure of his firm lips on hers was delicious. The heat of his body caused all the senses in her body to intensify in their reaction to him. She groaned as he held her tighter and their kissing intensified.

Eventually they broke slightly apart, but he held her tightly. 'Izzy, I …' he began, his voice husky.

205

'Oh, sorry.' Jess was standing in the doorway.

'You're home!' Izzy said, trying not to show how frustrated she was to see her friend. 'We were just, um –'

'I think it's pretty obvious what you were both doing,' Jess teased. 'Sorry. I didn't mean to burst in on you both.'

Izzy reluctantly stepped back from Ed, feeling the warmth of his arms slipping away from her. 'It's fine, don't worry about it.'

'Liar,' Jess whispered as she walked past Izzy to go to the kitchen. She stopped and turned. 'Luke called, he's not going to be able to come round tonight after all. He said he'll rearrange coming here in the next few days.'

'No problem,' Izzy said, disappointed that they wouldn't be discovering the contents of the mysterious room just yet.

'I'd better be going anyway,' Ed said, leaning forward and kissing Izzy on each cheek. 'I'll see you both tomorrow at the manor.'

'Bright and at sparrow-fart,' Jess said pulling a face.

'She's not a morning person,' Izzy said, putting her arm round her friend. 'Then again, I'm not that good if I'm honest.'

'I love the mornings,' Ed laughed. 'Though it's probably got something to do with spending so many years at boarding school and being woken so early.' He looked at Jess. 'What did you call it?'

'Sparrow-fart,' she repeated, making him and Izzy burst out laughing.

'Yes, that's about right.' He walked over to the door and pulled it open. 'Till tomorrow, then,' he said, smiling at Jess and giving Izzy a lingering look.

'Tomorrow,' she said, looking forward to being able to see him again. It had been a busy but fun day, and one she couldn't wait to repeat.

'I think it's all coming together nicely,' Jess said, giving Izzy a hug once he'd gone.

'What, me and Ed?'

'Everything,' Jess said, walking into the kitchen.

Izzy followed her, a warm feeling coursing through her. She didn't want to spend hours chatting so didn't tell Jess about Ed leaving the island. 'Yes, I think you could be right. The business is back on track, thanks to Ed and the Seigneur, and we're both happy.' She pulled out a chair and sat down, watching Jess make a cup of tea for herself to take up to bed. 'So, how was your afternoon and evening with my brother?'

'It was awesome.'

Izzy looked at her dreamy expression. 'He kissed you, didn't he?'

'No.'

She could see by the innocent look Jess was trying to give her that he had.

Jess forgot her tea and pulled out a chair to sit down next to Izzy. 'Oh, Iz, he's so lovely.'

Izzy groaned.

'Oh, I knew you'd be like that,' Jess said leaping up, grabbing hold of her cup and marching into the living room in a sulk.

Izzy followed, annoyed with herself for not checking her response. 'Sorry, Jess. I didn't groan because I don't want you to see my brother, but because I don't trust him not to hurt you.'

Soothed slightly, Jess looked at her. 'Fine, but I'm a big girl, Iz. I'm not a teenager who sees a wedding at the end of every kiss.'

'I realize that,' Izzy said. 'But you do like him, a lot. Even I can see that. And I just don't want you to forget all those times girls have turned up at my mum's house crying because he'd dumped them just when they thought things were getting serious.'

Jess leaned back in her chair and sniffed. 'I haven't forgotten.'

'But?'

'I'm just hoping that maybe he's grown up a bit and won't be so quick to do that now.'

Izzy hoped so too, but Alex would have to fall hard for Jess to be remotely reliable and not let her down. 'I hope so too,' she said. 'What about Roman, I thought you liked him too? Maybe if you see him again you'll realize you like him more than you do Alex?'

Jess thought about this idea and took a sip of her tea. 'Maybe, but I don't think so. Anyway, I think Roman has his life sorted in France. At least Alex is over here and I know he's fun and won't be going anywhere.'

Unlike Ed, Izzy thought, her mood dipping. 'Apart from travelling for competitions, Jess,' she said. 'Don't forget that. And we both know that Alex attracts a lot of attention from girls who follow the surfers on the tours.'

'I could go with him,' she said thoughtfully.

'During the summer, when our business is at its busiest?' Izzy realized her friend hadn't thought it through, but wasn't too worried. She knew her brother and doubted he'd stick to one girl long enough for Jess to have to make any difficult choices.

Jess lifted her feet and rested them on the thick footrest in front of her chair. 'I know you're only trying to pacify me.'

'A little,' she said honestly, aware Jess knew her too well for her to be able to fob her off with a lie.

Jess smiled. 'This is like when we were teenagers and used to wonder who we were going to marry.'

'Yes, and you changed your mind every time we spoke about it.'

Jess laughed. 'And you only ever wanted to marry that rotten David, even when we were back in secondary school. I remember the first time you saw him, all skinny in his school uniform.'

Izzy giggled. 'I was also in my school uniform and

desperately skinny with untameable hair.'

Jess patted Izzy's hand. 'He still fancied you though, didn't he?'

'Yes.' She remembered the day he'd asked her out. She'd waited the entire school year, sitting next to him during their history and English lessons, desperate for him to make a move. It was when she'd come first in their year for the hundred metres on Sports Day, and everyone in their school house had hugged and congratulated her. David's congratulations had been her first kiss. She'd never forgotten it, or him.

'Come along,' Jess said quietly, as she always did when the conversation turned to David. 'Time for bed, if we want to be alive enough to function tomorrow morning.

Izzy stood up and picked up her and Ed's mugs, carrying them through to the kitchen and placing them in the sink to wash in the morning. He was the first man she'd wanted to kiss since, well, since David. It was a new experience and for the first time in a very long time, Izzy felt truly alive.

Izzy was following Jess up the stairs to her room when it dawned on her what the perfect table decoration might be. She turned and ran down to get her phone and text Lacey to see what she thought of her idea.

'What are you doing?' Jess asked. 'Remember we've got a lot to do tomorrow, so don't spend hours texting lovely Ed.'

'I'm not,' Izzy shouted back up to her. 'What do you think of small lavender plants for the tables?'

'Bloody brilliant,' Jess agreed. 'Perfect. The colouring will go with Lacey's theme for our crockery and they aren't as expensive as roses.

'And if Lacey doesn't want to keep them all, we can plant some here and either use them at another party or sell them on elsewhere.'

Jess followed her back down the stairs. 'We can place

them into the older sugar bowls we've got, and mask the broken handles from old cups with greenery and use those too, if we need to.'

'Good idea.' Excited and with no thought of going to bed, Izzy send Lacey a text.

Chapter Nineteen

'It's looking perfect now the dance floor has been laid and the floral arch has been started,' Jess said, rubbing her hands together. 'Ed and the other gardeners are collecting roses from around the grounds to add to the hydrangeas that we've got to insert and I think it's going to look spectacular.

Izzy agreed. She looked at Jess's creation around the marquee entrance and put down the first couple of polystyrene trays of lavender plants just outside on the grass.

'Aren't these perfect?' she said as Jess came over to inspect her garden centre purchases. 'I was so relieved they had enough in stock and they're all blooming beautifully.'

Jess bent down to sniff the small purple plants. 'So fragrant too, clever you. I'm so pleased Lacey loved your idea.'

They walked over to the van to collect the rest of the lavender and the two boxes of crockery Izzy had bought to plant them in.

'Hey, don't you two worry about those,' Ed said, walking onto the lawn from the back of the manor house, pushing a wheelbarrow filled with hydrangeas and roses. 'You'll get your hands all mucky and you've still got your tablecloths and napkins to lay out yet.'

Izzy laughed. 'So you did listen last night when I waffled on about everything we still had to do today?'

'I did.' He waved the other two gardeners over. 'Can

you guys plant up the lavenders into those little bowls?'

They nodded, smiling appreciatively at Jess and Izzy. 'Thank you,' Izzy said, as Jess gave them both the benefit of her brilliant white teeth.

While the guys got to work, Jess carried on with dressing the marquee archway and Izzy began laying the tables and setting places with the crockery and napkins. She was sure Lacey would have a perfect day.

'It's looking incredible,' Ed said coming up behind her. 'And you haven't even finished yet.'

'I'm glad you like it,' she said honestly. 'It's good to get another opinion.' She lowered her voice. 'We need the photos to be as spectacular as possible. We're hoping to use them to advertise this year's parties for Lapins de Lune.'

He gave her a kiss on the cheek. 'You'll get many bookings on the back of these pictures, I'm certain.'

'I hope so,' she said.

He checked his watch. 'I'd better get on. I haven't got through half the jobs I should've been doing this morning. I don't want the grounds to let the pictures down.'

She shrugged. 'Personally I can't see that happening, but you'd better get on.'

A couple of hours later Jess and Izzy stood outside the marquee and smiled at each other.

'It's looking perfect,' Jess said.

'Isn't it?' Izzy gave Jess a hug. 'We've pulled this off in record time too. I knew we could do it.'

Jess puffed out her cheeks and blew a raspberry. 'I wasn't so sure, but after everything that's happened I'm so relieved it's looking this good.'

They finished packing the remnants of their crockery and linens away into the butler's pantry. 'This is in case there are any extra guests we haven't been told about,' Izzy said when Marie asked them why they had extra stock.

'Or in case there's a drama and we need to replace stuff.' Izzy narrowed her eyes. 'You'd be amazed how many times we've had to do that.'

Marie wanted to see their progress, so they all headed over to the marquee. 'Wow, you girls are seriously talented.'

'That's what I said.' Ed had come up to the entrance of the marquee behind them.

The roar of a car came towards them down the long driveway. Izzy turned as a beautiful pillar-box red sports car rounded the corner, driven by Ed's godfather.

'Hello!' Ed called, hurrying over to greet the Seigneur. Next to him in the passenger seat was a younger, more glamorous man who wouldn't look out of place in a theatre. It was Rick from the Encore.

Marie turned to Izzy and Jess and said, 'Good-looking, isn't he?'

'If you're talking about the Seigneur, I can't see it myself,' Jess murmured.

Ed and the two men came back towards them. 'The girls have done a brilliant job setting up the marquee for the wedding on Saturday.'

Izzy stepped forward to greet the Seigneur who smiled and nodded to her. 'We're incredibly grateful to you for agreeing to let us hold the wedding here. It's going to be amazing.'

He took her hand in his and almost crushed it in his grip as he looked over her shoulder at the floral archway. 'It looks pretty splendid from out here.'

Izzy was surprised that the Seigneur was being so pleasant, after his coolness at their initial meeting. She wondered if it could be because his friend was with him, or maybe it was because Catherine was home again.

Ed indicated the other man. 'Ladies, this is Rick from the Encore.' Rick grinned at them, holding his arms out as if he was about to take a bow.

'I'm delighted you girls were able to return from your trip with Ed and accommodate the young bride. Francesca and I were inordinately concerned when we had the fire and had to cancel her arrangements for Saturday,' he said in his southern American drawl.

'It's no problem, we were grateful to be given the opportunity,' Jess said, glancing at the Seigneur, 'and we were happy to be able to step in and save the day.'

Rick patted Ed on the back. 'Well it's young Ed here you have to thank, not me. Ed's the one who persuaded that chap there and insisted you could do it and Francesca and I were willing to agree to anything to help the kid. And look, you've pulled it off.'

'Not yet,' Izzy said smiling, 'but we will.'

'Of course you will,' Ed said, putting an arm each around Jess and Izzy. 'I have every faith in you,' he said tilting his head towards the marquee. 'What do you say, Marie?'

Izzy had forgotten Marie was standing with them, she'd been so quiet. She wondered if it was because her boss was here and maybe she felt she should be inside doing jobs or something.

'They've been very creative,' she said.

Izzy spotted the Seigneur glancing at Marie and, without saying anything further, she walked off back into the house. What happened there? Izzy wondered, hoping Marie was OK.

'We'd better go,' Izzy said. 'But thank you once again, Mr, er, sir.'

He shook his head. 'Just call me Ralph, everyone else does.'

'No they don't,' Ed teased.

He pushed Ed's shoulder. 'Haven't you got work to be getting on with instead of annoying these poor girls?' He looked at Izzy and winked. 'I'd better get on, too.' He looked over at the parking area. 'Catherine about?'

Ed shook his head. 'I haven't seen her today.'

The Seigneur stopped walking. 'I was sorry that Catherine's elopement caused you both so much inconvenience,' he said, sounding sincere. 'Ed was unimpressed to say the least.' He gave Ed a smile. 'He didn't really give me much opportunity to refuse this idea of you holding the wedding here, although he'll probably be furious with me for telling you as much.'

Ed didn't look pleased for this news to have been given out to them. 'That was because I wanted you to see how well something like this could work.'

'Yes, well, now you have.' Ralph patted Ed's arm before walking off towards the manor house. 'If I don't see you before, I hope your day is everything you hope it to be.' He motioned for Rick to follow him. 'Come along, I think we could do with a snifter, don't you?'

'He can be really lovely,' Jess said.

'We really need to get home and make any last-minute plans.'

Ed followed them over to the van and walked around to the driver's side to speak to Izzy. 'I was wondering if you'd want to come for a quick drink tonight?'

'I've got the wedding tomorrow,' she said, sorely tempted. She'd never ordinarily go out the night before a big event, but who knew how many times she'd be able to go for a drink with him before he left. She watched him waiting for her answer. 'Go on then, but just a quick drink.'

Ed smiled. He bent down and kissed her just as she was about to add something. She wasn't sure what, because his lips on hers wiped out everything she was intending to say.

'I'm going to have to go home and shower first,' she said, not relishing sitting in a pub after hours of toiling in the heat of the marquee.

'No problem,' Ed said, 'I'll meet you at the cottage in an hour and we can go somewhere close by so that you can go home whenever you choose.

That suited her fine. She reached up and kissed him once more, glad of the excuse to touch his perfect lips with her own once again. 'See you soon,' she said getting into the van.

It was only as they drove out of the gated archway on to the main road that Jess spoke. 'You're really crazy about that guy, aren't you?'

'What are you banging on about?' Izzy asked, trying to deflect the interrogation she knew was about to happen.

'Er, you know exactly what I mean, so don't pretend you don't.' She fanned herself with a notebook from the side pocket of the van. 'You never usually go out the night before we have a large job on.'

'Never mind me,' she said. 'I think there's something odd going on between Ed's godfather and Marie.'

'I didn't notice anything. What do you mean?'

Happy to have succeeded in changing the subject, she said, 'I thought the way Marie reacted to him was odd.'

Jess stared out of the window silently for a few minutes. Izzy was just beginning to wonder if she'd fallen asleep when she said, 'Do you think they're having an affair?'

Izzy wasn't sure if Jess sounded jealous or simply intrigued at this notion. 'I don't know what I think, but she acted very strangely when he arrived and couldn't get away from him quick enough.'

'So?'

'Well, I just thought there were unspoken messages going between them. I'm not sure what though, but something was going on.'

'I wonder,' Jess said, going quiet again. Then seconds later, slapping Izzy's arm, she shouted, 'Hey, clever cow, that was sneaky.'

Pretending not to understand what Izzy was accusing her of, she frowned at her. 'What was?'

'You're talking to me, don't forget,' Jess said. 'I know you too well and especially when you're trying to distract me, which only goes to prove that you are crazy about Monsieur Edouard, or Compte Edouard, or whatever his proper name is. Go on, admit it.'

Izzy shook her head, exasperated with Jess not leaving her alone with her thoughts. 'OK, OK! Happy now?' She narrowed her eyes. 'At least I can make my mind up about a guy. You've been flitting between Alex and Roman for weeks and it's not fair on either of them,' Izzy said.

Jess shrugged. 'Roman's not here, and Alex is gorgeous.'

'I think my brother likes you a bit more than he expected.' Izzy sighed. 'Now, rather than worrying about you, I'm more concerned about his emotions if you hurt him. It's an odd sensation.'

'It feels great to be the one with a little power,' Jess said thoughtfully. 'Although,' she poked Izzy in the shoulder. 'Your brother is so hot I think I'm falling for him.'

'Shit, that's terrible.'

'Why?' Jess asked sounding hurt. 'I'm your best friend, Iz, you should be happy for me.'

'I am, truly, but it's one thing you two falling for each other and being all loved up now – what happens if you fall out and one of you gets hurt?' She pulled a face. 'Think about it, whoever gets hurt will either be my best friend or my brother, and either way I'm going to be caught in the middle and whoever I comfort the other will feel betrayed.'

'Hmm, I hadn't thought of that.'

'Didn't think you had. Maybe you should be focusing your affections on Roman, at least that way we would be having relationships with two brothers.'

'If they wanted us to, that is.'

Izzy laughed. 'I hadn't considered that. We'll just have

217

to make sure they fall in love with us.'

'How?'

'I've no idea,' but she was going to think of something, she was certain of it.

Jess was concentrating on her mobile phone. Izzy drove, thinking about which summer dress to put on for her drink with Ed when, turning down the hill towards the slipway near the cottage, she spotted Alex's familiar motorbike. It wasn't like him to make two visits in such quick succession.

'What's he doing here?'

Jess didn't say anything, which was a little odd.

'Jess? Do you know why my brother is parked outside the cottage?'

'Maybe,' she said guiltily.

'Go on.' Izzy suspected she wasn't going to like what was coming next.

'He sent me a text earlier. I didn't mention it to you because I'm so confused about what to do. But after everything you've just said I quickly texted him back and agreed to go out with him tonight.'

Confused and aware there must be more, Izzy said, 'And?'

Jess groaned. 'I said I thought it was probably best if we stopped seeing each other, before either of us got hurt, and that maybe we should go out and discuss everything.'

Izzy was beginning to wonder how well she did know her best friend. 'But you just said … oh never mind.' They drew up next to his car and Izzy leaned her head out of the window. 'Hi.'

Not giving her the usual cheery banter, Alex scowled past Izzy to Jess. 'I was hoping to have a word with your friend.'

Izzy turned to see Jess getting out of the van. 'I'll go and park this on the hill, but I'll be back in a few minutes. Try not to kill each other in that time.'

She drove away, unhappy to see them both angry, but at the same time relieved that their fledgling relationship wasn't going to go any further. If this was how they were after only going out surfing once together, what would they be like ending a full-blown relationship?

It took longer to park the van than she'd expected, and when she arrived back at the cottage, Izzy could hear the shouting before she even stepped inside the front door.

'Your brother is so full of himself,' Jess yelled as soon as Izzy was inside.

'No I'm not!'

Izzy stood saying nothing as they bickered back and forth, but eventually she grew sick of listening to their petty rowing, she shoved herself between the two of them. 'I think you two need to take a deep breath and relax a little. This isn't getting you anywhere.'

Alex paced the floor, pushing his long tanned fingers through his sun-kissed hair. 'I only suggested we go out for a meal. I didn't ask her to elope, for God's sake.'

He frowned, looking more uncomfortable than she'd ever seen him before. It occurred to Izzy that her brother was always the one in control in any romantic relationship and his feelings for Jess were causing him to feel vulnerable.

'Right, you two,' Izzy began, only to be interrupted by someone knocking on the door.

'Who the hell is that?' Alex asked as Izzy waved for them to wait and went to answer it.

'Ed,' she said checking the time on her watch and realizing she was going to be late for their planned drink. 'Sorry, I didn't realize the time.' She looked behind her, hearing Alex's voice murmuring something to Jess.

Ed pointed behind him. 'Luke's here too. He's come to open a door?' He peered over her shoulder towards the living room, and asked. 'Have we come at a bad time? We can go if you'd rather.'

Annoyed at her best friend and brother being so childish, she waved them in. 'No. It's fine, come in.'

He followed her into the living room where Alex now held Jess by both shoulders and was whispering to her. He looked up when Izzy entered the room closely followed by Ed and Luke.

'Sorry, we were just trying to sort something out,' Alex said, stepping forward and shaking Ed's hand. Giving Izzy a quizzical look he said, 'Didn't expect to see you here tonight, mate? Hi, Luke.'

'Izzy and I were going out for a quick drink before the wedding tomorrow.'

'I don't get this,' Alex said to Jess. 'It's OK for them but not for us, why?'

Ed stepped forward. 'Why don't Luke and I try to open this mysterious door, leave you two to it?'

'Great idea,' Izzy said without waiting for Jess to react. She and Alex needed time alone that much was obvious.

'No chance!' Jess shouted. 'That's my door and I'm going to be there when it's opened.' She pushed past everyone to the bottom of the stairs. 'It's this way, guys.'

Izzy couldn't help being amused at the dramatic change in her friend's mood. She followed the others up the stairs, hearing Alex grumbling to himself as he walked behind her.

Pulling her mobile from her pocket, Izzy quickly sent her mum a text asking if she'd discovered anything new about Jess's great-grandmother and the reason behind her locking the door. She didn't have long to wait for an answer.

She read her mum's text standing at the doorway to her room. Letting the information sink in, she leaned against the doorframe, watching Luke and Ed crouching down as Luke worked on the lock.

'I can't make it budge,' Luke said, moving back out of the way and handing a long thin tool to Ed when he held out his hand. They all waited quietly. Jess chewed one of her little fingernails as she stared at Ed. No one made a sound.

Chapter Twenty

Ed tried to concentrate and not think about how close Izzy was standing behind him. When her mobile buzzed and she began whispering with Alex, he focused his attention more on the matter in hand. He used to pick the locks of unused rooms in the château. It had been fun entering the rooms after decades of them being locked up, and he could imagine how exciting this must be for the girls.

He rummaged around in Luke's tool bag and located another, thinner tool that he hoped would help. It took a bit of effort, but his patience paid off. Ed stood up and breathed a sigh of relief as he turned the ebony handle and pulled open the door, which creaked loudly in complaint.

'It needs a bit of an oiling, but who wants to go through first?'

Jess almost bowled him over. Flinging her arms around him briefly, she kissed his cheek and squealed. 'So exciting. Thanks, big man.'

He stood back to let Jess, then Izzy and the others, pass before following them up the narrow oak stairs to a room so bright he assumed it must have been a sun room at some point. There was a tattered cloth map of the world pinned to the back wall, a shelf of old hardback books, and a window seat with a striped pink cushion, but apart from that the room was empty. Everyone gawped in silence.

'There's nothing here,' Jess announced, her eyes filling with tears. 'Why lock a door with nothing inside? It doesn't make sense.'

'It doesn't to me either,' Ed said, studying the map of the world.

'It's very faded,' Jess said. 'Look at these pins stuck in little groups in France and Belgium. They make me sad. There's an odd sense of loss about this room, don't you think?' she asked.

'True,' Luke said. 'Look at that.' He pointed to the shelf. At one end there was a model of a boat, used as a bookend. 'A sailing boat.' He went closer and peered at it. 'I think it could be handmade.'

Ed walked over to the large square window, resting his hand on the cushion that seemed to have been made to fit the deep window seat. He stared across the calm sea in the Channel to the Brittany shores. 'Incredible view though.'

Izzy cleared her throat. 'And that's –' she began, before stopping, clearing her throat and saying. 'That's why the door was locked. Or so my mum believes.'

They all swung round to wait for her to tell them more.

'Go on, Iz,' Ed said.

Izzy held up her mobile. 'Mum texted me to say that she's discovered your great-grandad moved in to this house with your great-grandmother when they were first married, Jess.'

'Yes,' Jess whispered. 'Go on.'

Ed watched Izzy trying to remain unemotional and failing. She stood in front of them, her curly, platinum blonde hair wild and loose, her T-shirt and shorts dusty, and without a scrap of make-up – and he couldn't imagine ever seeing a more beautiful creature.

'It's OK,' he said. 'Take your time.'

She smiled at him and took a deep breath. 'Sorry, I don't know what's got into me today.' Clearing her throat again, she smiled. 'Right. Apparently, the Great War began soon after they moved in here and he signed up to be one of the Jersey Pals. When she was upset at the thought of him going he told her to come up here and look out of this window, because in that direction,' Izzy pointed towards the French coast, 'is where he'd be fighting and he'd look back towards her and even though they couldn't see each other, they would know that each day at some point, they would be looking towards each other.'

Jess gulped and began to sniff. 'Oh, that's so romantic.'

Ed watched Alex putting his arm around Jess's shoulder, and asked Izzy, 'How did your mum know all this?'

Izzy held up the phone. 'She asked a few of Jess's gran's friends to see if any of them had heard about this locked room and one of them remembered her mother telling her about it. Apparently, at the time, it was well known around here that every day at noon, Jess's great-gran would come up here and stare silently out of the window, thinking about her husband and they believe the only thing that kept her going was discovering she was pregnant with his child.'

'He bloody died, didn't he?' Jess asked, sniffing and wiping her runny nose on the bottom of her T-shirt. 'That's why she locked up the room. Poor Gran, I wonder if she ever came up here after?'

Ed waited for Izzy to answer. 'Yes, Mum said the poor lady lived here for as long as she could, until she had to go into a home, but she made your gran promise never to open the door to this room.'

Ed cringed. 'And now I've unlocked it,' he said quietly.

'We'll have to close it up again,' Jess said.

He looked around the dusty room, sun pouring in through the window even though it was early evening. 'No.'

'What?' Izzy asked, frowning. 'Jess is probably right.'

'No,' he repeated. 'Why close it up? It's been left empty for what, a hundred years now?'

'Yes, it must be,' Jess said, her eyes wide with shock. 'Do you think it would be OK then,' she asked him. 'You know, to use it?'

He nodded. 'I do.'

'Me, too,' Luke said. 'Look at that view, it's magnificent. Why would you not want to make the most of it?'

Ed watched Jess and Izzy stare out of the window.

'I think Ed's right,' Izzy said. 'We need the space and this is the perfect place to put a desk and sit quietly when we have to work on our books.'

Jess sighed, wiping away her tears. 'Yes. We need to make this room happy again.'

Ed smiled. He watched Izzy and Jess standing at the window, their heads tilted towards each other as they took in the view and he wondered if Izzy would ever come up here and think of him when he returned to the château.

She turned her head and looked over her shoulder at him, as if she'd had the same thought.

He smiled at her, committing her pretty face to memory when she smiled back at him, the sun lighting her from behind making her hair seem like an unruly, white halo around her head. Yes, this was exactly how he would remember her. He could picture them both very happy together, but it was a pipe dream. He wasn't in a position to give Izzy the future she'd want, any future for that matter. No, he needed to put a stop to this craving for her right now. She deserved to be happy with someone and he wasn't the right man for her. However much he might wish it to be the case.

Izzy walked down the stairs from the attic room to her bedroom and waited as the others filed through. Ed caught her arm as she went through the door.

'I thought that was a beautiful story your mum discovered.'

'So did I,' she said. 'I was thinking that I'll think of you when I'm up there and you're living back in France.'

He bent down and kissed her, taking her by surprise.

'What's that for?' she asked, not minding one bit.

'Because I was thinking the same thing when I watched you and Jess standing by that window looking out across the channel.'

Izzy wondered if she could ever stand not having him nearby. 'It's not going to be the same though, is it?'

'No,' he said.

A well of emotion rose through her chest. 'I'll need to shower and change quickly before we leave, if that's OK?' she asked desperate to change the subject before she made a fool of herself in front of him.

Ed smiled, but she could see he was trying not to show her that he was also upset. The thought that he was going to miss her too cheered Izzy a little.

'Why don't you grab some clothes, and come back to my cottage and shower. We can go out for a drink from there.'

'Great idea. I'll meet you downstairs in a minute.'

Grabbing a fresh cotton dress and pair of slip-on shoes, Izzy hurried back downstairs and walked into the silent room. The atmosphere had become heavy in the short time she'd taken to gather her things.

'Luke's had to race off,' Ed said.

She could see Alex and Jess glaring at each other and could understand why he wanted to go so quickly.

'Shall we?' she asked Ed, grabbing his wrist and pulling him willingly towards the front door. 'I'll leave you two, but please try to get on. We can't go on like this.' She smiled at Jess. 'Don't forget we have a lot on tomorrow.'

'I won't,' she nodded. 'See you in the morning.'

Ed slipped his arm around her waist as soon as they were outside. 'You OK?' He gave her a gentle squeeze.

She nodded. 'Fine, thanks, though I think I've started something with those two in there.'

'I think she's probably a little emotional after hearing about her great-grandmother's loss.'

'I can understand why,' Izzy said. 'I hope she and Alex find some way to get on. They're really attracted to each other, but I can't see them getting on well enough to actually have a relationship.'

'No?'

'No,' she shook her head. 'Then again, what do I know, I'm hardly an expert in romance.'

He led her to his Land Rover and opened the door for her to get in. 'You didn't mind me suggesting you shower at mine, did you?'

'Of course not,' she said honestly. 'But it'll mean we have to go back to the other side of the island now, with you driving.'

'That's fine, I'm from France and we're used to driving far bigger distances than crossing this small island.'

'I suppose you are.' Izzy laughed as she clipped in her seat belt. 'You must think us a bit silly sometimes, the way we complain about going "all the way to town".'

'No, I love it.'

'Sorry I hadn't had time to shower before you arrived just then,' she said, not sorry at all now.

'It's fine.' He smiled at her. 'I don't suppose you've had a chance to eat anything either?'

She looked out of the window as they drove along the rugged north coast of the island towards St John. 'No, and I'm starving.'

'Good, I can try out my culinary skills on you then, if you want?'

She nodded. 'I'd love that.'

'You've only had my cooking the once. I might not be any good this time. '

She didn't care. 'No, but however hopeless you are as a chef you'll have to be better than me. Mum despairs at my lack of talent in the kitchen.'

'You'll need to go through the bedroom to get to the

bathroom,' Ed said, opening a cupboard and handing her some towels. 'That door there.'

Izzy opened the door to his room, surprised to see how tidy it was and how few belongings he had. Alex's room had always been such a mess, with old surfboards resting against the walls and wet suits, shorts, and sunglasses strewn about among the surfing magazines. She picked up the top book from a pile on his bedside table, noting his choice of psychological thrillers.

'Lemon sole OK for you?' he called, the sudden sound causing her to almost drop the paperback in her hand.

'Yes, lovely,' she shouted back, placing the book back down on top of the pile and walking into the bathroom.

Once showered and refreshed, she returned to find Ed setting a small round table. 'That was wonderful,' she said brushing her damp hair a few minutes later. 'You really are very well house-trained, aren't you?'

He gave her a pointed stare. 'You thought I wouldn't be after being married to Marie?' He laughed. 'She's so bossy and organised, she soon knocked me into shape.'

'I'll have to thank her then,' Izzy teased. 'She's done a great job with you.'

He smiled and bent his head down to give her a kiss on the lips. 'I'm glad you approve.' Standing up and turning once again to give his attention to the cooker, he said, 'Please take a seat. I've opened you a bottle of rosé.'

She was doubly impressed with his powers of perception. 'Brilliant; I can't think of anything I'd rather have right now.'

He left the cooker and walked two steps to the fridge, taking out the cool bottle and pouring her a glass. He poured a glass of red wine for himself and sat down opposite her. '*Salut*, and thank you for coming here tonight.'

'*Salut*,' she said touching her glass to his. 'I'm pleased you asked me.'

He smiled. 'You're looking doubly pretty tonight, if I may say so?'

'You may.'

If this was what being with someone like Ed was like then Izzy suspected she could get very used to evenings like this. He was such a gentleman. Even David hadn't been so … what? Grown up? Then again, she thought, David had been so young when he'd died; their romance had been more of a teenage love affair that slowly evolved as they reached their twenties. She shook her head.

'Something wrong?' he asked looking concerned.

'No, sorry,' she said cross with herself for forgetting where she was for a moment. 'I was just thinking about someone.'

'Someone?'

'Um, yes.

'Someone you obviously care about.' he said, his voice gentle.

Could she confide in him about David, she wondered.

'Can you tell me about him?' Ed asked putting his drink down and knitting his fingers together.

'Yes,' she said. It was time to open up a little to him. 'If you like.'

She took a sip of her wine, not used to discussing David with anyone, mainly because those closest to her already knew what had happened between them and how utterly crushed she'd been by his unexpected death.

'We met on the first day at secondary school and he asked me out when we were fifteen,' she said smiling at the memory. 'He was my first and only boyfriend and I adored him. We were together for six years.'

Ed watched her, listening intently to what she was saying. 'Where is he now?' he asked.

'He died,' she said simply, adding before he had to contemplate asking the obvious next question. 'I waved goodbye to him one afternoon never dreaming that it would be the last time …' She cleared her throat. 'It was a motorbike crash.'

She said the words, but had long since learnt not to connect them with the picture of his final minutes and the next year and a half of her life when nothing mattered.

Ed didn't speak but continued to stare at her. Finally, he swallowed, then cleared his throat and reached out taking both her hands in his. 'I'm so sorry, *chérie*, I didn't realize I was asking you to divulge something so intimate and traumatic for you. Is that why you didn't want to go out with me? These were your personal reasons?'

'I guess so.' Izzy squeezed his hands back to comfort him. She was used to comforting others when the subject of David came up. It was as if it was her job to make sure she didn't disturb anyone with her emotional scarring.

'It's fine,' she could see he didn't believe her for a second. 'Well, actually it's not fine, far from it. I'd expected to be happily married to him by now. But it wasn't to be.'

Ed closed his eyes and took a deep breath. 'You're very brave. I can see that you've had to learn to be, but you hide your pain well.'

She opened her mouth to give her usual reply then his words sunk in and she realized he hadn't simply said the usual soothing words she'd become used to hearing. 'Thank you. There's only so many times people really want to hear how you are if you don't put on a brave face.'

Ed smiled. 'And you do it well. You're an incredible woman, Izzy.'

She looked at him properly for the first time, finally seeing through the surface rugged good looks, so different to David's gentle face and slight body.

'I have known loss,' Ed said quietly, 'but nothing as cruel or as heart-breaking as this. I wish I could soothe your pain, I really do.'

She didn't want him to think that she couldn't cope

about David, because she could. She'd learnt how to, with Jess's coercion over the past few years. 'Don't be upset for me, Ed. I'm fine now, really.'

When he continued to look deeply concerned for her, she pulled one of her hands from his and reached out to rest her palm against his cheek. 'I really am fine. I'll miss him for ever, but now I can think about him without feeling like there's nothing for me to live for.'

'Good, I'm pleased.'

'You've helped me do this,' she said honestly. 'You're kind and good, like he was.' Not wishing him to think she was only seeing him to replicate her time with David, she added. 'That's where your similarity ends though. You're very different from David physically and I've grown up a lot since he died. But we kissed, Ed. Don't you think that meant something to me?'

'I'm glad it did. It meant something to me too, Iz.' He stood up and pulling her to her feet took her in his arms and kissed her.

Relieved to have assured him that she did have feelings for him, Izzy kissed him back, her hands slipping up over his shoulders and around his neck. She murmured in pleasure, enjoying his reaction when he kissed her more thoroughly and held her tightly to him.

When he finally let her catch her breath, Izzy laughed. 'You see, I have moved on.'

He smiled and kissed her once again. 'I'm happy to be the man with whom you've chosen to move on,' he said kissing her quickly again. He gazed at her, his eyes glazing over as he stared thoughtfully. Then, clearing his throat, he picked up their glasses and walked through to the small living area just off the kitchen. 'Come through,' he said. 'Let's chat for a bit and catch up properly.'

Izzy didn't allow herself to show any disappointment at his change in attitude. And she was disappointed – extremely so. She followed him through and sat on the cream sofa opposite where he'd placed her drink on a glass coffee table.

'It's such a pretty cottage,' she said. 'Very contemporary décor too, which surprises me.'

He sat down next to her turning to face her, one knee raised up onto the seat. 'Catherine oversaw the revamping of the three cottages last year. She did a great job, don't you think?'

She had to agree.

'I enjoy living here,' he said, looking out of the window at the tree-filled wood beyond. 'It's peaceful most of the time, yet so close to the beaches.' He laughed. 'Well, everything is close when you live on an island,' he said. 'Especially Jersey, don't you think?'

Izzy giggled. He was right. Nothing was that far away. She'd always dreamt of living in England when she was growing up and having so many places to visit and things to do and see. 'When I first visited England, I thought that I could see all the places I'd read about and visit them. It didn't occur to me that England might have these places, but most of them take forever to get to.'

'Yes,' he nodded. 'It's very inconvenient when you have to travel hours between one place and the next.'

She slapped his leg lightly. 'Stop teasing me. I forgot you're French.' She narrowed her eyes. 'You really don't have any accent at all, apart from when you speak with your family or another French person. It's very strange.'

He pulled a face. 'Not really. I've been here for years, so I was bound to lose some of my accent.'

'Maybe, but not completely.' She thought of a few close friends who had lived on the island for years and still had kept their accents. 'I thought you were English when I first met you.'

'Disappointed that I wasn't?' he said, a glint in his blue eyes.

She tilted her face to one side and did her best to look

serious. 'No, but I would have liked you to sound a little more exotic. You sound the same as Alex,' she rethought this notion. 'No, not very like him, but you both have that cut-glass accent.' She smiled. 'Even though Alex does his best to hide it.'

'But you like where I live, though?' he teased.

'I do. It's cosy yet smart.' She looked at the warm cream wallpaper, coffee-coloured carpet, and contrasting purple curtains and nodded. 'Jess and I should do something with our place,' she thought of the floral curtains, carpet and wallpapers, each room different, all mismatched. 'When I first moved in I thought the décor was going to drive me nuts, but oddly enough I barely register it now.'

He picked up her drink and handed it to her. 'Probably because you're so busy.'

They finished their drinks and it seemed the most natural thing in the world for Izzy to take the empty glass from his hand and place it down next to hers on the table. She looked at him to try and gauge his thoughts. Fed up with waiting for him to make a move, she leaned forward and kissed him. The next thing she knew she was lying on top of him, kissing him like mad. Her brain vaguely took in his fresh recently showered smell, his hard chest, and stomach muscles. She stopped kissing him and, ignoring his groan of protest, pushed herself up to gaze down at a very pleasing bulge in his faded jeans. Maybe pleasing wasn't the exact word she was looking for, she decided, forgetting he could see her studying his crotch. Startling probably described how it looked to her right now.

She looked up at him, seeing the amusement on his face, and grimaced.

'I'd like to say something encouraging or amusing, but I can't seem to think of how best to make you forget my obvious enjoyment of you lying on me. Maybe you should kiss me again?'

Deciding he was right, Izzy, lay back down on top of him, pushed her hands in his wavy hair and kissed him again. He wrapped his arms around her, then moving one down to her bottom he squeezed lightly and groaned. She liked having this power over him, although if he stopped kissing her now she was liable to rugby-tackle him to the floor.

She moved her hands down to his chest and up under his white T-shirt, relishing the heat of his muscles.

His hands moved away from her bottom and taking her under the arms, Ed lifted her off him.

'Hey, what are you doing?' she asked sounding, even to her ears, like she was about to have a temper tantrum. Which she just might, she thought.

'I'm a bit big for this furniture.'

She saw how high his knees were now they were sitting. 'I suppose you are,' she said, wanting to kiss him again.

'Would you think it forward of me to suggest we go through to my bedroom?' he said. 'I think it'll be much more comfortable in there.'

Izzy didn't mind him being forward at all. She'd waited a long time to find another man she wanted to go to bed with.

'OK,' she breathed, trying not to sound too desperate.

He took her hand and led her through to his room.

Izzy wasn't sure what to do next, now that the spell of kissing him had been broken. She peeked up at him through her lashes, sucking in her breath at the sight of him standing silently in front of her, so tantalisingly close. She dropped her gaze down to the floor, her bravado seeping away from her.

Ed stepped forward and took her in his arms. 'If you'd rather we go back into the living room, just say,' he said, his tone tender. He placed one palm on the side of her face and kissed her lightly on the mouth. 'I don't want to rush you. I want you to want this as much as I do.'

Hearing him saying how much he wanted her made her forget her inhibitions. 'No,' she said taking his hand and kissing the palm that had just been against her cheek. 'I want this, very much.'

She stepped back from him and taking a few shallow breaths slipped her spaghetti-straps from her shoulders and let her dress drop to the floor, stepping out of it and standing in front of him in her white bra and panties.

He watched her. 'You're so beautiful.'

She smiled. It was so long since anyone had been this intimate with her, but unexpectedly it didn't seem strange. 'This feels so natural,' she said unable to keep the surprise from her voice.

He took hold of her, hugging her tightly against him. 'For me too,' he said.

They stood together for a moment. Izzy realising she was the only one who'd undressed, stepped back. 'Hey, I'm not going to be the only one standing here in my underwear,' she joked.

'You don't have to tell me twice to take my trousers off,' he laughed, undoing his jeans and letting them fall to the floor. He stepped out of them, kicking them away.

'Very nice,' she said, amused at her huge understatement. She stared at the bulge in his boxers, unable to help herself.

'Nice? Right, you beautiful woman, come and let me show you how a Frenchman makes love.'

'Even one who's lost his accent?' she teased.

He picked her up, carrying her over to the bed and laying her gently on top of the duvet. 'Yes, even one that's lost his accent.'

'Can't you even try to speak that way now?'

He pulled off his boxer shorts and climbed in next to her. '*Ma chérie*, kiss me,' he said in an exaggerated accent, kissing her shoulder.

'Shut up.' She pulled his head down to her and kissed him, trying not to giggle. She wasn't sure if it was excitement or nerves, but whatever it was, she was enjoying every second lying semi-naked in bed with this gorgeous man.

'I think this is a little one-sided, don't you?' he asked.

'What do you mean?'

He touched her mouth with his finger, kissing her. Then, tracing lightly down from her mouth, her chin, her neck to her bra, he kissed each of her breasts. 'Are these going to stay encased in this?' he asked, indicating her lacy bra.

Izzy giggled, shivering when his finger, followed by his mouth moved lightly down her stomach to her knickers. 'Can I take these off?'

'No,' she said, enjoying the look of disappointment when she sat up. 'I want to.' She unclipped her bra, threw it off so it flew through the gap in the curtains and rested on the inside of the window. 'That was close,' she laughed. 'I hope no one can see it on the windowsill.'

'I doubt anyone will be walking by this cottage tonight.' He put one hand behind her head and lifting it slightly towards him bent to kiss her.

She couldn't stand the tension a second longer. 'OK,' she said. 'I've changed my mind. You can pull down my knickers.'

He reached out and did so.

'So beautiful,' he said looking appreciatively at her body as she lay there in front of him. 'I've wanted to do this since we first went riding at the château.'

She couldn't help grinning like a fool at his admission. The pressure of his firm lips on hers when he kissed her once again made her insides clench. His tongue found hers. Boy, he knew how to kiss. She wanted this kiss to go on for ever.

He moved from her mouth, kissing her neck. Izzy

squirmed involuntarily at the exquisite touch. He was on top of her, but she only felt the firm pressure of his body, and his pleasure at being with her pressing against her stomach. Unable to resist, Izzy reached down and took him in her hand.

He groaned, reminding her that he could feel everything she was doing and this wasn't just a fantasy she was experiencing.

'Sorry,' she whispered, not letting go and kissing him hard on his lips.

'If you keep doing that I'm not going to be able to contain myself.'

She giggled. 'I don't care, I'm enjoying this.'

He placed one hand on her left breast and, taking her nipple in his mouth, tugged it gently between his teeth. Izzy forgot what she was doing, opened her legs, and put both hands on his buttocks, annoyed when she couldn't get low enough to get a proper grasp of them.

'You are one sexy lady,' he murmured. Reaching down he touched between her legs lightly.

Izzy groaned. 'Please, don't do that.'

'Why not?' he asked.

Was he smiling she wondered, looking up into his eyes and seeing tenderness shining from them. 'What do you want me to do?'

Oh hell, she thought, not caring how unladylike she sounded. 'Please, get on with it before I lose my mind,' she whispered, barely able to speak with the sensations he was causing between her legs.

'You're sure?' he asked, his voice husky.

She was. 'You want me to say it twice?'

'What? That you want me to …'

She giggled, embarrassed. 'Shut up and do it.'

He did.

She arched against him, consumed by him wanting him inside her. Wrapping her legs around his waist, she writhed against him as he thrust into her. Oh God, this was beyond anything she'd ever experienced before. Desperate not to come before him, she tried to hang on, but unable to resist, gave in to the most almighty climax she'd ever experienced, heightened by the guttural groan as he came seconds later.

He kissed her neck and then her mouth for a few minutes before resting next to her, her legs tangled in his. Their breathing slowed back to normal and she relished lying in his arms.

She felt his body tense.

Had he just heard something too, she wondered. 'What was that?' she asked. 'Was someone outside the window just then?'

He shook his head. 'Probably just one of my godfather's dogs, out before being shut in the boot room for the night.'

She snuggled back into his arms. 'You were right, you know.'

He gave her a brief squeeze. 'Go on, what was I right about?'

She held back a giggle. 'About showing me how Frenchmen make great lovers.'

He laughed, loudly. 'What, even those with very English accents?'

She pinched the skin on his waist, making him flinch. 'Ouch.'

'Yes,' she said bending down to kiss him where she'd just inflicted pain. 'Even then.'

They lay in silence for a few moments.

'Tell me about your father?'

She couldn't understand why he would ask such a random question. 'Why?'

He propped himself up on one elbow looking down at her and kissed her on her forehead. 'I want to know more about you. Do you mind me asking?'

She shook her head. 'It's just an odd question to ask. I mean, right now.'

He frowned slightly. 'I suppose it is.'

'My dad was eccentric, but lovely.'

'You must miss him very much,' he asked thoughtfully making her think that he was relating it to himself somehow.

'I do. I don't have as many memories of him as I'd like and I suspect some have been altered in my mind. I wish I still had him in my life to be able to get to know him as one adult to another. '

He thought about this, then nodded. 'I can imagine.'

'He wasn't in my life as much as I would have liked, and I suspect Mum secretly wanted him to be a bigger part of our lives, but he had a family. That was before I came along.' She thought back to the birthdays and Christmases since losing hers at ten years old, where she had watched friends being spoilt by their fathers and secretly wishing for the same closeness with her own. 'I suppose that's what comes from being an unexpected surprise.'

Ed scooped her up in his arms and cuddled her. 'You deserve to be loved.'

'Thank you,' she said, meaning it. She reached up and kissed him.

Moving so that he was on top of her once more, he grinned and said. 'I think I should show you how I make love when I've got a bit of self-control.'

She smiled, happy to let him know how much she approved of his idea and even happier to be changing the subject away from her and her strange childhood. 'Now that is a good idea.'

As Izzy drifted off to a contented sleep in his arms, she thought for a second she heard distant rumblings of a thunderstorm. 'I hope that passes us,' she said sleepily, closing her eyes.

Chapter Twenty-one

She wasn't sure if it was the screaming that woke her or Ed leaping out of bed.

'What on earth's that?' she shouted, but Ed was tugging up his jeans and out of the doorway before she'd finished speaking. Izzy grabbed her dress, shoved it over her head, and ran out of the door after him. The crying was coming from around the other side of the manor house somewhere. Izzy ran but as she neared the first corner she came to a sickening realisation. She knew that sound.

'Jess!' she shouted, running faster. She turned the corner to see Ed standing at the door to the marquee, a sobbing Jess in his arms.

'What's happened?'

Jess pointed into the marquee.

Izzy saw the arch Ed had hung so carefully above the opening. Almost all the roses had been blown off and the ivy hung untidily from the frame.

'It's fine,' she said, hugging Jess. 'We'll fix that in no time.'

'Not the bloody arch,' Jess pushed her away. 'Look inside.'

Izzy stepped forward, but Ed grasped her arm. 'You don't want to look in there.'

'It's bad, isn't it?' she said, trying her best not to panic.

'We'll sort it out,' he said, his voice cracking. 'Try not to worry.'

Izzy gently disengaged his fingers. She had to see.

'No,' she whispered as she stepped inside, her heart pounding at the sight of the devastation. The lining was torn and hung in strips, and almost all the crockery had been smashed.

Unable to move, she stared from one destroyed setting to the next. It was ruined. They were ruined. She checked the time on her watch. Five hours until seventy-five people would descend on this place, and there was nothing here for them at all.

She felt Ed's firm arms go around her from behind. 'I'm so sorry, Iz. I can't imagine what could have happened.'

Jess stepped inside, spluttering. 'It's perfectly clear what happened. Catherine. I'll bloody kill her.'

'No, Jess,' Ed said gently. 'She isn't capable of this.'

Izzy was shaking her head. 'You have to understand that Catherine has had it in for us since the day she let us down and we had the gall to mind about it. So much for her apologising to us.'

There was a long silence as Ed stared at her.

'I'm sorry,' she said, embarrassed by her outburst. 'It's not your fault. I shouldn't be screaming at you about this. You've been nothing but helpful to us.'

'It's OK,' he said quietly, resting his hand on her shoulder. 'We'll do our best to fix this. We still have, what, five hours? We can achieve a lot in that time.'

'One of us needs to phone Lacey and break the news to her that we can't host her reception after all,' Jess said, sniffing loudly.

Ed folded his arms across his chest and stared at the shambles. 'Not necessarily,' he said.

Jess narrowed her eyes. 'Are you nuts?' She waved her arms around taking in the area. 'You think we stand any chance at all of making this chaos vanish?'

'Yes, we can do this,' he said, puffing out his cheeks. 'The first thing we need to do is clean up this mess. I'm going fetch the gardeners and a couple of wheelbarrows and start picking up the broken shards of crockery. We don't want guests standing on anything sharp and cutting themselves when they're dancing, do we?'

'Guests,' snorted Jess. 'Not much chance of them dancing here today.'

Izzy agreed with her, but seeing Ed hurry out of the marquee with so much determination she turned to Jess. 'Listen, he's right. We have to give this our best shot. It's the only chance we have of not letting Lacey down.' She hesitated. 'Or ourselves.'

Jess sighed, wiping away her tears with the backs of her hands. 'Fine, but what do you suggest we do?'

Izzy tried to straighten out her thoughts and make some sort of plan. 'Firstly, the place needs to be tidied up, which the gardeners will do. Thankfully, the floral arch can be sorted out easily with some more flowers.'

'That's something, I suppose. Go on.'

'The most important thing we need to do is assess how much of the crockery we have left. Don't forget we have a couple of extra boxes in the butler's pantry in case of breakages. Hopefully they haven't been damaged.'

'The linens are a bit creased but they're just about OK,' Jess said, the colour seeping back into her face slightly.

'We have to find a way to hide that,' she said, pointing to the huge tears in the silky marquee lining. 'It looks horrendous. I'm phoning the marquee hire company. One sec.' She dialled their number on her mobile and spoke to a flustered woman who said that nothing could be done for several hours as everyone was out working.

Izzy relayed the conversation to Jess. 'We have to think of some way to cover this ourselves. Then we need to beg, borrow, or magic up more crockery from somewhere,' Izzy said, wracking her brains to come up with people who might own vintage crockery that would suit this occasion. 'My mum will have some more, but not too much, unfortunately,' she pulled a face.

'We have a couple more boxes at home,' Jess pointed

out. 'They're not the best stuff, but we can't afford to be picky today.'

She was right. Izzy hated the thought of using less-than-perfect china for the event, but it couldn't be helped. 'I don't think there'll be nearly enough though,' she said. She heard voices coming from outside the marquee.

'I've asked Catherine to find Marie and come up with as much suitable crockery from the manor and cottages as she can,' Ed said, leading the gardeners inside and directing them towards the mess, then heading out again, muttering something about fetching another wheelbarrow.

Jess glowered after him. 'He wants us to let her back in here? What, to see what other damage she can do to wreck this wedding?'

Izzy didn't care who helped, as long as they managed to secure enough stock to get through today successfully.

'Let's worry about her tomorrow, shall we? Ed will be here and I doubt she'd try anything with him around.

Remember, the best way to get back at whoever did this will be to make a brilliant success of today.'

'If you say so,' Jess said sulkily. 'Though personally a hard smack in the face is my favoured form of getting revenge.'

Izzy wasn't certain. She remembered Lacey's concerns about Jack's ex-girlfriend and her threats about their wedding.

'Maybe Ed's right and it wasn't Catherine,' she said.

Jess gasped. 'Are you for real?'

Izzy shook her head. 'Remember Lacey telling us about Jack's ex? What if she's responsible for this?'

Jess frowned. 'Oh, I'd forgotten about her.' She considered it, then added. 'I suppose you could be right.'

'Look, we don't have time for pondering about who did this,' Izzy said. 'We need to re-arrange this marquee and worry about it later.'

'Saris,' someone called from the lawn area.

'Jess, Izzy?' Ed hurried back into the room, closely followed by Catherine. 'Catherine has come up with a brilliant idea to help cover the torn lining.'

Izzy eyed Jess warily as Catherine entered the marquee. 'Go on,' she said.

'A friend of mine married a guy from India and we had a huge hen party for her.'

'So?' Jess said, glaring at her.

'So,' Catherine replied sarcastically, 'I've given her a call and she said we can borrow the saris she bought for the occasion. They're in vibrant colours and perfect to cover that hideous mess up there.' She grimaced when she looked at the torn lining. 'She's dropping them off in about ten minutes.'

Ed raised his arms and looked up to the ceiling area. 'The guys and I can put them up. I think they'll look amazing and completely cover the damage.'

Izzy and Jess followed his gaze. Izzy tried to picture the scene and had to admit that the bright colours would go well with the rest of the décor.

'They will add a dash of summer colour to the place, I suppose,' she said. 'I love the idea. Jess, what do you think?'

Jess gave Catherine a withering look. 'I suppose so.'

'Great,' Izzy said. 'Let's do it.'

Catherine coughed. 'I've also managed to collect quite a bit of crockery. Marie is washing it now.'

'You work quickly,' Jess said icily.

'That's great, thanks.' Izzy linked arms with Jess, hoping this would remind her to watch what she said. If Catherine did turn out to be the person behind today's drama, she would have no problem sorting her out, but for now, at least, they had more important priorities on which to focus.

'We're going to phone around our friends and family and collect as much as we can. We don't have long, especially as we need to set up all the tables again.'

'Not all of them, some are still as you left them last night, and none of the glasses are broken,' Ed said. 'Maybe the culprit was interrupted.'

'Probably,' Izzy said, looking at the tables that hadn't been touched and grateful for that at least. She counted how many placc settings remained intact. 'Sixteen out of seventy-five,' she murmured. 'We need to come up with fifty-nine other sets, less what Catherine's found, and what's hopefully left in the pantry. Oh, and we're missing a saucer from there, that you broke.'

Izzy sighed, and realizing she'd left her mobile in her bag at Ed's cottage, pointed at Jess's hand to borrow hers. She called her mum, telling Cherry what had happened and what they needed from her. 'We'll be round in the next half an hour.' She handed the phone back to Jess.

'I hope we can do this,' Jess said, sighing heavily.

'We'll do it,' Izzy assured her, not feeling as positive as she sounded.

'Right,' Ed said. 'I'll get the guys to help me put up the saris. Catherine and Marie can sort out the crockery they've put together,' he said. 'I'll go and source more roses and ivy for the garland and I'll catch up with you two when you get back.'

'We'll need to come into the manor and count up how much we have inside for the place settings,' Izzy said.

They left Catherine and Ed standing in the marquee and ran in to the manor house and through to the kitchen where they saw Marie washing the crockery.

'How many sets do you think you have there?' Jess asked.

Izzy stood near the sink and did a quick tally. 'Twenty-six cups,' she said to Marie. 'Do you know if they all have matching saucers?'

'Yes, they do, and plates.' She pointed to a pile in the sink.

Izzy patted her shoulder. 'Thanks, Marie, we owe you.'

Izzy, followed by Jess, went through to the butler's pantry. She breathed a sigh of relief as she saw that everything was as they had left it. They quickly unpacked the two extra hampers they always took to each event in case of damage.

'We never thought we'd have to cover this many breakages, did we?' she said.

'I've got twelve cups and saucers in here.'

Izzy quickly counted the contents of her box. 'Twelve plates here. So we have another twelve complete sets and that's ...' she calculated the amounts in her head.

'Not enough,' Jess groaned. 'Still twenty-one more sets to find.' She slammed her palms down on the worn table and lowered her head. 'We may as well give up now. We're never going to do this.'

'Don't be like that, Jess,' Izzy shouted. She heard a crash on the floor. 'What the hell?'

They turned to see Marie, hands clasped over her mouth staring at the remnants of three plates scattered on the flagstone floor.

'I'm so sorry,' Marie cried. 'One slipped out of my hands and caught the others lying on the drainer.'

Izzy stared at the bare stone drainer and winced. 'It's fine,' she fibbed, wondering how Marie could have been so careless just when they needed all the plates they could get their hands on.

Jess turned to Izzy, her mouth open in shock, but for once she didn't say anything.

'Look,' Izzy said, 'We might not make it, but we have to give it our best shot, so stop being negative. Twenty-four more sets to find.'

She grabbed Jess by one of her wrists and went outside, waving to Marie as they passed her. 'We'll be back as soon as possible,' she said. 'If we're longer than an hour, please can you ask the guys to help you take this crockery out to the marquee so we can start setting up the places as soon as we get back?'

'No worries,' Marie assured her, immediately racing back to the sink.

They raced to the van and drove as quickly as the speed limit would allow to Cherry's home.

'Mum, where are you?' Izzy asked bursting in through the front door with such force that the door slammed back against the hall wall.

'Careful!' Cherry shouted. She wiped her hands with a small towel and spotted Jess over Izzy's shoulder. 'Hi, Jess, good to see you again. Right, come through here, you two. I've got five of my mother's old tea sets that I was keeping for best – you can borrow them for now, but please look after them.'

They followed her into her dining room where on the table she'd stacked the mismatched crockery. 'It's very pretty, don't you think?' she asked holding up a yellow and black cup. 'I know you said preferably pink, but this is the best I could come up with.'

Izzy hugged her mother gratefully. 'This is brilliant,' she said. 'So that makes, um, nineteen sets we still need to find. Do you have a box we can pack them in Mum?'

Cherry nodded. 'In the utility room, I think.'

Izzy left the room, almost bumping into her mother's neighbour as she came through the back door carrying two shopping bags.

'You've been out and about early,' Izzy said stepping aside so the woman could make her way into the dining room.

'Come in here, love,' she said. 'I've got something for you gels.'

Izzy did as she was told and followed the elderly lady back into the room she'd just left.

'I knew you'd come up with something,' Cherry said, smiling at her friend. She looked at Jess and Izzy and smiled. 'Margaret has brought you two more sets for your wedding. Let's unwrap them.'

They did, and although they didn't match the pink chintzy theme Lacey had wanted the design was fresh and sunny.

'Thank you so much, Margaret,' Izzy said giving the lady a kiss on her powdered cheek. 'We really are very grateful. She had an idea. 'Could you hold up one of the plates from each set, so I can take a picture with Jess's phone and make sure you get the right set back?'

Margaret did as she asked and then so did Cherry. The four of them hurriedly packed up the sets.

'How many more cups, saucers, and plates do you still need?' Margaret asked the girls as they walked out to load their new stock into the van.

'Seventeen, I think,' Izzy said. 'Not many, but we need to find them and soon if we're going to be ready for this wedding reception.'

'What about the food?' Cherry asked as Izzy clipped on her seat belt.

'The caterers are doing it, and they shouldn't need the crockery till they're almost ready to serve.'

'Right. You'd better get on now girls,' Cherry said. 'Let me know how it all goes, won't you?'

'We will,' Jess said, carrying the bags of china out to the van with Izzy.

Izzy started the ignition. 'Thanks again Mum, Margaret.'

They drove off, waving to the two women.

'We're nearly there,' Izzy said, glancing at Jess sitting thoughtfully and resting her chin on the back of her hand. 'Where shall we try now?'

'We don't have time to start phoning and waiting for friends to find stuff,' Jess said. 'And we don't have time to sit through the traffic to get to Rozel to go through the crockery we might have at home.' She groaned. 'Turn left at the next junction and let's go to town and pop into some of the charity shops. Maybe we can find the remaining sets in there?'

'Let's hope so,' Izzy said hopefully.

They managed to find a parking space not too far from three charity shops.

'I can't believe I didn't think to bring my bag,' Izzy moaned, angry at her thoughtlessness. 'Do you have any money on you?'

Jess pushed her hand in her bag and pulled out her purse. 'Twenty-six quid,' she said. 'And my debit card. We'll use the card first. Then if one of the shops won't take it, we can use the cash.'

The first shop had enough crockery to make two reasonable sets, with an odd saucer, so they paid for them and hurried to the next one a couple of doors down the back street. 'Those are quite nice,' Jess said pointing up on to one shelf where three mismatched sets were displayed. 'Can we see those, please?' she asked the assistant.

Checking the crockery quickly, and trying not to panic when Izzy noticed the shop clock telling them that they'd already been nearly an hour and a half, she paid the cashier and packed the purchases into another bag.

'Twelve more,' Jess moaned. 'We're never going to find another twelve sets, not now.'

Izzy hoped she was wrong, but doubted it.

Jess wasn't wrong. 'If some people cancel at the last minute then we'll need fewer sets,' she said hopefully.

'Never mind that now,' Izzy said as Jess paid. 'We need to get back to the manor and start setting up the tables.'

Jess and Izzy thanked the shopkeeper and hurried back to their van.

'But what will we do about the last place settings?' Jess asked. 'I think people will notice if they don't have anything to eat off.'

As Izzy drove through the morning traffic, Jess made a few phone calls. They recalled one more charity shop on the way home and found four more mismatched sets there.

'Eight more,' Jess said tapping the black plastic dashboard. 'We still need more.'

'Shit,' Izzy said, indicating to turn into the manor driveway through the huge stone pillars and under the granite archway towards the marquee. 'There's nothing we can do now,' she said. 'We can ask them to check the manor kitchens again, or the cottages.'

They parked the van near to the manor house and hurriedly carried their new stock in to the kitchen. Jess unpacked while Izzy washed the newly bought crockery. They dried everything and set it out on the bleached table top to see what they had to work with.

'We've done all we can now,' Izzy said, trying not to feel too deflated at their failure to come up with all the china they needed. 'Come on, let's get this lot into the marquee, we're running out of time.'

Chapter Twenty-two

They rushed into the marquee, immediately taken aback by the glorious array of saris hanging from the walls. Ed and the gardeners had done a brilliant job.

'Look Jess,' she whispered, unable to help smiling at the difference it made.

'What?' Jess grumbled, carrying the heavy hamper and placing it on the table closest to the door. She turned to see what Izzy was talking about. 'Holy crap, that's stunning.'

'You like it?' Ed asked, coming in behind them.

Izzy looked over to him, noticing his happy expression. 'Very much,' she said honestly. 'It looks better than it did before.'

'How will we explain away the Indian saris in an English country vintage wedding setting though?' Jess asked.

'In colonial times the British people in India epitomised the art of drinking tea. Just explain that the wedding setting is taking them back to the days of the Raj.'

Izzy liked it. She smiled at Jess then looked back at Ed. 'I doubt anyone will ask. You've all done an amazing job here, thanks.'

He bowed his head briefly. 'I'm glad you're happy.' He lifted his arm and tapped the face of his large watch. 'You're running out of time to set everything up in here. Tell me what you want me to do and I'll get on with it.'

'Me, too,' Catherine said from the doorway.

Jess groaned. 'Really? You want to help us?' She glowered at her nemesis. 'Or is it more that you want the opportunity of accidentally damaging some of this stock?'

Catherine glared at her, hands on her slim hips. 'I didn't do it, Jessica Moon. Now do you want my help, or not, because unlike you I have a life and can be somewhere else today that'll be far more interesting than helping you out.'

'Then why don't you just –'

'Jess, that's enough,' Izzy hadn't missed the concerned look Catherine had given Ed before remembering herself and making it vanish instantly. Izzy didn't know what Ed had said to Catherine, or why, but she obviously knew that getting everything perfect for Lacey's day mattered to him and she was grateful.

'We need all the help we can get, so yes please, Catherine.'

Catherine smiled, the first genuine one they'd seen. 'I also found another five sets going through the cottages again, and I've washed them up ready for you.'

Izzy and Jess headed for the kitchens, astounded. They heard the caterers arriving and Marie telling them to take everything through to the kitchen. Izzy was very grateful for her enthusiasm.

'Have you seen inside those portable loos?' Marie asked, coming into the marquee with a tray of glasses and a large jug of elderflower juice for them all. Placing the tray on a clear area at the end of a table near to where Izzy was standing, she added. 'They're more luxurious than my mum's bathroom in Devon.'

Izzy hadn't, but she had seen others at events they had organised and she'd also been surprised at how smart they were.

'I know,' she laughed. 'Jess and I thought the same when we first saw one of them at a party. We'd love it if our loo at the cottage was half as beautiful.'

'Drink?' Marie asked holding up a glass.

Izzy nodded and Jess came to join them. 'I really need this,' Jess said. She wiped her forehead with the back of her hand. 'It's so hot today. I pity poor Lacey in her wedding dress, don't you?'

Izzy nodded. 'Rather her than me.'

'You don't want to get married?' Ed asked, picking up one of the glasses and downing the liquid quickly.

She looked over at him and couldn't make out if he looked relieved or disappointed at her comment. Watching him standing there, patiently waiting for her to reply, she couldn't help remembering his taut, tanned torso beneath his grass-smeared T-shirt. 'I'm not sure, but I know I wouldn't want to have to go through it on a day as hot as this one.'

'You're sensible,' Marie said. 'When we got married I wore a little cotton summer dress, not too different to the one you're wearing today, Izzy. It was perfect for the Parisian summer. Mind you, we didn't have a church ceremony.'

Izzy watched her looking over at Ed and realized he hadn't taken his eyes of her.

'Did we, Ed?' Marie asked, holding the half-filled jug in one hand and an empty glass in the other.

'What? Oh, no. No we didn't. You wanted to keep things simple, I seem to recall.'

Izzy didn't ask if that had been what he wanted. She didn't really want to know anything much about their wedding at all. In fact, standing here with them both, aware that she and Ed had spent the previous evening making love, made her feel distinctly uncomfortable.

'That juice looks delicious,' she said, reminding Marie about the drink she'd offered to pour for her.

'What?' Marie said, looking surprised to still be holding the glass and jug. 'Sorry,' she poured a glassful and passed it to Izzy.

'Thank you,' Izzy said noticing that Ed was holding something very sparkly and pink. 'Is that my mobile?' she frowned, wondering what he was doing with it.

He held it up and stared at it for a second. 'Yes, it is,' he said walking over towards her. 'I heard it ringing when I was passing the cottage just now and thought I should bring it to you. It might have been an urgent call.'

He handed her the phone. His finger grazed hers lightly and his warm touch sent shivers through her body. 'Thank you.'

He didn't take his eyes off her, but cleared his throat and said quietly. 'Your bag is still back at the cottage. I can go and fetch it for you if you like.'

Unwilling to pass up an opportunity to return to his cottage, however briefly, she said, 'No, that's fine, I can collect it after the reception is over.'

'No problem,' he said, the hint of a smile on his perfect mouth.

She breathed in his musky scent and only just managed to stop herself reaching up and pulling his head down to hers, desperate for their lips to connect once again.

'Er, hello?' Jess interrupted the moment, 'Izzy, when you've quite finished, I think we need to press on.'

Izzy checked the missed call on her mobile. 'I'll just make a quick call to Lacey, see what she wanted to speak to me about.'

She pressed 'redial' and hoped this wasn't Lacey telling them she'd discovered what had happened and called off her wedding. Lacey's mum answered her phone.

'Hi, it's Izzy,' she said, listening as the mother of the bride passed on a message from Lacey.

'Thank you,' Izzy said, relieved beyond belief. 'And please thank Lacey for asking you to let us know. I hope the wedding ceremony goes well. Please send her our best wishes and say we're looking forward to seeing her at the manor soon.'

She disconnected the call and turned to Jess. 'That was Lacey's mum wanting us to know that two couples have had to cancel. Apparently chicken pox is going round the island and their kids have come down with it.'

Jess frowned. 'She's telling us this why?'

Izzy laughed. Jess was always easily baffled whenever she was stressed. 'She doesn't want us to have empty places set at the tables.'

Jess smiled, realization dawning on her. 'And that we have too many settings rather than too few, is that what you're getting at?'

Izzy clapped her hands. 'It is.'

She sighed loudly. 'Such a relief.' Checking her watch she added, 'We have one hour before they'll be here and we're not nearly ready. Come on, Jess. Let's move our bums and get this place ready to rock.'

Three-quarters of an hour later, after checking each place setting, and straightening the pretty table decorations Lacey had chosen, Jess and Izzy stepped back to take in the scene in front of them.

'We actually did it,' Jess said, her face puce and hair standing up in all directions. She draped an arm over Izzy's aching shoulders.

'I have to admit that this morning I thought I'd never see this moment.'

'You're not the only one, babe.' Jess waved her free arm out to encompass the vintage-themed room. 'I actually think it looks better than anything we've ever pulled off before.'

Izzy thought so too. 'Do you think it's the added colour from Catherine's saris?' she asked, half-expecting a snappy retort.

She shrugged. 'I do, actually. Much as I hate admitting it, it was a brilliant idea of hers to hang them over the torn lining.' She turned to Izzy. 'You know, I think that whoever tried to wreck everything for us today has probably done us a favour in the long run, don't you?'

'Yes,' Izzy agreed. 'And I think we need to speak to Catherine about buying the saris from her friend. Maybe incorporate them in a more colonial theme rather than this vintage one.'

Ed arrived behind them, freshly showered and carrying the elaborate, flower-covered wedding cake. 'Where do you want me to place this?'

'Over there, please.' Izzy indicated the only round table in the room that they'd positioned underneath the central sari. 'Lacey certainly loves her colours,' she said, going over to inspect the bright creation. 'This looks like a cottage garden to me.'

'I think it's supposed to,' Ed said smiling at her and straightening the cake on the table. 'There. Now everything is ready.' He studied the room. 'Impressive. You girls are very good at what you do. The caterers moved their van to the back of the manor house a short while ago and Marie informs me that everything is now ready.'

Izzy thought about this and mentally ticked off everything that they needed to do. She nodded. 'Yes, I think that's it.' She checked her watch again. 'And only just in time, too. Come on, Jess, we'd better freshen up and make ourselves respectable.'

'Use my cottage,' Ed suggested. 'You won't be disturbed in there and I'll keep an eye on this place so that nothing can be touched while you're gone.'

Several hours later, Izzy and Jess watched the photographer take his final photos of the wedding party.

'We want a couple of you two next to the bride,' he said, waving Jess and Izzy over. 'I'll send you copies of the photos taken earlier that my boss said you wanted to use for your website,' he said. 'Don't forget to accredit them to us.'

Jess assured him they wouldn't and smiled sweetly.

Lacey, holding hands with Jack, came over to them and giggled. 'This is proper amazing; we can't thank you two enough.'

'Yes, it was brilliant,' Jack said.

'And no sign of that horrible ex of his either,' Lacey said.

Izzy heard Lacey's mum calling them over. 'You two had better go, or you'll be late for your flight out.'

They watched them go.

'I'm so tired I think I'm going to collapse,' Jess said. 'I could sleep right here on this grass if they'd only all bugger off.'

Izzy laughed. After her night at Ed's and then the exhaustion of the day, she understood what Jess meant. 'Me too.'

The girls waved goodbye to Lacey and Jack as they were driven away in her uncle's vintage Mercedes. They then helped Lacey's mum pack up what remained of the wedding cake. As soon as the last guest had driven around the bend at the top of the long driveway, Jess ran to their van to bring it round to the entrance of the marquee.

'Marie did offer to help us wash this lot up,' Jess said, 'but I just want to get home and collapse. We can tackle it all in the morning before returning the sets to their rightful owners.'

'It's a good thing we're used to doing this,' Izzy said, scraping the remnants of the food from the plates into the small bin they always brought for this use. 'Mind you, this lot didn't leave too much.' She kicked off her sandals and wriggled her toes to ease her aching feet. 'I'm shattered,' she said.

'Probably because you didn't get much sleep last night,' Jess giggled, holding up a fork and winking at her. 'It's not like you to stay out all night.'

Izzy carried on scraping and piling plates. When she had a full crate, she carried it out to put it into the back of the van. She wasn't surprised at Jess's amusement. It was the first time her friend had ever known her to spend the night with someone since David's death. She returned to the marquee.

'You don't mind me teasing you, do you?' Jess asked.

Aware she hadn't replied to her earlier comment, Izzy shook her head. 'No, of course not, I was just thinking, that's all.'

'So, was it good?' Jess asked.

'What?' It was her turn to make Jess feel uncomfortable now.

'Izzy, you know exactly what I mean,' Jess groaned. 'Was Ed any good in bed?'

Izzy laughed, but before she could reply, she felt a change in the tension in the room and glanced at Jess to see her staring at the doorway, her cheeks reddening. She knew without looking that Ed must be standing there having heard every word.

'Well, Izzy?' he asked. 'Was he?'

She turned to look at him, a wide smile on his face. 'I refuse to kiss and tell,' she said.

'Do you need any help with clearing away?' he asked, laughing.

'No thanks, we're used to doing this and have a system.'

'I'll get the guys to help clear away the tables and take down those saris for you,' he said, locking eyes with her for several seconds. 'I'll leave you to it; I need to go and do something in the manor.'

'Spoilsport,' Jess whispered as Ed walked away.

They finished the clearing up and loaded the van.

'Phew, that was a lot of work,' Jess said. 'I hope we get more bookings out of it.'

'Yes,' agreed Izzy, 'I can't wait to see the photos. He took loads, didn't he?'

Jess yawned. 'I just want to get home and chill in front of the telly with a glass of rosé.'

'Me too, but I'll just need to get my bag,' Izzy said.

'Turn the van round, I'll only be a second.'

She hurried across the parking area to the cottage, grabbed her bag and was walking back to the van when she heard Ed's voice. He sounded angry and sterner than she'd ever heard him before. She followed his voice and walking into the kitchen spotted Catherine and Marie glaring at each other. She stepped back, not wishing to let them see she was within earshot.

'I think your time here is over, don't you?' she heard Catherine saying to one of them.

'Why did you do it?' Ed's voice was quiet, but he sounded devastated.

Izzy strained to hear if he said anything more. She couldn't imagine what was going on in the room but waited to hear more.

'Because she's jealous,' Catherine snapped. 'Aren't you, Marie?'

'Of her?' Marie laughed. 'He's had other girlfriends since me and I've never been bothered about them. Why would I care about some cutesy little Jersey girl he's been interested in for five minutes?'

Marie's words stung and she moved slightly closer to the doorway.

'Because he's in love with her and if I can see it you certainly can.' Catherine said. 'So, Ed, are you going to tell her?'

Izzy stepped forward to make her presence known. 'He doesn't have to,' she said taking in the picture of the two antagonistic woman standing at either sides of the room with Ed scowling between them.

'Oh here we are, Miss Perfection,' Marie spat, narrowing her eyes and glaring venomously at Izzy.

The spite in her gaze stunned Izzy. She'd only ever known Marie to be friendly and accommodating before.

'So you are still in love with him?' she asked, aware it was a stupid question.

'What do you think?' Marie sneered.

'Tell her,' Ed said, glaring at Marie. 'Or I will.'

'Do what you like,' Marie shouted, throwing a glass at him and narrowly missing his face when he leaned away. Catherine walked slowly up to Marie, her nose almost touching the other woman's.

'If you think that after this my father would have anything to do with you then you're sorely mistaken.'

Marie threw back her head and laughed. 'Oh, Miss Spoilt Brat, who are you to tell me what I can and can't do? You're only jealous because Ed married me.'

Izzy held her breath, suspecting this notion did have some truth in it.

'I don't deny that I was jealous.' Catherine looked up at Ed. 'You know how I feel about you. Felt,' she corrected herself, probably, Izzy suspected, because she was now married to someone else herself. She focused her attention back at Marie. 'But that doesn't give you the right to have your own way all the time. I'm going to tell my father what you've done.' She smirked. 'You're welcome to come with me if you want. I can guarantee that however much I frustrate him with my behaviour at times, he will believe me over you and instead of moving in with him at the manor house, you'll be packing your bags and leaving.'

Izzy could tell Marie believed everything Catherine was telling her. She did too.

'You bitch,' Marie shrieked, pointing in Catherine's face.

Catherine smirked at her, looking very self-satisfied with Marie's reaction. 'Yes, and I think you're about to discover quite how horrible I can be.'

Marie glared at her. 'Do what you like, I'm leaving.' She pushed past Ed and rushed out of the back door, slamming it as she left.

Izzy looked at Catherine. 'So it was Marie who trashed

the marquee.'

Catherine nodded. 'It was, although after my behaviour towards you and Jess before and during the French trip, I can understand you both suspecting me.'

'Are you going to tell Izzy why you eloped?'

Catherine looked unsure and she and Ed stared at each other thoughtfully for a few seconds, before she addressed Izzy. 'I overheard Ed and my father discussing finances and discovered that Dad has problems. I couldn't bear for him to have to pay for my wedding, so thought the best thing I could do would be elope.'

Izzy's mouth fell open. 'I never thought …'

Ed walked over to Izzy and took her by the shoulders. 'She just didn't think of the consequences of running away and how it would affect Lapins de Lune.'

'No,' Catherine said. 'And I really am sorry about that. When Jess went on about it, I was so humiliated to think that my father could end up losing all this that I reacted nastily and turned on you both.' She hesitated. 'I'm sorry, truly.'

Izzy could only imagine the fear of losing everything when you had only known this sort of luxury. 'It's fine, I understand.'

'Ed has been trying to persuade my father to hold more weddings here. Large, lavish ones that will make him some money and maybe help clear a few of his debts.'

'I thought you were doing this for us,' she said quietly to Ed, unable to help feeling hurt that his motives hadn't been about her and Jess after all.

He tilted his head to one side. 'I thought you holding Lacey's reception here was perfect timing to show him that it didn't need to be invasive having a wedding in the manor grounds, while at the same time helping you two out of a tight spot.'

She couldn't blame him. It had helped save them after all. 'It was a good idea,' she said. She heard a car starting up outside and remembered Marie's part in everything. 'I can't believe Marie could be so vindictive though. After everything she's said.'

Catherine groaned. 'So you thought she was being friendly when she kept reminding you that she and Ed were married, where they were married, and what she was bloody wearing, did you?'

Now that Catherine mentioned it, Marie's constant reminders had been a bit much. She thought back to seeing Catherine and Ed in the cabin and decided that while all this was coming out, now was the time to ask Catherine about it.

'And you,' she hesitated unsure how to put it. 'Undoing Ed's shorts in the cabin when your new husband was on the boat; what was that all about?'

'Go on,' Ed said to Catherine. 'You may as well spit it out.'

Izzy listened while Catherine admitted to having been in love with Ed since they kissed as teenagers. 'He's never seen me as anything other than some sort of cousin though,' she narrowed her eyes and smiled at him. 'Have you, spoilsport?'

'Get on with it,' Ed said, shaking his head and giving Izzy a reassuring smile.

'I got into a bit of trouble, but I'm not sharing the details with you. Ed helped me out and I'd never intentionally hurt him. The cabin thing was me being an idiot and he told me off in no uncertain terms.'

'Fine,' Izzy said. 'But why are you so antagonistic towards Marie? I know I am now, but what's she done to you?'

Catherine closed her eyes as if trying to refrain from losing her temper. 'She's set her sights on my father and when I came back this time I could tell she'd been working on him, because he was far more interested in her than he's ever been before. I'm not having that cow involved with him.'

Izzy could completely understand her reasoning, especially now she'd witnessed what Marie was capable of. 'I think you're right to send her packing,' she said. 'We're going to have to ensure she makes amends for the stock she's ruined, not to mention pay for the damage to the marquee; I don't see why we should claim through our insurance for what she's done.'

'Too right,' Jess said from the doorway. 'I don't mind her having her mega-tantrum, but the cow is going to pay for it.'

Izzy agreed. 'I think we're going to have a bit of a battle on our hands to resolve this, but we won't back down.' She looked at Catherine. 'Marie's incredibly manipulative and I think your father's had a lucky escape from her. She would only cause him grief in the long run.'

'My sentiments entirely,' Catherine agreed. 'You had a lucky escape when she dumped you, Ed, and thinking about it, maybe that was when she'd decided to make a play for my father.'

'Thinking back, I guess it must have suited her to have me out of the way on the trip, because while I was here he wouldn't get involved with her out of respect to me.'

'Exactly,' Catherine said. 'Then you went and spoilt it all by racing back here from the yacht, chasing after Izzy.'

Izzy liked this other side to Catherine. She was relieved she and Jess had been wrong about someone so close to Ed. Not that there was any future for them, however much she and Ed might be in love with each other.

'And now you're going back to live at the château anyway,' Izzy said miserably. She was vaguely aware of Catherine and Jess leaving the room. She looked across at Ed to see he was watching her. 'What are we going to do?' she asked.

'I've been trying to figure that out,' he said, taking her in his arms. Holding her tightly against his chest, she could feel his heartbeat against her face. 'I love you, Izzy. I don't want to lose you, but I need to go back and help my parents and you look like you have a lot to contend with now where your business is concerned. You've worked so hard to build this up,' he said frowning. 'If you need me to help in any way with Marie, you must let me know.'

She put her arms tightly around his waist. 'I will,' she said. 'About you returning to France and me staying here in Jersey, it's a bit of a dilemma, isn't it?' she said. Tears were welling up in her eyes.

He lifted her chin gently with his finger so she had to look at him.

'You're crying,' he said, bending to kiss her.

'I'm not,' she lied.

'Listen, Iz,' he said, holding her by the shoulders. 'I know it isn't perfect, but neither of us can back out of our obligations. We're committed to other people right now, you to Lapins de Lune, and me to my father and the château.' He smiled at her. 'But I'm only in France and your island is only fifteen miles off the French coast.'

'True. But we'll still be apart.'

'But Izzy, catching the ferry from St Helier to St Malo to spend a few days together is nothing. It only takes seventy minutes to get there and after a ten-minute walk to the train station you'll have an hour and a half on a train to the station near the château.'

'But if it's such a quick trip why did you arrange for Jess and me to be collected in Paris, rather than take a train to the station near your home?' It didn't make sense.

'Because it was Bastille Day,' Ed explained. 'The usual rail trip you'd have taken to get there was fully booked up.'

'Oh, I see.' It had been incredibly busy wherever they'd gone on that day, she recalled. She thought about it. Her mother used to go to lunch in London some days with Alex's dad, and that was further. 'Sounds OK,' she said, warming to the idea.

He smiled, happy with her reaction. 'If I come to you here when I have a quiet couple of days and you come to see me when you can, we could spend a fair amount of time together.'

His expression was filled with hope that she'd agree and it didn't take her long to nod enthusiastically.

He lifted her by the waist and swung her round, kissing her as he lowered her feet back onto the ground again.

'We're actually going to do this, aren't we?' she asked laughing and knowing the answer already.

He nodded. 'We are. You can stay here with me in the cottage when I'm in Jersey and at the château when you're in France, that way we won't get in Jess's way when I'm over.'

They heard the van horn bursting into life several times. 'I think Jess has had enough of waiting for me,' Izzy laughed, leaning into him and breathing in the freshly showered smell of his body.

He held her tightly to him. 'I think we'd better go before she interrupts Catherine's rant to her father.'

'Yes, good point.'

They walked around the corner to the van.

'Hurry up, I want to get home and change.' Jess stared from one to the other of them and shook her head slowly. 'I might have guessed. If you can put him down for long enough, we can go home and I can get an early night. I'm dying here.'

Ed laughed and opened the passenger door, holding it while Izzy stepped in and opened the window down fully. He leaned in and gave her a kiss, then looked across at Jess. 'Funny that.'

'What?' she asked, half-glancing at Izzy.

'Roman called me earlier and told me he was picking you up at seven thirty.'

Izzy gasped. 'Jess?' Izzy said, taken aback at this turn

267

of events. 'What about my brother?'

Ed winked at her. 'It appears she's decided to go out with mine instead.'

Jess laughed. 'I like Alex, but I realised that it could make things difficult having a relationship with my best friend and business partner's brother.' Izzy widened her eyes. 'Imagine if we fell out, it could makes things uncomfortable between us.'

Izzy pushed Jess's shoulder. 'Well, I appreciate it.'

'Yes,' said Ed, 'now can we agree that I'll pick you up in two hours?'

Izzy thought back to their enjoyable time the night before that had gone by far too quickly. 'Yes, I think that's a great idea.' She leaned out of the window and grabbing him around the neck, pulled him to her and kissed him hard on his smiling mouth. 'I'll see you very soon.'

Georgina Troy

The Jersey Scene

A Jersey Kiss
A Jersey Affair
A Jersey Dreamboat
A Jersey Bombshell

For more information about **Georgina Troy**
and other **Accent Press** titles

please visit

www.accentpress.co.uk

Lightning Source UK Ltd.
Milton Keynes UK
UKOW02f1019121015

260340UK00001B/39/P